IRISH GOTHIC
FAIRY STORIES

Let us go forth, the tellers of tales, and seize
whatever prey the heart long for, and have no
fear. Everything exists, everything is true, and
the earth is only a little dust under our feet.

William Butler Yeats

IRISH GOTHIC

FAIRY STORIES

FROM THE 32 COUNTIES OF IRELAND

STEVE LALLY & PAULA FLYNN LALLY

The
History
Press
Ireland

THIS BOOK IS DEDICATED TO PAULA'S MOTHER AND STEVE'S FATHER,
WHO ARE NO LONGER WITH US

CAIT FLYNN
(1947 – 2016)

PATRICK LALLY
(1945 – 1993)

First published 2018

The History Press Ireland
6–9 Trinity Street
Dublin 2
D02 EY47
Ireland
www.thehistorypress.ie

British Library Cataloguing in Publication Data.
A catalogue record for this book is available from the British Library.

ISBN 978 0 7509 8698 4

Typesetting and origination by The History Press
Printed and bound by TJ International Ltd

CONTENTS

About the Authors   7

Foreword by Liz Weir   9

Introduction   11

'Fireside Tale' by Steve Lally   19

1   The Province of Ulster   23

2   The Province of Leinster   79

3   The Province of Munster   145

4   The Province of Connacht   183

How to Keep on the Right Side of the Sidhe   215

Acknowledgements   219

Bibliography   220

ABOUT THE AUTHORS

PAULA FLYNN LALLY grew up in Forkhill, Co. Armagh. From a young age she would pack her small bag with a notebook and pencil and go through the fields and find a nice tree and sit under it and write for hours. Paula is a singer-songwriter who once upon a time had a hit with David Bowie's 'Let's Dance'. She is now back in the recording studio. She is a graduate from Dublin City University, and when leaving was awarded the Uaneen Fitzsimons Award. She worked for a spell in radio. Paula loves reading a good thriller, watching a scary movie and a decent BBC drama, and she loves nothing more than a good country song. She admires the work of Salvador Dali, Sean Hillen, David Shrigley, and Minton Sparks. She loves the poetry of Edna St Vincent Millay and Emily Dickinson and the music of The Carter Family, the Moldy Peaches, Gram Parsons and Nick Cave. The child inside her loves vintage doll's houses and Blythe Dolls. She has a 7-year-old son called Woody who keeps her heart young. He is an aspiring writer who sells his books from a stand made by granddad Sean and uncle Micky Flynn at the front of the house. Paula loves her cats, going to the seaside, and spending time with Steve. She appreciates the darkness and the light and she believes in the fairies.

STEVE LALLY was born in Sligo, the Kingdom of the Fairies; he later moved to Dublin and then settled in Rathcoffey, Co. Kildare. This is where his imagination flourished, fired by the landscape, ancient sites and stories. As a teenager he developed a love of gothic horror litera-ture, music and film, spending the long, dark winter nights reading Edgar Allan Poe and H.P. Lovecraft and writing stories with the music of Bauhaus and The Sisters of Mercy filling the night air. He is a gradu-ate of Limerick College of Art and Ulster University, and now resides in Ulster. Steve is an international storyteller and successful writer who has already written and illustrated three books on folklore. He loves classic horror movies. He enjoys the work of Arthur Rackham, Harry Clarke, Jean Michelle Basquait and Neil Gaiman. He admires the poetry of Patrick Kavanagh and Patrick Mac Gill and the music of Einstürzende Neubauten, David Bowie, Nick Cave and Planxty. He is kept on his toes by his 7-year-old daughter Isabella, who constantly asks him to tell her stories based on the wonderful characters that she creates. Like Paula, Steve appreciates the darkness and the light and he too has great respect for the 'Good People'.

FOREWORD

Long before I became a storyteller I learned to have great respect for the 'Good People', those from the otherworld.

I grew up in Co. Antrim listening to the story of how my eldest brother encountered a banshee the night before the death of his friend's grandmother. I had to walk home from school past the very spot where it happened but I was always careful never to do it after dark. This was a tale he retold to me before his death some sixty years after the incident, and it was as vivid to him then as when it took place. How could I have any doubt?

As a child I was brought up on stories of magic and enchantment. My favourite film was *Darby O'Gill and the Little People*, even though the pooka and banshee terrified me and the fairies were very tricky. Little did I know then that I would end up becoming a storyteller, based in the Glens of Antrim close to Tiveragh, a hill famous as a fairy stronghold. Folk in the Glens do not like to talk about the 'other crowd', as my friend Eddie Lenihan calls them, but they know better than to cut down a lone thorn tree or to give away milk or a light on May Eve. Although we live in a world where scepticism is rife, tales of fairies playing hurling still survive and those of us who live here are proud of the rich folklore of the area.

As I travel throughout Ireland sharing stories, members of the public regularly tell me their own tales of magical encounters. There are many cautionary accounts about what happened to foolish people who cut down lone thorn trees. I have even been asked for advice about building a house on a site with a fairy tree and on one occasion how to deal with one that blew down in a storm. Even references to people who are

'away with the fairies' refer back to tales of changelings that were left when human babies were stolen from their mortal homes. So, even in our hi-tech world, stories of the otherworld are still being told.

It is therefore very appropriate that we now have a collection of tales of the good folk gathered from every county in Ireland. This is no light-hearted Disney-like account of flittering winged creatures; these stories have been collected with respect by two people steeped in tradition. As an author and storyteller Steve Lally has proven his dedication to folklore, not simply by preserving the tales but by performing them to audiences of all ages. His co-author and wife Paula, a talented singer, grew up in the Ring of Gullion, an area of outstanding natural beauty, rich in mystery and fairy lore. By combining their talent and background knowledge they present a very readable collection, which will give a greater insight into the magical world of Irish fairies.

Liz Weir
Storyteller and Writer

INTRODUCTION

Over the centuries such folklorists and storytellers as Seamus MacManus, Francis McPolin, Joseph Campbell, Henry Glassie, Patrick Kennedy, William Butler Yeats, Sinead De Valera, Eileen O'Faolain, Ruth Sawyer, Michael J. Murphy, Sean O'Sullivan, William Carleton, Katherine Briggs and Eddie Lenihan (to name only a very few) have been like butterfly collectors searching for stories of Ireland's mystical people, the 'Sidhe'. Only they set them free again for others to go and find them for themselves.

As the storyteller Eddie Lenihan told me when I asked him about collecting stories:

> These stories are not yours or mine, they belong to the people who were kind enough to tell them to me while they were still able to. I in turn regard it as my duty to share them with others. Through this process, hopefully, the stories will live on.

These enigmatic creatures go under many names, such as the good folk, the wee folk, the gentle people, the fey and even the other crowd. The term 'fairies' is merely an Anglicisation for something that cannot be defined or pigeon-holed, just like the Sidhe themselves.

But the fairies of Ireland are not the magical or elaborate fairies that we know from stories such as *Cinderella* or *Peter Pan,* or the paintings created by the Victorian and Edwardian artists Richard Dadd and Edward Robert Hughes, or the photographs of the Cottingley Fairies fabricated by Elsie Wright and Frances Griffiths during the reign of King George V (1910–1936), nor are they the delicate sweet fairies we see in a Disney film.

The Sidhe lend themselves more to the imaginings of Edgar Allan Poe, H.P. Lovecraft, Harry Clarke, Sheridan Le Fanu and Bram Stoker, hence the title of the book *Irish Gothic*. In fact, Bram Stoker, an Irish man born in Clontarf, Co. Dublin, in 1847, listened to many strange and disturbing stories about the Great Famine of Ireland (1845–1849) and the good folk from his dear mother. It was such stories that helped create the literary landscape for Stoker's 1897 masterpiece *Dracula*.

In fact, it was believed that the Famine was indeed caused by the Sidhe. According to folklore historian Simon Young:

> There was the belief among some Irish potato growers that it was the fairies' disfavour that brought down the blight on the land. Fairy battles in the sky – fairy tribes both fought and played hurling matches against each other – were interpreted as marking the onset of the famine: a victorious fairy army would curse the potatoes of the enemy's territory.

In Eamon Kelly's beautiful fairy story 'The Golden Ball' there is a brief description of one of these fairy hurling matches.

I grew up listening to my grandmother, from Co. Galway in the West of Ireland, tell me stories about the 'good folk', and she was also a huge fan of the Hammer Horror Franchise. This fascination with the sublime and the strange stayed with me throughout my life in the literature, film, visual arts and even music that I loved. As a teenager I was fascinated with the gothic rock sub-culture of the late 1970s and early '80s with bands such as Bauhaus, who penned a song dedicated to the Sidhe entitled 'Hollow Hills'. The Virgin Prunes from Dublin were an androgynous and bizarre otherworldly group that emulated the mystery, beauty and horror of the Sidhe, and then there was Siouxsie, who literally incorporated the Sidhe into her own realm with 'The Banshees'.

These artists, along with many others from the genre, were the soundtrack to my life at a time when I was living in a very remote and rural part of Co. Kildare, surrounded by ancient castles, forts and folklore. Their music still resonates with me today.

I have written three books already on folklore: *Down Folk Tales* (2013), *Kildare Folk Tales* (2014) and *Monaghan Folk Tales* (2017). The research for these books gave me a great insight into folklore, folk tradition and, of course, the Sidhe. This is my first collaboration and I felt Paula was a good choice for she helped me research *Monaghan Folk Tales* and she comes from a magical place and is a true believer in the fairy folk.

It was through storytelling that I and Paula first met; she has always had a keen interest in what lies beyond the ethereal wall that separates our world from theirs. Since Paula was a young child living beside the mountains she would sit and wait for the fairies to come and keep her company.

Her brothers were older than her and, as she lived in an isolated area, there were no kids her own age to play with. As a result, her imagination was her playground. Paula had a powerful imagination from a young age and this helped her song writing in later years. She would sit in her garden wishing and hoping the fairies would come and visit her. Although she has never seen one, she felt a powerful connection and belief towards them. As she grew older her connection to the fairies did not fade and this caused many people to think she was herself 'away with the fairies'!

But she remained true to her belief and remained very much an individual. It quickly became apparent as she got older that not many share her belief in fairies, yet when she asked those people if they would cut down a fairy tree they would always reply, 'No way!'

Paula's love of storytelling did not come out of nowhere for her cousin was the late great John Campbell (1933–2006), one of Ireland's most celebrated storytellers. His son John Campbell Jnr was for a time Headmaster at Forkhill Primary School, where Paula was a pupil. She still has many happy memories of being taught by Mr Campbell, whom she states was one of the best teachers she ever had.

When Paula and I met, we shared our belief in the Sidhe and this is a bond we feel is sometimes more powerful than ourselves. Writing this book has been a wonderful experience but has also had many drawbacks, for we feel the fairies interfered with our plans on several occasions and did not make this journey easy for us, both as story collectors or as a couple – testing our faith in both them and each other.

During the writing of this book huge obstacles were put in our way to see if we would falter or give up. Initially we found it difficult to get people to share their experiences with us. We found this both interesting and disturbing, as many individuals today still talk of the Sidhe in hushed tones, for fear of being heard and quite possibly punished. It is for this reason that the Sidhe are often referred to as the 'Good People' or the 'gentle people', so that they will not take offence or umbrage if they hear mortals speaking of them. Some folk did not want to speak of them at all and it proved quite difficult to gather stories from each county.

At two crucial stages in this process we lost all our work due to computer problems, we managed to recover most of it but some of the material had to be rewritten and re-documented. In the early stages all of Paula's research was wiped from her iPad. The camera that I used to document my illustrations for the book completely packed in and a new one had to be purchased.

Paula had lots of sleepless nights and bad dreams while writing this book, and a few times questioned if we should keep going. She felt for a time that maybe the fairies were telling us not to write the book, and that we were involving ourselves in something that we really do not understand.

I had read and heard of accounts of individuals being sabotaged by the fairies whilst trying to get close to them, and I was beginning to think it was a bad idea myself. However, after consulting some people who are lucky enough to have met them, they assured us that the 'fairy folk' would want us to write this book so the people of Ireland know about them. It's natural and important to fear them, but it's much more important to respect them. It is also true that anything worthwhile is never easy.

These are only a few examples of the struggles we faced while writing this book. We believe the fairies were testing our belief to see if we were serious, and maybe to see our motives for writing a book about them. We did not give up despite everything that was put in our way; we still believe in the fairies and each other – maybe even more than ever. Our belief in them and each other has become stronger as a result of writing this book.

It has been a labour of love and part of the process in creating this book has been the artwork. It has indeed been exciting, trying to imagine the Sidhe and their world visually. My old Art College friend James Patrick Ryan has been a wonderful support throughout this project. His contribution has been instrumental in the layout of the artwork. He created a set of wonderful coats of arms, one for each county, and a series of ornate borders that pay tribute to the plates of the great master of fairy illustration, Arthur Rackham (1867–1939).

James, a native of Co. Limerick, provided us with a chilling fairy story told to him by his grandmother. This story provides the chapter for Co. Limerick and is complemented by his own illustration. He also created a beautiful and intricate illustration featuring all the characters featured in the book.

The one question that I always ask while interviewing folk about the Sidhe is, 'What do they look like?'

Some people have told me the fairies are just 'wee folk', who seldom grow more than 3 feet tall, but resemble ordinary human beings in every other way. Their clothing is old-fashioned and their features plain, rather more ugly than handsome. Others have said that they look just like us and one could be standing beside you and you wouldn't know it, but there is a strange look in their eyes that gives them away. Some have said that they are beautiful beyond belief and when you see them your life will never be the same. I have heard tell of them being terrible monsters and creatures from your wildest nightmares. Many believe that the fairies are fallen angels that had nowhere to go, for they could neither enter Heaven nor Hell, and some say we can't see them at all.

I have spoken with many people, old and young, who have experienced first-hand the mischievous ways of the fairy folk. Some have been trapped in fields for hours and days and some have been tormented after cutting a bush or a tree, but what I have found is that most people, whether they believe in fairies or not, both respect and fear them in equal measure and don't tempt fate by interfering with what they feel is fairy property.

According to Co. Down folklorist Francis McPolin (1897–1974), most of them lived in underground caves, having secret entrances into the fairy forts, which can still be seen in varying states of ruin and preservation on most of the hillsides in the surrounding countryside. It's believed that there was a definite hierarchy or aristocracy among the fairies and these nobles lived in underground palaces that could only be entered via the larger forts that stood upon the higher hilltops.

The general consensus is that the fairy world is composed of the original fairy people known as the Tuatha Dé Danann, or 'The People of the Goddess Danu'. According to the Armagh folklorist Michael J. Murphy, these were an early Irish race who were skilled in magic and they were able to escape the physical death of mortal man. They were, however, compelled to dwell in fairy forts or rassans. They entertained themselves by showing off their superiority over ordinary people by playing tricks on them. This tended to take place at certain times of the year such as the 1st of May; probably the best known is the 31st of October, Halloween, when the ethereal wall between the human world and the fairy world is at its thinnest.

On these dates humans were carried off or abducted by the fairies and kept in fairyland permanently; these humans are known as 'changelings'. To protect themselves from such abductions, Murphy stated that the old people would place iron tongs across a cradle. Apparently, fairy folk cannot perform any magic when confronted with either iron, steel or the Bible.

In fact, all the knowledge we have today about the Sidhe has been passed down by storytellers going back centuries when the written word and literacy was only a pleasure of the privileged classes and stories existed through the oral tradition.

As a storyteller myself, I have had the privilege and a pleasure to work with other storytellers and hear their tales of the Sidhe. It has been particularly fascinating to hear first-hand accounts of experiences that people have had with them. Paula and I have spoken to folklorists, musicians, priests, academics, artists, poets, farmers, fishermen, mountain folk, storytellers and characters from every background imaginable with regards to this book. Our conversations have been both enlightening and enriching and have brought so much to this book.

Our aim was to find the best stories from each county and we hope we have done just that. We feel it is important to preserve these stories and share them with everyone.

We have always felt the good folk brought us together. Since we began writing this book we have got engaged and by the time it is published we will be married.

Steve Lally
July 2018

'FIRESIDE TALE'

by Steve Lally
In memory of 'Granny in Galway', Margaret Power King

Well folks come gather round
And listen to a tale
From a long time ago
I heard it from my Grandmother
It must be forty years or so
Well she sat me on her knee
Beside the fire, burning bright
And when my Granny told a tale
You would listen to her carefully
Deep into the night.

She looked me in the eye
All her wisdom shining through
And I knew…
She was going to tell me
A thing or two
About a thing or two.
'Now what time do you think it is?'
Her voice all hushed and low
'Well, tell me now…
Don't you know?'

Of course, I did not know at all
But the shadows dancing on wall
Told me it was very late
For the only light there was
Came from the fire
Flickering in the grate
'It's midnight,' she said to me
'It's the witching hour, oh yes!
And who comes out at this time?
Go on now, take a guess!'

Well I racked my brains
And I thought real hard
And then it came into my head
'Mam and Dad, they stay out late
And they'd be angry if they knew I was not in bed.'
'No, they go out, but these come out
Two very different things,
Some have fangs and fly with wings
Others howl and growl and bark
And their eyes, they light up in the dark!'

'But the worst of all are very small
And play tricks on little boys
When they don't eat their dinner
Or put away their toys!'
'Who are they?' I had to say
My voice was just a choke
'Oh! They are the Fey
The Sidhe
Better known as…
The Fairy Folk!'

Well I looked at her
And she looked at me
As I sat that night upon her knee
She told me of the the Fairy Tree,
The Pooka Horse,

And the Banshee, of course!
Now as the fire grew dim
As the shadows danced upon the floor
Suddenly! We were startled
A sound! A rustling at the door...

'Oh no!' I screamed 'It's them I bet!
Coming to see what they can get
We better run we better hide
It's the Fairy Folk,' I cried
Then the sitting room door, opened with a creak
My heart was pounding, my knees were weak
The cry of the Banshee rang through my head
That's it we're done, we're dead!
And the howling figure before me said...
'Ah! Mammy, why is that child not in bed!'

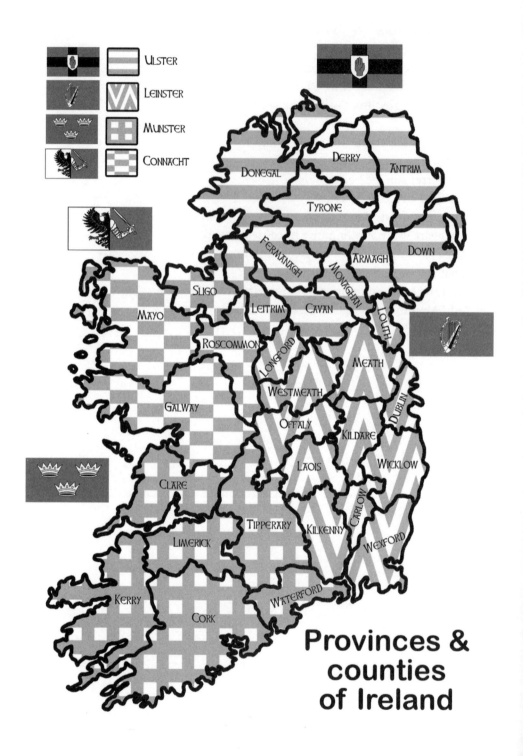

Provinces & counties of Ireland

ULSTER

LEINSTER

MUNSTER

CONNACHT

DONEGAL

DERRY

ANTRIM

TYRONE

FERMANAGH

ARMAGH

DOWN

MONAGHAN

LOUTH

SLIGO

LEITRIM

CAVAN

MAYO

ROSCOMMON

LONGFORD

MEATH

WESTMEATH

DUBLIN

GALWAY

OFFALY

KILDARE

LAOIS

WICKLOW

CLARE

CARLOW

TIPPERARY

KILKENNY

WEXFORD

LIMERICK

KERRY

CORK

WATERFORD

1

THE PROVINCE
OF ULSTER

Co. Antrim: From the Irish *Aontroim*, meaning 'Lone Ridge'. Antrim is a county renowned for its natural beauty and mythology. One of the world's most famous landmarks can be found along the coast of Antrim, the Giant's Causeway, built by the legendary hero and giant Fionn mac Cumhaill. The famous hexagonal stones are known as *Clochan na bhFomharach*, which means 'Stones of the Formorians'. The Formorians were an ancient demonic race that were defeated by the Tuatha Dé Danann. Also in Portballintrae in Co. Antrim you will find the Lissanduff Circles, which are originally thought to be fairy forts. Part of an ancient road was found near the upper circles and it is believed that it once went south from Lissanduff all the way to Tara. Ella Young (1867–1956), the poet and Celtic mythologist and member of The Gaelic & Celtic Revival, was born in Fenagh, Co. Anrtim. Ethna Carbery (born Anna Johnston) (1864–1902) was a great folklorist and songwriter born in Kirkinriola, Ballymena, Co. Antrim.

THE FAIRY TREE (CO. ANTRIM)

Co. Antrim is indeed a fine place to find wonderful stories – from the Giant's Causeway to Deirdre of the Sorrows. Indeed, what better place in this magical county to find stories of the good folk other than the Glens of Antrim. There are nine glens altogether and they all have many stories to tell.

According to Michael Sheane in his book *The Glens of Antrim: Their Folklore and History*, the nineteenth-century poet Harry Browne collected many stories of the good folk from around the Glens of Antrim for *The Ulster Journal of Archeology*. We too have collected some of these stories and would like to tell them to you now…

Many years ago, a young man from Glenarm told Browne about his grandfather, who had seen the good folk many times. In fact, on one occasion his grandfather had seen a fight take place between the wee folk. They were certainly aggressive wee craythurs when they got going. The old man told his grandson that he had met a fella from Cushendall with his head facing the wrong way around; 'Be jeepers, what a sight it was!' When he asked him what had happened, the poor chap told him that he had cut down a fairy tree. He had thought nothing of it despite all the warnings, and he went to bed as usual that night. But when he woke up he was shocked to find that his face was at the back of his neck!

Another person told of an experience he had whilst he was living in Glendun. He had wanted to cut down a *Skeogh* or fairy tree that was on his farmland. Well now this fella went like the Hammers a' Hell at this lone bush with his axe and after a couple of strikes, didn't the blade bend or turn (as they say in Co. Antrim) and he had to get another one. So when he came back with his nice new sharp axe he let out a big strike at the tree. As soon as the blade hit the trunk of the tree, blood started pouring from it. Now the poor fella got an awful shock from all this and he decided to give up on the job. He went home and went to bed, and when he woke up the next morning, sure there was not a hair upon his head, and he was as bald as an egg. After that the poor man had to wear a wig and his hair never grew back.

Now you don't always have to cut down a fairy tree for the wee folk to get upset; in fact, if you try and build or dig near one, this can cause problems too, as you are more than likely on a fairy path. Browne talks about a chap whose son wanted to build a rabbit hutch for his pets. So he started to dig near where there stood a Skeogh, then out of nowhere he could hear a voice calling to him 'Don't dig here!', but he just thought it was the wind and he paid no heed and kept on digging away. Again, the voice cried out, only louder this time, 'Don't dig here!', now this time he figured it was one of his friends trying to play a trick on him, so he stopped and went to find the culprit. But lo and behold there was no one there at all and the young fellow went on about his digging, only this time the voice screamed out **'Don't dig here!'** and he felt something fly past him, which sent him head over heels on the grass. When he looked up he saw a strange ghostly figure that looked like a pile of rags blowing in the wind standing over him. It had no face but had eyes of burning red. It pointed a ragged finger at him and screamed once more **'Don't dig here!'** Well with that the young chap jumped up from the ground and took to his heels. After that he made sure to build his rabbit hutch in a far safer place away from any fairy trees.

In Emyr Estyn Evans' classic book *Irish Folk Ways* he states that, 'A fairy thorn (fairy tree), as one not planted by man, but which grew on its own, typically on some ancient cairn or rath'. It is true that the fairy tree is not grown by man; in fact it is the birds and the fauna that plants the seeds. When they eat the haws or berries of the hawthorn or whitethorn tree, they then pass the seeds in their droppings all over the countryside and that is why we see so many fairy trees all over the rural and wilder parts of Ireland.

But that is not to say that they are not sacred and possess great power – in fact, it only adds to their mystique and their total freedom from the constraints of man and modern agriculture. The poet Harry Browne states in Michael Sheane's book that he remembered a fairy tree in Glens of Antrim, growing inside a hedge by the roadside. It stood there for a very long time and no one ever tried to clip it or prune it, for fear of a retaliation from the good folk. But after a while the tree was becoming a problem as it started to hang out over the road and it was declared that it could cause an accident or just block the road completely. So, with that a decision was made to have the tree cut down altogether. The road-man who was asked to take care of it refused point blank and would not have anything to do with such desecration. Well the old road-man eventually died and a younger fella took his place. He had no belief in such superstitious nonsense, so he went ahead and cut down the tree. Not long after this the road-man's daughter died. It was said that some of the local people took the branches of the tree and put them under the road-man's hay-stacks and it was this that had put the *piseog* (curse) upon him.

The fairy tree is part of a greater family of plants that grow in the wild and are associated with the supernatural. For example, foxgloves are a very common flower in the Glens of Antrim; they are sometimes called fairy thimbles or fairy hats because of their unique conical shape. The ash tree or ash plant is said to have great powers and was used by Druids in the ancient world as part of their rituals. Ash rods are placed in the ground overnight before building a house. If they are moved or damaged at all the house must be built elsewhere, as this is a sign of obstructing a fairy path.

There are many plants and herbs that grow in the wild that were used by wise men and women, or fairy doctors. These people were both feared and revered by the country folk. Two very famous fairy doctors were Moll Anthony, the Wise Woman of Kildare, and Biddy Early, the Wise Woman of Clare. These women were also known as witches or *Cailleaghs* but eventually they were simply called hags, which seemed to lessen their power and influence on the country folk. The hawthorn or fairy thorn is also known as the hag thorn; its berries are said to be associated with sacrificial drops of blood.

It is believed that the fairy tree is the watchtower to the Tuatha Dé Danann. These were a powerful race of magical people who ruled Ireland long before humans arrived. When the humans did arrive in the form of the Gaels or the Celts they were defeated by these mortal intruders. So they made a pact that the Gaels would live above the ground and they would dwell below. They used the whitethorn tree to look out across the land, to make sure it was clear to go on their nightly excursions and dances.

On the 1st of May, or Lá Bealtaine (this symbolises the beginning of summer and also the day that the fairies came to Ireland), the May bushes are put out in front of people's houses and decorated. They symbolise the fairy tree and bring good luck to anyone who leaves out a May bush.

The fairy tree is indeed an ancient and powerful thing and not to be treated with disregard or contempt. The well-known Co. Antrim story-teller Liz Weir told me once that she met a very well-to-do Co. Antrim farmer who believed that all this fairy business was a load of nonsense.

But when she asked him would he ever cut down a fairy tree on his land he quickly replied, 'I most certainly would not!'

The following is a poem called 'The Fairy Tree' from South Armagh bard Marie McCartan (*née* Murphy), a good neighbour of Paula's from Forkhill. Marie is a wonderful character who hails from a family of bright and creative people who offer much to the area. Her mother was Brigid Murphy, a story and song collector. Her stories are kept safe in the Folk Museum in Cultra and the songs she collected are in the archives in Dublin.

Marie has published her own book of poetry, also entitled *The Fairy Tree*. As well as being a Bard of Armagh finalist, she was the recipient of the 2012 prestigious Gerry Watters Hall of Fame Award at the Bard of Armagh Competition.

The Fairy Tree
By Marie McCartan

He was born along the border
On wet and boggy land
He got started at the smuggling
And bought himself a van
He shifted pigs and cattle
It was profit without pain
He bought himself a lorry
And started moving grain

He was known for sharp dealing
A smart mover, a cute hoor
Money changed how people saw him
You're no one when you're poor
But when you're rich, you're not a smuggler
You're an entrepreneur

On a mansion he decided just as big as it could be
He had found the site he wanted
Out near Dromintee
A meadow of five acres
Where the corncrake used to be

But growing in the middle
Was a little fairy tree

He bought the land and paid in cash
And had the plans drawn up
To him it was a hawthorn bush
His plans it wouldn't stop
He brought his aging mother
His dream site for to see
She stood awhile then sighed and said
You bought a fairy tree

He said he planned to build there
Just where the tree was stuck
She said, you'll have to leave it
It will only bring bad luck
He said, all that oul talk is piseogs
It's just a hawthorn bush
There's no such thing as fairies
It will fall down with a push

She says, I have to warn you
That if you touch the tree
The luck that kept you going till now
Never more will be
You can't cut it, you can't push it
You must wait till it falls down
A fairy tree is sacred
For it grows on fairy ground

Although he didn't heed her much
He began to have some qualms
The fairy tree would have to go
But he'd have to change his plans
He resolved to dig around it
And hired a JCB
But the roots remained embedded
And the fairy tree stood free

He thought he'd try and burn it out
Sure they'd have to let that pass
The fairies couldn't blame him
For a fire in the grass
As he sprinkled on the kerosene
And waited for to see
A voice from out of nowhere warned
Don't burn the fairy tree

He looked around saw no one
Thought, it's all in my oul head
But, the voice from out of nowhere said
Destroy it and you're dead
He lit the match and dropped it
Then out of there did flee
The fire burnt everything in sight
Except, the fairy tree

He thought he'd try explosives
He brought experts from afar
You won't find that kind of expert
In a place like South Armagh
They carefully laid the charges
Blew up stones and lumps of wood
But when the smoke and dust had settled
The fairy tree still stood

He thought he'd try and flood it out
To Hell with the bad luck
He brought the digger in again
Diverted a large shuck
The water poured around it
And flooded the big field
But the fairy tree still stood its ground
It wasn't going to yield

He built the house around the tree
It was finished safe and sound

What happened is a mystery
One night the house fell down
The field was filled with rubble
Burnt, blew up and then the flood
But right there in the middle
The fairy tree still stood

If he'd listened to his mother
And left the fairy tree
He'd still have all his money
House and wife and sanity
Social position doesn't matter
To a fairy, young or old
But underneath the fairy tree
They store their pots of gold
So if you happen to pass by a fairy tree
Between dusk and early dawn
Don't look back or linger
Just bless yourself and go on.

Co. Armagh: from the Irish *Ard Mhacha*, meaning the plain or height of Macha. Macha was a Sovereignty Goddess. Navan Fort or Eamhain Mhaca was the ancient realm of King Conchobar or Conor Mac Nessa, the High King of Ulster; it was named after the Sovereignty Goddess Macha. St Patrick's Church of Ireland Cathedral is the burial ground of King Brian Boru, who was known to have tamed and rode upon a pooka horse. There you will also find a stone carving (thought to date back to the Iron Age); it is a helmeted figure with its right arm clutching the left one. It is known as Nuadha of the Silver Arm or The Tandragee Idol. Nuadha was the King of the Tuatha Dé Danann, who lost his arm in the First Battle of Magh Tuiredh when they fought the Fir Bolg (the fourth group of people to settle in Ireland) for the kingship of Ireland. Because he was disfigured he could no longer be King. His physician, Dian Cecht, made him a silver arm and so he became known as Nuadha of the Silver Arm. The great storyteller John Campbell (1933–2006), the renowned Folklorist Michael J. Murphy (1913–1996), Sarah Makem (1900–1983), who was an important traditional singer, and her son Tommy Makem (1932–2007), a world-famous singer and member of the eminent Clancy Brothers, were all from South Armagh.

WISE WITH THEIR YEARS (CO. ARMAGH)

Paula grew up in South Armagh, the backdrop to her childhood was Slieve Gullion mountain. The townland was Shean, in the village of Forkhill.

This story was given to us by a man called Eugene McCann from Mullaghbawn, Co. Armagh. It was written by Michael McManus, who went by the name Clia Staca. He was from the townland of Adanove, which is in Ballykeel, Mullaghbawn. These stories where published in the *Frontier Sentinel*, which was a newspaper based in Newry, Co. Down. He was born on the 29th of September 1896 and died on the 25th of November 1935. He was only 39 years old.

Clia Staca told many stories about the 'Cailleach Beara', who he and many believe lived up on the very top of Slieve Gullion mountain. The word 'Cailleach' has come to mean 'hag' but in old Gaelic it means 'veiled one'. She is associated with winter, and the creation of the landscape. Stories of the Cailleach can be found in Loughcrew, Co. Meath (the Hag's Mountain), Cliffs of Moher, Co. Clare (one cliff is named the Hags Head). Co. Galway has the Hag's Cliff and Co. Cork has the Labbacallee Wedge Tomb, which is known as the Hag's bed. But it is in Co. Armagh on the top of Slieve Gullion mountain that you will find the Calliagh Beara's house.

The Calliagh Beara is said to be the Goddess of Winter. Sometimes these burial mounds are referred to as 'womb tombs'. Ali Issac, storyteller, says that 'from the darkness of the womb the light of life is born, and the dark silent inner chamber of the cairn can be likened to the womb'.

A wonderful website we would recommend you visit (ringofgullion. org) has a lot of information on the area, from archaeology to geology. This is a great source for finding detailed and accurate information about the famous passage tomb on the top of Slieve Gullion mountain. The passage tomb, sitting at 570m above sea level, is the highest surviving passage tomb in Ulster. It consists of a circular cairn some 30m in diameter and up to 4m high. The earliest documented investigation of the passage tomb dates back to 1789, when it was opened by locals who were apparently looking for the Cailleach Beara, but only a few human bones were found.

It was opened again in 1961 by students from Queen's University and all that was found was a few pieces of worked flint, a single scraper and an arrowhead. Two of the stone basins, commonly found in passage tombs, were also found and a third was discovered and is now housed in Armagh County Museum. Also in 1961, on the same mountain, a small round cairn was found and excavated, revealing two small cist graves and fragments of distinctive early Bronze Age pottery.

Clia Stacca wrote a lot about the Calliagh Beara and the landscape and fairy dwellings of his home place that he obviously admired and held dear: 'Around my own country from Narrow-water to Culloville, I know hundreds of little "forts" and "rings", where fairy dances and meetings were held, or, at least, we were told and believed.'

Shean Mountain was credited with being the place of banishment of the fairy king. Stacca tells us he was expelled from the fairy circle because of his unjust war on humans – he often committed offences such as stealing butter from the crocks of the nearby farmers. He was tried by the fairy court and sentenced to remain in solitary exile on the Shean Mountain until the court decided he was deserving of release. The only one he was allowed to make conversation with was the Calliagh Beara on Slieve Gullion, and only when she desired.

When the Calliagh Beara first addressed the fairy king, he complained to her that his sentence was too severe. She laughed at him and said she once felt the same way when she first came to Slieve Gullion, but with time she got used to it:

'I am here now one hundred and fifty years and when I first came here the western slope was growing hay almost to the shore of the lake, and I was annoyed at daybreak and until dark at night with the people working and shearing and saving the crop. Now I have peace, for the years have brought a change; the humans are getting too weak or too lazy to work; they are wiser and wickeder; there is no hay now only heather and wild grass, and the hens and old straggling sheep are all I see on my rambles.'

The fairy king laughed and said, 'Well, one thing I am sure of, you never remember hay growing here or people working on Shean Mountain; if there was a lake here I could sit and admire my own beauty in the reflection of its waters.' The Calliagh Beara replied, 'Well, if you are so fond of looking at yourself, you will have plenty of time to do so. Don't let me stop you, for I'll never speak to you again.'

And she kept her word. The one and only person he was allowed to talk to refused to speak to him ever again. He was so lonely he would sit up all night long wailing to try and attract her attention. He wanted her sympathy and conversation so badly. He was desperate for company and companionship. It was said that his cries were heard by men out late at night, men walking home from pubs and ceili houses, but eventually his cries stopped. It was believed that the fairy council granted him release.

Clia Staca said it was thought that the fairy king made the journey to Scotland, like a lot of the fairies were meant to have done many years ago. He also said that some people maintain that he was reinstated with his old title as 'Fairy King' and went to live in Dorsey (also in South Armagh) where all his fairy friends (who refused to leave Ireland for Scotland in the 'bad times') also went.

The Calliagh Beara on Slieve Gullion was once a beautiful little girl who was stolen by the fairies from a well-to-do family in Killeavy and held prisoner. The family were distraught and sought the help of someone who was credited with witchcraft. At the time they felt it may have been the only way to get their daughter back. The old woman was known as the Witch of Carriba. She told the family that on Halloween night the fairies were to hold a dance in Killen and that the little girl would be there with them. She told them that if they wanted to retrieve their only child then the nearest family member who was not afraid to make the journey alone on Halloween night was to go there and take with them three quarts of new milk, fresh as it comes from the cow (and this was the vital part – the milk had to be pure) and as soon as they saw the child they were to throw the milk on her, grasp her tightly, and carry her off home and let nothing or no one interfere.

Halloween night came and the anxious and hopeful father made the journey and did what he was told by the old lady. But it didn't go to plan for when he threw the fresh milk into the fairy ring where his little girl stood – the child disappeared. He went home, deeply upset. His wife was waiting for their return and broke down when she saw he was alone.

When the old woman went to the house the next day and asked how the father got on he told her what happened. When she asked, 'Was the milk pure?' he told her that someone else had fetched it for him, but he was sure it was.

However, it was revealed that a cousin of the child, who the family had taken in after their own child was taken, fetched the milk and somehow managed to water it down, so the milk was not pure. It is not known if this was deliberate on the girl's part, or she may have been unaware of the strict instructions.

The parents still held out hope and asked the old woman to help them for a second time. The witch told the family that for every drop of water that was placed in the milk their daughter would spend a year with the Good People.

A short time afterwards the parents died, and the house was visited by the fairies. Their well went dry, their cattle died and everything that could go wrong, went wrong.

It is said that the little girl grew up to become a beautiful woman and went to live in the cave on Slieve Gullion. She became known as the Calliagh Beara and was said to have many powers and wonderful charm.

Slieve Gullion plays a central role in many folk tales. One well-known story involves the Cailleach Beara and Finn McCool.

Clia Staca wrote a story about when Finn McCool hunted deer from Kildare to Slieve Gullion. When he lost deer on the mountaintop he heard crying and saw a beautiful girl weeping by a lake. He walked over to the girl and asked her why she was so sad and if he could help her. She told him that she had lost her ring in the lake when she was bathing. So, in Finn dived and searched for her ring. When he arose to the top for air the beautiful girl was replaced by a cackling old hag. She said to him, 'I am the Cailleach Beara. You chased my deer, you will chase no more.' When he looked at his reflection in the water he saw an old man staring back at him. When his followers caught up with him on the mountain they did not recognise him, but for his voice they wouldn't have believed it was him.

Clia Staca said that the stories he shared came from those before him, from those who were 'wise with their years'. He said he didn't doubt them, for the proof was there for all to see. The mountain still stood, with the cave and the lake. He said he often drank from the lake after the long journey from Mullaghbawn. He spoke fondly of the 'fairy forts' and 'gentle bushes', and he finished by saying if you require proof of my story, come in summer and see them, and if in the meantime any further stories come to light, I will let you know.

Co. Cavan: From the Irish *An Cabhán*, meaning 'The Hollow'. Co. Cavan was founded by the King of East Breifne, Giolla Íosa Ruadh O'Reilly, during his lordship between 1300 and his death in 1330. O'Reilly was such a wealthy and well-to-do man it was from his lavish lifestyle that the term 'The Life of Reilly' came. On Shantemon Mountain where the inauguration of the O'Reillys took place you will find 'Fionn Mac Cumhail's Fingers', the great giant lost them in battle and they are preserved there in the form of five standing stones. They are 'cursing stones' and are turned traditionally sun-wise to extend a blessing towards someone and reverse a curse. Co. Cavan is home to the mysterious 'Pooka of Cuilcagh'. Séamus P. Ó Mórdha (1915–2005), an Irish teacher and historian passionate about Irish culture and folklore, came from Scotstown, Co. Cavan.

THE FAIRY HORSES (CO. CAVAN)

We found this magical tale in The Schools Collection UCD, Vol. 0986, pp.1–2. This story from Co. Cavan was collected by Cathal O'Ragallagih, from his father, who was 56 years old when this story was recorded in 1938. Cathal was a pupil at Lough Gowna National School, Co. Cavan. We took it upon ourselves to recreate the story in our own words.

Fado, fado (Long, long ago) a girl went to the Sallaghan bog near Lough Gowna in Co. Cavan for a bag of turf. It is a very treacherous place and it is not advisable to go there when the light is bad, for there are many bog holes and marshes that cannot be seen in the dusk. But the poor child did not take heed of this fact and she fell into a bog hole and drowned.

There was great commotion and concern when she did not return home. The bog was searched and her poor little body was found.

After the body was brought home and the wake and funeral were over, her older brother went to the same bog for a bag of turf. Unlike his sister he took heed of the warnings, especially careful after the tragic death of his wee beloved sibling.

He went early in the morning when the light was good and he began to collect the dried turf and put it into the potato sack he had taken with him. Whilst he was collecting the turf, he heard a voice being carried on the wind; it was a child's voice and it was calling his name ever so mournfully: 'Michael, help me, please help me. Michael looked around and he almost fell over when he saw his little sister standing before him. Poor Michael did not know what to do and he ran home. He was very shaken by all of this and he did not say anything to his parents. That night he lay in his bed unable to sleep when a short while later he heard a troop of horses riding by his window and he could hear the sad voice of his sister calling out his name once again.

He was terrified and frozen to the spot, his heart beating in his chest like a drum. He did not dare go out and see what was going on. He felt guilty about this and the fact he had also run away after his sister had asked for his help, but he was scared stiff. When he woke up the next morning he was filled with dread. He kept wondering if it was a nightmare, or if he was so badly affected by the loss of his sister that he was experiencing a stage of grief he had heard people talk about. But he wasn't sure, so he decided to return to the bog in the hope he could maybe talk to his sister. Sure enough, his sister appeared to him again. He went to reach out to her but she disappeared right before his eyes.

This time when he went home he told his parents, who were very concerned, but they had heard of such things happening before. His father said that they should go and see Tommy the Sideog, a fairy doctor or wise man who lived in Mullahoran, Co. Cavan. Tommy claimed to have lived among the Sidhe for over twenty years and was an expert on their ways.

So the father and son headed off to see Tommy the Sideog. When they got to his wee cottage in Mullahoran, they could hear him talking away to someone inside the house. On entering they thought that Tommy must have been talking to himself for there was not a soul besides himself in the place. They asked him who was he speaking to and he replied 'the Good People'. They looked at each other and knew fine rightly he was referring to the fairy folk.

Michael and his father explained to Tommy what had happened and how the wee girl had appeared before Michael in the bog twice and how he had heard the sound of horses running past the house and his sister calling out to him the night before. They then asked what was going on and what should they do.

The wise man thought it over and told them that the body they had buried was not the man's daughter nor the boy's sister, it was a fairy. He explained to them that the fairies take children and replace them with one of their own, called a changeling. He said that sometimes they even leave behind an inanimate object like a broom or a shovel after they steal a human and this is called a 'stock'.

Well, as you can imagine the father and son were very perplexed with all of this and they were eager to find out what they should do.

Tommy told Michael he had to go to the bog the following day alone and talk to his sister but not to try and make any physical contact with her.

That night Michael lay awake again and at the stroke of midnight he heard a troop of horses running past the house and the sound of his wee sister calling out his name. 'Michael, Michael, Michael …' This time he wanted to run out and save her but he stopped himself because he remembered the advice he was given by Tommy the Sideog.

Sure enough he went to Sallaghan bog the next day on his own. When he got there his sister reappeared again and Michael spoke to her, asking where she was and if she was alright.

She told him that she did not drown at all, that she was only spirited away by the fairies, and that every night at twelve o'clock she would go past the gable of their family house riding a white horse along with a group of horsemen.

She then told him that there was only one way she could be saved, and that was if he would stand at the gable of the house as she rode past and make a grab to catch her. If he missed they would both die instantly, but if he was quick enough he would not lose his grasp.

With that, the wee girl disappeared and poor Michael was left standing alone in the bog not knowing quite what to do.

When he got home he told his parents what their daughter had said to him and they were very concerned indeed. In fact, they were not going to allow their son to go out that night for fear that they would lose him too. But he pleaded with his parents and said that he heard the horses and his sister running past his room at the end of the house every night and he would surely lose his mind if he did not do something about it.

His father took pity on him and he also admired his son's courage and selflessness. He told him that he would help him that night. He gave his son a black-handled knife, which is protection against the fairies, and he told him to stand his ground and he would catch onto his legs if he was taken by the fairies.

Well it was getting close to midnight and the father and son waited at the gable end of the house, as the mother looked out the window, with a candle lit on the sill. There was a great tension in the air and the three of them were very frightened. Then they heard something in the distance: it was the sound of thundering hooves approaching. Michael's heart was beating hard and his father was saying the rosary for he knew their lives depended on it. And unbeknownst to them the mother was inside the house rhyming off a decade herself. It was then that they saw the white chargers coming towards them and there on one of the beautiful horses was the little girl. They could see the other riders and they were fearsome-looking creatures with faces so terrible that words could not describe them. But Michael focused only on his beloved sister's precious face. Right there and then he made a promise to himself that he would make sure both of them would be safe in their beds that night.

As the wee girl rode past, Michael jumped up and grabbed her. He faltered for just a second but his father grabbed his legs and together they pulled the child from the horse. One of the riders stopped and gave Michael a fearsome look. He was about to dismount and attack the boy when Michael's father told him to take out the knife. Michael took the black-handled blade from his belt and thrust it into the rider's stomach. A gush of green blood spewed from the wound and the rider let out a terrible scream and both he and his horse disappeared before their eyes.

Michael was still holding on to his sister and he was relieved to see that she was unharmed. His father told him that he was very proud of him and that they should take the child inside and put her to bed. They all watched over her that night.

After that the wee girl never went to the bog on her own again and Michael's father let him keep the knife and told him he had earned it for he was a man now.

Co. Derry: From the Irish *Daire* (modern Irish *Doire*), meaning 'Oak Grove' or 'Oak Wood'. The world-renowned poet Seamus Heaney (1939–2013) from Bellaghy, Co. Derry was a champion of folklore, folk tradition and mythology; he translated the Anglo-Saxon saga *Beowulf*. Tirkane Sweat House stands beside a hill called Sidhe Fionn, which means 'The Fairy Mound of Fionn'. Co. Derry is also the home of Abhartach or Abhartaigh (from *Abhac*, the Irish for dwarf), an ancient Celtic demon dwarf who played a harp to seduce his victims (women) and then drink their blood. This story is believed to have inspired Bram Stoker's 1897 gothic novel *Dracula*. Some say the dwarf was killed by Fionn Mac Cumhaill, other sources say it was a Chieftain called Cathrain who pierced him through the heart with a sword made from Yew wood. He was buried upside down (so his evil seductive music could no longer be heard) beneath Slaghtaverty Dolmen, outside Garvagh, Co. Derry. The Dolmen is better known as *Leacht Abhartaigh*, meaning 'Abhartaigh's Stone'. His tomb lies in the shadow of a fairy tree.

THE DERRY POOKA (CO. DERRY)

We had heard of the Kildare Pooka – of Wicklow and Galway too. There may be a pooka story from every county but one of the best stories we have heard is from Co. Derry.

We borrowed books from many friends for this project and one book was called *The Middle Kingdom*, which was given to us by Eamon Keenen, a storyteller from Belfast. The book, written by Dermot MacManus, is all about the fairy world of Ireland and we learned a lot about fairy lore, including fairy trees and pookas and even magic cures. Dermot had an aunt called Lottie and she was a friend of Douglas Hyde. He would spend a lot of time with him and he also knew William Butler Yeats in his later life. Hyde and Yeats had great respect for fairy stories and collected many, and as a result of their work those stories remain alive today. Dermot admitted that without the influence of both those men he would not have written this book. In his preface he says that, 'I have written all these stories with entire sincerity, and I am satisfied that they have been given to me in full sincerity. I feel sure they will be read with equal sincerity.'

We feel the same about the stories within this book.

This story came from a friend of Dermot McManus. His name was Mr Martin, a prominent Civil Servant in the east of Ireland until he retired at the general handover after the war. But the experience we are referring to happened when he was a young man. At the time, Mr Martin was in his final year of university at Trinity College Dublin, 1928, and he was at home visiting his father in Derry. It was Easter time and he didn't have long to go before he completed his degree.

There was a river near his father's house and, due to the dry weather, the water was low. The river was known for its trout and so on one of the warm sunny days over Easter he headed off down to try his luck. He liked the idea of relaxing by the water and not having to worry about exams – for the time being anyway. As he was standing on the gravel next to the river he was taking in all the sounds and smells and really was in a peaceful state of mind when something compelled him to look to his right. He could see something black in the distance and when it came nearer he saw that it was some sort of animal. The animal was paddling slowly along in the shallow river. He squinted to make out what it was but wasn't sure – all he knew is that it wasn't small. Was it a large dog, or a panther, maybe? Whatever it was he didn't like the look of it, later describing it as 'intensely menacing'. He started to become fearful and so he dropped his rod right where he was standing and ran to the nearest tree and began to climb up as high as he could. He could get a good view of the animal from way up high and as it passed him by it looked up at him. The animal didn't get any faster or slower, it just maintained

a steady pace, looking up at Mr Martin in the tree. The beast looked at him with almost human intelligence. It bared its teeth with a mixture of a snarl and a jeering grin, its eyes a fearsome, blazing red. The animal was savage and dangerous and Mr Martin was frightened and felt unsafe. He hoped the animal wouldn't attack him but knew if it really wanted to it was well fit to run up that tree and drag him down. He wondered if the animal had escaped from a circus.

A while later, when he felt it safe to climb back down, he did so and collected his rod and ran like the clappers home to his father's house. His father wasn't home so he grabbed his shotgun, loaded it up and went in search of the animal. He knew the community was in danger with that thing on the loose. He asked everyone he met if they had seen the wild beast but they replied no, and soon enough he started to think he had imagined it. When his father returned home later that evening they had a good chat about the animal and neither of them could imagine what it could have been.

The next morning Mr Martin was due back at university and so off he went. He finished his studies a few months later and returned home for the summer. He had forgotten about the wild animal for a few months but when he was back in the countryside he began to wonder whatever came of it. Mr Martin was a smoker and one day as he opened up a new packet of cigarettes he took out a card that came with the pack and couldn't believe what he saw. Right there on the card was the very same animal that he had seen in the river back at Easter time. Underneath the picture were the words 'The Pooka – the great black fairy dog'.

When Dermot MacManus first heard this story, he went in search of a card just like the one Mr Martin found in his cigarette packet many years before. When Dermot finally found one he went back to Mr Martin and showed him the card and asked him: was it the same animal?

'Yes,' he said, 'that is just what I saw, except that it does not show the red eyes or the wicked teeth. It was as tall as a mantelpiece. That picture is so true you'd think it was drawn from life.'

Until Mr Martin returned home that summer and saw the pooka on the card he had no clue what he had encountered. It was a mystery. So he was curious and went about talking to locals and trying to see if anyone else had a similar experience. To his surprise the pooka was quite well known in the area and had been sighted over the years. It was always seen in the glooming, in or by the river. He was told that it was over fifty years since anyone had seen it in daylight. He had no idea whether this was a good thing or not. He left the story behind in Co. Derry because he soon moved abroad to take up a new post. He may have left the story behind but we are sure he thought about it quite a few times over the course of his lifetime.

Co. Donegal: From the Irish *Dún na nGall*, meaning 'Fort of the Foreigners'. It was at one time known as Co. Tyrconnell, from the Irish *Tír Chonaill*, meaning 'Land of Conall'. Co. Donegal is rich in folklore and stories of the Sidhe, from 'Jamie Friel' to 'Balor of the Baleful Eye'. It was in Glencolmcille that St Colmcille held a race to see who would become the 'King of all Birds' after the Dodo had died. The little Wren won by hiding under the Eagle's wing and flying out once the Eagle had exhausted itself, hence becoming the 'King of all Birds'. Tory Island (from the Irish *Tóraidhe*, meaning outlaw or pursuer), off the coast of Donegal, was believed to be the last outpost of the ancient demonic race known as the Formorians. Seumas MacManus (1867–1960), the great Irish folklorist, hailed from Mountcharles. Also the 'Navvy Poet' Patrick MacGill (1889–1963) came from Glenties. He was a great writer and poet and he penned some of the finest Fairy Poetry of the twentieth century. William Allingham (1824–1889), Ireland's most famous 'Fairy Poet', was from Ballyshannon, Co.Donegal.

THE FIDDLER AND THE FEY
(CO. DONEGAL)

This story was originally told by the legendary Donegal fiddler Mickey Doherty (1894–1970) and was passed on to us by another great Donegal fiddler, Domhnall McGinley, from the Irish punk/traditional band The Pox Men.

This was our first introduction to the music and stories of Mickey Doherty. Doherty was a fiddler from a well-known family of Irish Travellers from Donegal. They were also well-respected musicians; his older brother John Doherty (1900–1980) was a renowned fiddler too. Mickey was a true believer in the fairy folk and told stories about how they would give us mortals tunes to play. Some of these tunes are still in existence.

This is a story he told about a man who had an encounter with one of the good folk.

A man lived in Glen Finn and his name was Fearon and he only had one tune. In that time fiddlers were very scarce. If a man back then could play a tune he was appreciated and even idolised. People would look at musicians in amazement.

There was a wedding in the locality and this fiddler was asked to attend and play a few tunes. He was delighted to be asked but sadly he only had one tune and there was no way he would be able to learn something new before the big day.

He sat and pondered over his predicament for a few days, tossed and turned in bed at night, but he knew he would have to decide as to what he would do. The wedding day was approaching and all the neighbours would be there and so he picked up the fiddle and began to play it, but still only the one tune came out. He tried to play others he heard over the years but what he had in his head just wouldn't come out on the fiddle. He was upset and ashamed and thought he would have to tell the wedding party he was ill.

The wedding day came and for some reason he awoke with some courage in his heart. He took a drop of whisky and made off with his fiddle, hoping the mixture of courage and alcohol would see him through the day.

He was walking along the road and as he drew nearer to the house where the wedding was taking place he started to feel his stomach jump a little, as if he'd swallowed a box of tiny frogs. He thought about something nice to take his mind off the task in hand. He was walking down a lonely part of the road – 'a gentle place', he thought. To the old folk a gentle place was one that was 'full of fairies'. His head was bent and he was kicking stones and whistling the only tune he knew. He was a kind old man and he didn't want to refuse the neighbours, so he kept on walking and there in the distance was the house and he could see that

47

people were beginning to gather around the gable. Just as he was about to take a step out popped a wee red-haired man who saluted him. 'Well my young man, are you heading out for a journey?'

'I am,' said the old man. 'I am going to a wedding.'

'I see you play the fiddle – I love that instrument.'

'Aw I play the fiddle in a way,' said the man. 'Aw and I don't play it in another way.'

'Whatever do you mean sir?' said the wee man.

'Well I was asked to play at a neighbours' wedding over beyond that tree and as I walk my courage is failing, for I only know one tune.'

'Show me your fiddle,' said the wee man and he took the fiddle and he tried it out. He didn't play a fancy tune but instead he just ran his fingers over the strings three times, almost like he was checking to see if it worked. He handed the fiddle back with a cheeky grin and a glint in his eye and said, 'Now man you go ahead to that wedding and enjoy yourself. I promise you there will be no one there tonight that can play a fiddle like you.' The old man was a bit wary but thanked the stranger and off he headed.

He arrived to a crowded house and the celebrations were under way and sure he took out his fiddle and to be honest the crowd were as nervous for both him and themselves because they knew as well as he did that he only knew one tune. Settling into their seats the crowd made themselves comfortable and ready to hear the same tune they had heard from him for many years. 'Ah here we go again,' they thought and sure you couldn't offend such a kind-hearted man so they smiled and give him their support.

But when he picked up that fiddle to play his fingers worked a kind of magic we don't see every day. The crowd and the old man himself were beyond shocked because he was the best fiddle player they had ever heard. They must have been thinking he had practised since the last time he played for them. He played over a hundred tunes, never getting tired or bored in himself. He was loving the music and the crowd were shouting for more. The roof nearly came off the house.

After the wedding he walked home along the same road, looking out for the wee man to thank him, for whatever he did to that fiddle it sure made him the best fiddler in all the land and not to mention the most popular man for miles around. The whole place far and wide were talking about him.

Years had passed and he spent many happy times playing for pleasure and for friends. But one day he took sick and was confined to bed, and the old fiddle was hung on the wall above him. The day came when he passed on and the moment he died the family heard a crack on the wall and the fiddle smashed into a hundred bits.

It's believed the fairies did that – they didn't want anyone else to get their hands on that fiddle. The red-haired man he met on the way to the wedding many years before enchanted him and gave him the gift of playing the fiddle. Before the wee man left him on that magical day he whispered in his ear, 'You will be the best fiddle player in this land.' He was right. The man was never forgotten.

Co. Down: From the Irish *An Dún*, meaning 'The Fort'. Down is a mysterious county full of wild beauty, legend and folklore. Ireland's patron saint, St Patrick, is buried in Downpatrick. This county has a great number of ancient dolmens (megalithic tombs). Outside Finnis is the Legananny Dolmen, one of the finest in Ulster; the area that surrounds it is scattered with magnificent fairy forts and fairy trees. The ghost of the diabolical Squire Hawkins still haunts the grounds of Drumballyroney church, where Patrick Brontë (father of the Brontë sisters) once taught. On the old road from Rathfriland to Poyntzpass stands Bonnety's Bridge, which is guarded by a fairy called Bonnety, who wore a huge bonnet on her head. The great folklorist Dr Francis McPolin (1897–1974) hailed from Hilltown in Co. Down; he dedicated many years of his life collecting and archiving folk and fairy stories from his native Hilltown and other parts of the county.

BILLY AND THE CHANGELING
OF GLASCAR (CO. DOWN)

Come away, O human child!
To the waters and the wild
With a faery, hand in hand.
For the world's more full of weeping,
Than you can understand.

(From 'The Stolen Child' by William Butler Yeats, 1889)

This beautiful and melancholic tale was first recorded by the Revd J.B. Lusk of Glascar, Co. Down, in 1925. This story features in Steve's collection *Down Folk Tales*, which is also published by The History Press Ireland. Steve had the privilege of finding this story deep in the archives of Co. Down's rich folk history.

Over 200 years ago the desire for news, gossip and stories was as strong as it is today, but for the majority of the people living in and around Glascar in Co. Down, there were neither newspapers nor novels available. Even if they did obtain such items, the ability to read evaded most of the population. So how did they gain knowledge of the world around them? It is hard to imagine in today's culture but information and news was supplied by the beggars who travelled the country roads. Beggars were a common sight, even before the Famine, as ordinary folk were dependent for their food supply from their own harvests; in bad seasons many were driven by the fear of starvation to beg for a living. Few who took to the roads returned to the humdrum ways of hard, loveless labour. What they at first looked on as a curse they came to regard it as a blessing in disguise. At every home, with few exceptions, beggars received a handful of oatmeal or a few spuds. They carried only their beds with them, consisting of a pair of blankets and a quilt.

These beggars were made welcome to a night's lodging in any of the more modest, less affluent homes. They paid for their accommodation by the news they related, news they had gathered on their wide travels, the songs and ballads they collected and, of course, wondrous stories. Indeed, their arrival was looked forward to by young and old. Some of the beggars saw themselves as entertainers, some even as celebrities, and felt that houses and homes had been honoured by their company.

According to Revd Lusk, by the end of the eighteenth century the recognised chief celebrity of this ragged fraternity was Billy the Beggar-man. Billy occasionally visited the Glasgar neighbourhood and Lusk states that his visits were like a royal progress, in which he received the homage of his subjects and the offerings of his admirers. His sophistication and elegance were the wonder and envy of many and, like today's pop culture where young people try to emulate their favourite rock star or actor, the younger generation at the time wished to imitate him.

According to this illustrious vagabond, there were few countries in the world where he had not fought and fewer still that he had not visited. When asked how foreigners spoke, which was always a great subject of curiosity, he would reply, 'Some make a kind of rumblin' noise and others make a sound like cats spittin.' And not to mention the wild beasts, strange creatures and terrible monsters he encountered – and he had scars to prove it. He had a grand, majestic manner about him, like some hobo monarch, but was described as being a big, affable, kind, jolly, hairy-faced man with a powerful voice and grand company to be in.

Unlike his peers, he visited only the more respectable houses, but on the rare occasion where lady luck was not smiling on him, he went to men of low estate. His method of breaking new ground was to stop some yards from the door of the abode and chant this piece of his own composition:

> Pity kind gentle folk, friends of humanity;
> Cold blows the wind and the night's coming on;
> Spare me some food for my mother and charity;
> Spare me some food and bid me be gone.

The reference to his mother is either for the sake of rhyme or some class of poetic licence as he always travelled alone.

Lusk speaks of a very old man named Jimmie he knew when he was a young man, who claimed to have heard some of Billy's stories during his boyhood. One might think that the story was told to rattle a young and innocent minister arriving in a new parish, but Lusk states the old man showed all the signs that he believed every word of it. And the old man told the story with such conviction and zeal that the tale had stayed with

Lusk all his days. This is the story about Billy the Beggar-man and the Changeling of Glascar.

Early one cold and windy morning in December, one of the local lads of Glascar was startled to see Billy the Beggar-man running towards him out of the woods, like a man possessed.

'Oh Jimmie,' cried Billy, 'I got the most desperate scare I ever got in my life and if ye listen I'll tell you, but you must never tell it to another man or mortal.'

Billy had been on his rounds over in the Ballynafern side and had called to a house with 'decent folk'. They gave him two good handfuls of meal and wee bit of bacon. As he was leaving the master gave him a kind of half wink and told him he could get him something that would warm his heart on this cold night. He knew a man not far from there who was making a drop of the rare auld mountain dew 'Poteen' and would give Billy a dram on his account.

The man brought Billy to a wee sod house. Inside a man was working a still. The brewer gave Billy a mug-full of the stuff and said, 'No clash o' this in the country, and what's more you need never show your nose in this side again or you'll get me in trouble.'

'Oh you can trust Billy,' replied the man who brought him in.

Well they had a great time taking a sup of the good stuff and before Billy knew it was coming up on eleven o'clock. Although the company was good and the drink was flowing, Billy had the sense to make his excuses to leave.

He decided to take the higher ground and come around by the west, as there had been a lot of rain and the river down in the glen would have been too difficult and dangerous to cross in the dark.

When he got up to Ballynaskeag Hill it was a grand night. There was a touch of frost and Billy knew this by the throbbin' and the leppin' o' the stars, and the mist that lay like dark loughs in the hollows.

Billy was in no hurry; the sights and sounds were wondrous all around him. As Billy later explained himself, 'I was feelin' comfortable and content, indeed sometimes the stars was whirlin' round me, and I sat down once or twice to look at them.' But with all Billy's stargazing he missed his turning for Glascar and it wasn't long before he found himself lost.

After a time he came to a big hedge and he figured that his right road was on the other side of it. He decided that his best course of action

would be to jump over the hedge, rather than lose himself further by following it to its end and going around it. So he proceeded to climb the hedge, which was not an easy task in the dark and under the influence of strong alcohol. When he got to the top he grabbed a branch to steady himself. As he lowered himself over the other side the branch gave way and Billy landed heavily on his back, hitting his head on something hard. The last thing he remembered was rolling down into a deep hollow and then everything went black.

How long he lay there he couldn't tell, but when he came to he could not move either his hands or his feet, it was as though he was tied down with threads. It also appeared that he must have grown miles and miles in length for it seemed to him that his head was resting up against Glascar Hill like a pillow and his feet were laying a few miles away down in Loughbricland. After a while he felt that he was swelling up, rising upwards towards the stars as though he would eventually fill the whole world.

Whilst he was lying there pondering all of this, the most beautiful music he had ever heard started playing all around him. It sounded like flutes and fiddles with birds singing in between. 'Oh! It would have wiled the heart out of ye,' said Billy to Jimmie. 'I opened my eyes, and there was a light all about me like a lot o' candles seen through thin paper. I saw then where I was and my heart stood still for a minute, and then it raced like a gallopin' horse. I was that scared I must have fainted for a bit. Well Jimmie, there I was on top of Derrydrummuck fort, and I swear on my soul, the fairies were out at their diversions. If I had been outside the ring all the chains in Ireland wouldn't have held me.'

Billy explained to Jimmie that if you are outside a fairy ring when you hear the music, you're safe enough, but if you're inside they can do what they like with you. So there he was inside the ring and there was nothing he could do except lie there and look on.

After a while the fear left Billy and he figured that they would not hurt him, sure what would they want with a poor beggar man who never harmed anybody? He lay there gazing around and saw a hole in the far side of the ring that he hadn't noticed before. As he looked at it, out trooped a whole host of wee men. They came out like bees from a hive. The men were about 2 feet tall, and they wore cocked hats of all colours and green or dark-coloured coats with long tails and pockets and long waistcoats with gold buttons. They had white knee-breeches and blue stockings, and shoes with silver buckles. The lassies were hardly as big as the men; they had beautiful shoes that shone like gold and wide skirts that came down to their ankles and bodices that were laced across with coloured ribbons. Around their shoulders they had shawls of lace that glistened, as they had been laid out in the frost. Their hair was piled up on top of their heads, and when they turned their heads it looked as if a lot of wee stars had got mixed up in their hair.

Last of all came a girl that looked younger than any of them, maybe 5 or 6 years old, but she was of enormous size. She was dressed like the rest, but she had a long rod in her hand with a light at the top of it that shone one minute green, then yellow, then blue and red. She gave it a wave and they all made a ring around her and began to dance. It was a breathtaking sight, all the wee crathurs circling round her, keeping time to the music and dancing as light as feathers. As they danced they sang a song that went like this:

> By the sheen of the stars
> By the light of the moon
> Under these our rights are done.
> The still night and muffled streams
> Gleaming frost and whitened earth
> O! These are for our mirth.
>
> Hence! Ye earth-born mortals, hence!
> Come not near our wonted haunts
> Taint ye not our ancient homes!

Then Billy saw one of them lifting up his hand and suddenly they all stopped. In a powerful voice for such a small creature the wee man shouted, 'Our gentle thorn is injured – look! And see what has per-formed this heinous act.'

They rushed over to where Billy was lying. The fear came back on him like a wave and he began to gasp as if he were drowning. As they gathered around him they let out a terrible screech that turned Billy's blood to ice.

Billy knew well enough not to open his mouth until he was spoken to, for if you speak to the fairies before they speak to you, you'll never speak again. The one who stopped the dance stepped up to him and said, 'Rash mortal, why do you dare disturb us?'

Billy tried to explain how he had got lost and meant them no harm or disturbance.

With that, one of the fairies rushed forward crying, 'O King! It is he who has broken our gentle thorn.'

The wee man, whom Billy had just learnt was their king, looked at him severely, then raised his hand and shouted, 'Punish him!' With that, the rest of them pointed their fingers at Billy and wherever they pointed an agonising pain surged though his body. Every bone in his body felt like it was being wrenched out of its socket. This seemed to last for an awful long time, and he thought he could take no more, as he said to Jimmie, 'I gave a groan, thinkin' I was departin'.' But just when Billy was about to give up hope of survival the big lass came up near him and cried out, 'Oh King, I must speak to him!'

'No, no,' replied the king.

'Oh I must,' the girl implored.

The king relented and told the girl she could have a wee while, but mustn't be long. With that they all scuttled back into the hole and the girl sat down on the grass beside him. She put out her hand and touched him, and instantly all pain left his body. He looked at her with gratitude – she was just a child, but she spoke as well as an educated adult.

The girl asked him what had brought him there and he explained that he had got lost and did not realise he was so close to the fort, let alone a fairy ring.

'Did you come here to spy on the fairies?' asked the child. 'Tell the truth, it will serve you best.' Billy swore on the Bible and the 'Question Book' that he was no spy. When he mentioned the 'Question Book' he saw that the child believed him. She asked Billy if he had any children and he told he her had none, 'What would a poor beggar-man be doing with children?' he asked.

The girl seemed saddened by this and said it was a pity as she would have liked to talk about the children. She told Billy that he should not have come to this place, but she was glad that he did.

'Who are you child?' asked Billy, bewildered.

'I am a changeling,' she explained. 'You see, when I was a wee baby the fairies saw that I was going to be badly treated all my life and have an awful hard time, so they stole me from my mother and father and left some wicked creature in my place that caused them awful bother and then left when there was nothing left to take. I can see you're wondering how I know, and think I couldn't remember such a thing. Babies that stay with humans forget as they grow older, but babies that come to Fairyland remember everything. I remember how they petted me and cared for me, though it's so very long ago. Babies that come here never grow bigger than I am now. I have had a beautiful time here.

'I can go where I like and often play with children among you, though they don't see me and don't know that I am with them. I make every-thing go wrong for bad-tempered and peevish and cruel children. They fall and hurt their heads, bite their tongues, and the really bad ones I frighten in their sleep. But the good-natured ones, who try to help others, I make contented and happy, and when they are asleep I bring them to Fairyland and show them the beautiful things I have. I tell the fairies to help the grown-up people who are generous and kind with their work and to watch over their homes and protect them from all harm and evil spirits. But I plague the ungenerous, unthankful and unkind. I open the gaps and make their cattle stray, I make their watchdogs sleep and I send rats and mice into their haystacks and houses. I have such powers to help and hinder the good and bad of this world, but I sometimes miss talking to those who know nothing about Fairyland and tell them all about it, as I am talking to you now.'

The changeling explained to Billy that the fairies didn't like her talk-ing to other humans in case she decided to leave them. But she said she would never leave, and wouldn't go back even if she could.

'What will they do with me?' asked the poor beggar man as he heard the trooping fairies returning.

'They hate anyone who spies on them or who digs about a fort, and they will always punish them. But they always keep a changeling like me who understands something about humans; for fear that they should become harsh and cruel and punish mortals too severely. I will speak to the king on your behalf and you must do what I bid you, or something terrible will happen to you. If he says "Be gone", make a mighty effort, though you may think that you are tied down, and jump to your feet and run for your life. Don't under any circumstances look behind you and never go near the fort again as long as you live.'

Well Billy took everything in and thanked the changeling profusely for her clemency. Within seconds the fairies were all about him. He could see the changeling speaking to the king, but he could not make out what was being said.

Suddenly the king stepped up towards him and shouted 'Be gone!'

With all his strength, and although it was agony, Billy leapt to his feet and took to his heels. He didn't care about the ditches and hedges but just tore over and through them. They were after him like a swarm of bees, prodding him all over with tiny spears. From the corner of his eye Billy could see one wee ruffian driving a spear into his hip joint. He could have easily walloped him across the head but his fear and prudence made him think it wiser to do nothing except run. He only stopped when he came across wee Jimmie, out of breath and out of his mind.

Well some years later Billy the Beggar-Man passed on and many of his stories went with him and are now lost. Some of the old-timers say that his ghost can be seen on a certain night of the year at the fort, sitting on a rock with a ring of little lights dotted around him, telling stories and singing songs, and that there can be heard the sound of a wee child's laughter. But if you ever witness this for yourself do not get too close; instead make a wish, keep it to yourself and quietly go on about your business.

Co. Fermanagh: from the Irish: *Fir Manach* or *Fear Manach*, meaning 'Men of Manach'. Fermanagh is a county steeped in ancient history and myth. On Boa Island (named after Badb, the Irish Goddess of War), off the coastline of Lower Lough Erne, stand two carved stone statues. One is the Janus Figure, which stands 3 foot tall and has two figures standing back-to-back, the other is the Lustymore Man, who was moved to Boa in 1939. They are believed to have been carved between AD 400–800 and are meant to have been based on ancient Celtic Gods. In the townland of Drumco stands Crom Cruach, a large standing stone that represents the ancient Celtic God *Crom Cróich*, meaning the Bloody Crooked One'; he was a cruel God more feared than revered and was appeased with human sacrifice. The award-winning folklorist and collector of fairy stories Eddie Anderson (1897–1960) was from Corragun, Kinawley in Co. Fermanagh.

WEE MEG BARNILEG AND THE FAIRIES
(CO. FERMANAGH)

This great tale about a mischievous little girl who was taught a lesson by the fairies was given to us by the Co. Down storyteller Doreen McBride. She first heard it in New York City, being told it by her friend Sharon Saluzzo. She was surprised to hear that it was from Co. Fermanagh and that she had never heard it before. The story was originally collected by the great American storyteller Ruth Sawyer (1880–1970) in her book *The Way of the Storyteller*. According to Saluzzo, Sawyer had a nursemaid called Johanna, who had emigrated from Ireland and brought her stories with her.

Sawyer was a magnificent storyteller and the children's literature expert Mary Hill Arbuthnot said of her, 'There is no one else who can relate Irish stories as she does.' This a fine example of one of those stories written using the authentic local dialect – so here it is, the cautionary tale of Wee Meg Barnileg and the fairy folk.

A long time ago a rich farmer and his wife lived beside Lough Erne in Co. Fermanagh. They were a kindly, good-hearted pair who had one daughter, a wee terror called Meg. She was spoilt rotten. Whatever she wanted, she got. Her parents doted on her and as far as they were concerned she could do no wrong. Wherever they went they took Meg with them, to fairs, weddings, wakes and festivals, and she was guaranteed to behave badly. The neighbours hated to see them coming because she was a destructive child who would smash your best china and it was said she had a tongue fit for clipping hedges. When she went visiting she'd stand in the middle of the floor and look around, then turn to her mother and make comments such as, 'Do you see they've still got them old torn lace curtains at the window. Thon chair still has a broken leg and look at that – the dirt from the floor's been brushed into the corner under yon brush! Thon's a disgrace.' She was even worse at a wake, passing remarks such as, 'Listen till auld Aggie coughing her head off. Another clean shirt'll do her. I'll bet hers is the next wake we'll be enjoying. She's got consumption, so she has.' And when not encouraging people into the grave she'd say things like, 'Didn't Barney Gallagher say before he died that Barney Maguire was the meanest man in the whole of Ireland? I remember father telling mother he'd rather strike a bargain with the auld Devil himself than with him. Do ye remember saying yon Father?'

When Meg wasn't pestering the neighbours, she was pestering animals. She took delight in pulling the cat's tail and whiskers, in beating dogs with sticks, pulling feathers out of chickens and the wings off flies. She was a terror who had her poor mother worn to the bone. Her mother was a fussy woman, who took pride in her tidy house and well-dressed family. She spent her days cleaning up after Meg, who trailed mud into the house and went through clothes like a dose of salts. She was a genius for becoming covered in dirt and tearing dresses. Every night her poor mother sat mending and sewing by candlelight. Meg often refused to eat what was set in front of her. 'I can't stomach that rubbish!' she'd shout, before throwing perfectly good food on the floor. Her mother's soft voice was often heard wheedling, 'Meg, darling, tell me what you'd like to eat? You've got to keep your strength up. Please put that bowl down before you break it and stop annoying the dog. Now come on, be a good girl and your Da will take you to the shop and buy you some sweeties.'

In other words, Meg's mother, without meaning to, encouraged her to behave badly. The neighbours said, 'It's a disgrace what thon wean puts her mother through, and her such a nice, gentle woman.'

One day Meg's mother decided to take Meg next door to the neighbouring farm to borrow a bowl of sugar. When the farmer's wife saw them coming she let out a cry that could have been heard over the whole of Ireland. 'Bless us! Here comes Meg. Quick, hide the new butter crock in the loft, put the best platter under the bed. Tie the pig in the byre, hide the hens' eggs in the churn and pray to the Holy Virgin we survive with nothing broken.'

Meg came into the house and looked around. 'Mother,' she said, 'do you see auld granny sitting in the corner there. She looks greyer than ever. I'll bet she's not long for this world. She'll soon be pushing up the daisies. Just look at thon boil she has on her eyelid! Have you ever seen anything so ugly? And do you see they've still got that old faded rug on her knee – they mustn't be doing too well or they'd get her a nice new one.'

Meg ran around the kitchen like a wild thing. When a hen walked in through the open door, she kicked it and the poor thing squawked and rushed back outside. Old Jack, the gentlest dog in the whole of Fermanagh, lay asleep in the street outside. Meg kicked him awake. Jack groaned, stood up and wagged his tail. Meg pulled his whiskers. Then she began to tease him by holding a bar of chocolate out and jerking it away as he went to eat it. Eventually Jack accidentally bit her and she went off like a siren before running back into the house screaming, 'Old Jack bit me! Old Jack bit me! He should be shot, so he should. He's a dangerous dog.' She climbed on to her mother's knee and sobbed.

'There, there,' comforted her mother. 'Let me kiss you better. My poor wee darling! Did that nasty dog hurt you? You're right, he should be shot for biting my wee sweetheart.'

The farmer was attracted by the commotion and came into the kitchen. 'That child should be shot, not Jack,' he said firmly. 'Jack's the gentlest dog in the whole of Fermanagh, if not in the whole of Ireland. That child's a cruel wee brat. If Jack bit her she deserved it.'

Meg peeped through her fingers. The farmer looked very angry. He scowled at her. Would he really shoot her, she wondered? She felt uneasy and sat quietly on her mother's knee, then, when nobody was looking, she slithered down and sneaked out through the open door. 'That nasty old farmer'll never catch me!' she chortled as she struggled through a hole in the hedge and into the field. She ran and ran, aiming to get as far away from the house as possible. Eventually, after running through several fields, she saw men making hay. She watched for a few minutes before going to hide behind a haystack. She found their food in a pail covered with a dish in the shade there. She felt hungry and devoured everything she fancied. She threw the rest of the food on the ground before stopping and thinking, 'Maybe the men'll be angry when they see I've eaten their lunch. Perhaps they'll help the farmer catch and shoot me. Maybe I'd better hide.' She went into another field, found another haystack and sat down behind it. The sun was very warm, Meg had had a lot of exercise. The drowsy sound of bees humming as they collected honey made her feel sleepy. She closed her eyes and fell into a deep slumber. The men finished their work, went home to milk their cows, the sun set, bats flitted against the moon and Meg woke up with a start. She heard tinkling voices and felt confused. Who was there? Where was she? What had happened to her? She peeped round in the direction of the voices and saw a troop of fairies dressed in green jackets and red hats and dragging small rakes. A small voice complained, 'That terrible child's a blithering nuisance scattering hay like this. We'll never get the place ready in time to have a decent dance before dawn.'

'Somebody should teach her a few manners,' scolded another. 'Yes, and to be more thoughtful. I hate the way she wastes food and do you see how she destroys clothes. She has her poor mother worn to the bone what with cleaning and washing and ironing and mending. It's a crying shame. I hope we catch her some night and have a chance to knock some sense into her. Ye'll see! We'll teach her a lesson she won't forget!'

Any other child would have been frightened to hear such a conversation, but not Meg. She was used to having her own way and getting into the middle of everything. 'What can those silly wee fairy men do?' she thought. 'They're old and feeble. I'm bigger and stronger than they are. I'll teach them a lesson. I'll knock them down like ninepins before I go home,' and with that she jumped out from behind the haystack. 'Come on!' she shouted. 'Who's going to teach me a lesson? You and what army?' She ran around knocking the melt out of the fairies and laughing her head off.

The night suddenly became very silent. The wee men didn't say a word. They just looked solemnly and quietly at Meg. Then one shouted, 'Make the fairy ring! Make the fairy ring! Fairies dance and fairies sing!' The wee men quickly formed a ring round Meg and began to dance, their tiny feet weaving complicated patterns on the green, green grass. Meg felt confused. The fairies moved so quickly they appeared like a blur. She couldn't see one to catch. They raised their small voices in song. It was a lovely tune but somehow threatening.

Ring, ring in a Fairy Ring, Fairies dance and Fairies sing.
Round, round on soft green ground, never a sound, never a sound.
Sway, sway as the grasses sway, down by the lough at the dawn of day.
Circle about as we leap and spring, Fairy men in a Fairy Ring.
Light on your toe, light on your heel, one by one in a merry, merry reel.
Fingers touching, fingers so round and round and round we go!

When the song was finished the wee men clapped their hands, kicked their heels and spun round like a hundred green spinning tops. Then they shouted, 'Move hand or foot if ye can wee Meg Barnileg.' Meg found she couldn't move a muscle. 'Open your mouth and come out with some of those fine statements you're famous for making,' jeered the fairies. Meg opened her mouth to scream and found her tongue was stuck against the roof of her mouth. She couldn't even squeak! 'Now have a look at your substitute,' the fairies laughed. 'He'll make a fine changeling.' With that the fairies went and brought out the ugliest wee man you could imagine. Meg was horrified. She'd heard of changelings but hadn't believed such things existed. She felt sick as she watched the fairies weave a spell. In the wink of an eye the ugly wee man grew and grew until he was the spitting image of Meg: face, hair, dress, boots, the lot. He stretched out in the hollow where Meg had been lying and was fast asleep before you could say 'Jack Robinson!'

'Now,' shouted the wee men, 'it's time to take you below.' A hundred pairs of fairy hands grabbed her, carried her over to a fairy thorn and threw her up in the air. Suddenly she was falling, falling, falling, down, down, down through a dark hole until she tumbled at the bottom onto a pile of soft leaves. She looked around and found she was at the heart of a fairy mound or fort. A soft light shone from what looked like thousands of glow worms hanging from the walls and ceiling. The place was beautiful but the floor was filthy, covered in scraps of food.

'You dirty clarts,' shouted Meg. 'If you'd any sense you'd keep this place clean and tidy the way my mother does at home!' The fairies laughed heartily. 'Meg,' said their leader, 'that's all the food you've wasted in your life. Here's a rake. Brush it up. Eat it when you're hungry.'

'No! No! No!' yelled Meg, stamping her foot in rage. 'I'll never eat that rubbish. I'm hungry. I want a drink of milk and a piece of currant cake.'

'Tough luck,' said the fairy leader firmly. 'You can't have anything fresh while all that wasted food lies uneaten. The quicker you eat it the quicker you'll have something fresh. It's up to you. You may starve if you choose. Here's the rake. Tidy the floor. Come on, get moving! We can't dance on it the way it is.'

So Meg found herself with a rake in her hands. The floor was covered as far as the eye could see with cold spuds, bits of wheaten bread, lumps of stir-a-bout, soda farls, potato bread, crumbs of cake, half-eaten apples and whatnot. She raked the largest pieces into a corner and swept the smallest into tidy piles. She worked and worked until she was exhausted. Every joint in her body ached and she grew hungrier and hungrier. 'My belly thinks my throat's cut,' she yelled. 'If you're going to force me to work like a slave for ye, ye could at least have the manners to bring me something to eat.' The fairies laughed. 'You've wasted all that good food and we've told you that we'll not give you a morsel until you use what you've wasted.' In the end Meg was forced, by hunger, to eat her own leavings. At last, weeks later, she'd finished her task and was given a piece of fresh bread and a drink of milk. It tasted wonderful and she vowed she'd never waste food again!

'Now, we've another wee job for you,' said a fairy as he led her into another wide, open underground space. It was cluttered with dirty, torn dresses, every stitch she'd ever worn since she could first crawl around the floor. Meg looked about her, kicked one of her dresses and snarled, 'What do you want me to do with this lot?'

'Wash, iron and mend your clothes. You had your poor mother worn to a frazzle running around after you.'

'I won't!' yelled Meg. 'I won't! I won't! I won't!' She stamped her feet and stuck her tongue out as far as if would go.

'Meg,' said the wee man quietly. 'It's up to you. We can wait a thousand years for you to make amends.' And with that he disappeared. Meg walked around in a temper, kicking clothes, banging walls with her fists and saying bad words. She threw herself on the ground and had a temper tantrum. Nobody came near her and she began to feel foolish. She picked herself up and thought, 'Maybe I should start washing, ironing and mending. At least it'd be something to do.'

The minute that thought crossed her mind an old fairy woman appeared, took her over to a wash tub and showed her how to wash clothes. Meg began to scrub her dirty dresses. Her hands became red and sore as she washed and scrubbed. Then she had to starch and iron them. The iron was heavy and very hot and she burnt herself several times. She hated mending. It was a boring job and the task seemed unending. The fairies were not sympathetic. 'Think of the trouble you gave your poor mother,' they said. 'Now that you're here she has peace and quiet to rest and the neighbours are enjoying life for the first time in years!'

At last Meg finished the task and the fairies took her into a large space filled with the ugliest plants she'd ever seen. They looked like nettles with the thorns of a thistle. Every now and then there was a pretty flower. 'What's all that about?' asked Meg.

'Those weeds are all the nasty words you have ever spoken. You must pull them out and put them over there on the compost heap.'

'I won't!' yelled Meg. 'I won't! I won't! I won't!' Immediately three large ugly plants appeared at her feet.

'You were shouting,' said a fairy. 'You must learn to guard your tongue or you'll never finish this task.' Meg looked around her. Had she really been that nasty? 'What are those pretty flowers?' she asked. The fairy smiled. 'Sometimes you made a mistake and said something pleasant like telling your mother you loved her. They're all the nice words you have ever spoken.' Meg felt ashamed for the first time in her life. Had she really said so few nice things and been so nasty? She got down on her knees and began weeding. It was a terrible job. The stings caused her hands to become swollen, her knees felt like two red lumps of burning turf, her back ached, her joints became sore and she learnt to control her tongue. Every time she said something nasty another ugly weed appeared. She began playing games with the space. When a fairy appeared, she said something pleasant and watched as pretty flowers grew. At last she was finished. She looked around her and for the first time since she'd gone to live with the fairies she felt happy. The room looked really pretty with all those beautiful flowers. She lifted her skirts and began to dance with joy. fairies love dancing and when they saw Meg bending and swaying like a flower and pointing her toes so nicely they clapped their hands and cheered.

'Meg,' they asked, 'would you like to come above ground tonight and dance with us by the light of the silver moon?'

'I'd love to,' said Meg. That night, for the first time in a year, Meg smelt new-cut hay and fragrant roses blooming round cottage doors. She felt a soft balmy breeze caressing her cheek and saw the green grass under her feet. It was wonderful. Then she remembered her mother had once said, 'Anyone taken by the fairies can escape by finding a four-leafed clover and wishing to go home.' Meg lifted her skirt and began to dance, taking every chance possible to bend low and look for a four-leafed clover, but to no avail. She became very homesick and her heart was in despair as the moon sank behind the mountains, then she saw it outlined against her shiny, black patent shoe. A lucky-four leafed clover!

'Look!' she shouted in delight, as she held it up. 'Look what I've found! I can have a wish! I wish I was at home!' With that she woke up in her own wee bed with her mother sitting beside her.

'Mother,' cried Meg, 'I hope they didn't shoot the dog. He'd never have bitten me if I hadn't tortured the life out of him.'

Her mother looked at her in astonishment. 'Meg,' she said, 'you don't sound like yourself. What happened to you? We found you fast asleep behind a haystack in Nobel's field. That was a year ago today.' Meg explained how she had been captured by the fairies and how they had taught her to behave herself.

From that day until the day she died Meg was a changed person. She was thoughtful, kind and gentle. She helped her mother tidy up, kept a civil tongue in her head and ate everything put before her. When she grew up she got married and had seventeen children. Today, if you walk along the banks of Lough Erne and see a well-behaved child, the neighbours will probably tell you, 'That child is the great-great-great grandchild of wee Meg Barnileg.'

Co. Monaghan: From the Irish *Mhuineacháin*, meaning 'Hilly Land' or 'Place of Little Hills'. Co. Monaghan is a county full of stories and folklore. It is home to the 'Graveyard Bride' who lurks in the cemetery of Errigal Truagh, looking for a groom to take to her grave. There is a banshee that still haunts the ruins of Rossmore Castle' Énrí Ó Muirgheasa (Henry Morris) (1874–1945), the writer and folklorist, was born in Castle East, Donaghmoyne. The Giant's Grave in Corlealackagh is an ancient cairn, which is also a beautiful example of a fairy fort. This county is also the home of one of Ireland's greatest poets, Patrick Kavanagh (1904–1967), who was a master at turning the mundane and ordinary into the mythical and extraordinary.

JOHNNY MCKENNA AND THE KING OF THE FAIRIES (CO. MONAGHAN)

Whilst travelling around Co. Monaghan I met many people and these people told me all sorts of wonderful stories about the fairy folk and what they get up to. I am delighted to tell you this one, the bare bones of which I got from an anonymous writer for the 2005 *Tydavenet Journal*. This story can also be found in *Monaghan Folk Tales* by Steve Lally.

Tydavnet, Co. Monaghan, was always well known for its 'Dealin' Men' or 'Wide Boys'; in other words men that knew how to buy and sell everything and anything, and always get a good price.

Now Johnny McKenna was one of these Dealin' Men and he was one of the best and he claimed to only ever work with the best of stock and breed. But he was also known to dabble with lesser stock to cater for the less affluent clients, for a sale was a sale after all and Johnny would travel to all the Fairs and Marts in Monaghan and the surrounding counties to get what he was looking for.

Well it so happened that the Parish Priest was looking for a new pony (as this was a long time ago before we had motor cars or buses and maybe even trains). So when Johnny heard about this he wasted no time at all – he set out on foot for the Fair of Fintona in Co. Tyrone.

When the bold Johnny got to the Fair in Fintona, all the good stock had gone and there was nothing that caught his eye so he decided to cut his losses and head for home again. On the way back he met a wee man who told him of a great shortcut over the mountain. Now anyone who knows anything about wee men and shortcuts will tell you to avoid such advice and stick to the road that they know themselves.

The wee man told him if he took this shortcut it would save him 8 or 9 miles on his journey. Now anyone who knows anything about walking long distances will agree that this is a massive saving indeed. Well, Johnny decided to take the shortcut and it was not long before he found himself lost; there he was, gone astray over the mountain not knowing if he was coming or going.

Well now poor Johnny must have been wandering about the lonely, dark and winding mountain roads for over half the night, when all of a sudden he saw a light in the distance. Now he was relieved to see this beacon of hope and he wasted no time making his way towards it.

As he got closer to the light he soon realised that it was coming from a wee cottage, thatched with heather and no more than about 4 feet high. It was a strange-looking little building but Johnny was glad to be outside of it and not wandering aimlessly around the mountain. Johnny knocked on the wee half-door and an old woman answered by opening the door and poking her withered face out at him.

'Who are ye?' asked the old woman in a shrill voice.

Johnny answered by stating, 'I am a poor man who is off his pad.'

'Come in,' says the auld one.

Well, Johnny stooped down and nearly had to crawl into the house. Well, he got the fright of his life for right before him lying on the floor of the old shack were dead sheep. Now Johnny gasped and let out a bit of a shout.

'Hould your whist and speak easy!' growled the old woman, and went on to explain her anxiety. 'I am afraid that the men will hear and they might come in. They are a bad lot and the work they do – I don't like it one bit, they are stealing sheep and killing them!' She then pointed towards the back of the house and said, 'Now go down to the room there, there's a bed there where you can rest yourself.'

Well poor Johnny made his way down the hall to the room and he was bewildered at how big the house was inside, for outside it was nothing more than a tiny hovel. Johnny opened the door to the room and was surprised to find it to be a fine big room with a very large and comfortable bed in it. Well he lay down and rested his weary bones on the soft feathered mattress. Now he was not long in the bed when he heard a loud knock on the front door coming up the hallway. He sat up and could hear the old woman say, 'Speak easy, for there is a man down in the room and he is trying to get a bit of rest.' Johnny was terrified, for he knew she was talking to the terrible sheep-stealers and he knew such men would not be happy to think that there was a stranger in the house who knew of their dealings and would make sure he would not tell anyone of their existence.

Well Johnny's fears were confirmed for a gruff male voice replied to the old woman, 'He won't be long in it!' and Johnny heard the sharpening of a knife. He jumped up from the bed and out of the open window. He was only out the window when three men came down to the room. When they saw him, they were hot on his trail as they bounded out the window like wild dogs after him. As he ran for his life, Johnny eventually came to a big river. He got in under the banks and when the men reached the river they searched up and down, poking the riverbanks with knives and sticks and whooping and howling like wolves.

Then Johnny heard one of them speak. 'Hey, didn't I tell you, the thief is away with the flood.'

Johnny stayed under the riverbank for two long hours when out came a wee man about 2 feet high on the bank opposite. He looked at Johnny with great puzzlement and called out, 'Well now, what happened you?'

'I have been out all night and what a terrible night it has been, I was nearly murdered!' cried out Johnny. Then the moonlight shone on the river, revealing a footstick, which is a makeshift bridge made from a log thrown across the river. The wee man crossed the footstick to where Johnny was and took him back over to his side. He asked Johnny if

he was hungry and Johnny replied that he was starving and the wee man produced a loaf of wheaten bread and a jug of fresh buttermilk, of which Johhny was very grateful for and he consumed them with great haste and appreciation. The food made him feel powerful, giving him the strength of two men. The wee man then produced a whistle, which he blew with great ferocity, and as soon as he did, two magnificent horses (the likes of which he had never seen in all his years as a Dealin' Man) wearing fine saddles and bridles appeared out of nowhere. The wee man mounted one of these beasts and told Johnny to get on the other, which he did. 'Watch yourself now!' said the wee man, 'for we have very rough and dangerous roads before us.'

Well the horses galloped like the wind for a couple of hours until Johnny found himself in the Bog of Allen. The atmosphere was strange and haunting; although he knew that the horses were walking on the soft peat of the bog, the sound of their hooves was one of clattering as though they were trotting along a hard and stony road, and above his head flew flocks of wild geese in their thousands; the sky was black with them like swarms of giant midges.

It seemed like an awful long time that they trotted and galloped through the haunted bog, but eventually they came out of it and Johnny saw before him a mighty plain covered in thick snow. But before he had a chance to admire this beautiful sight before him, he found himself galloping across a wide and magnificent lough. The horses galloped across it as if it were a broad highway. When they got across the lough they soon reached a dark and mysterious underground tunnel. They entered the tunnel like they were entering the mouth of a giant worm; it twisted and turned down deep into the earth. The riders were in total darkness the whole time – you could not have seen as far as the end your nose. They trotted along in silence and darkness for a very long time indeed until they saw a light in the distance.

Now Johnny and the wee man arrived at a great gated entrance that was adorned with burning lamps. The gates were huge and made from a dark wood decorated with impressive carvings. Then all a sudden the gates opened before them and the two men trotted inside. They were greeted by two rows with over a million men all about 2 feet tall, dressed in the richest of finery. These strange men took them into the grandest hall that Johnny had ever seen; it was massive, like someone had put a roof on the world and decorated it with all the jewels of nature. In this magical hall there were tables covered in every type of food and drink that you could think of and quite a few that went beyond the imagination.

Johnny was treated like royalty; he was told to take a seat and make himself comfortable and eat and drink as much as he liked. He was also told to take his time and enjoy the feast, 'for the man who made time, made plenty of it!' Forty fiddlers appeared out of nowhere and they started playing mighty jigs and reels, there was wild dancing and singing in the great hall. Then the wee man, whom Johnny had travelled with, put up his hand and all the dancing and music stopped right then and there.

He pointed at poor Johnny, who was quite caught off guard as only a second ago he was dancing and singing to his heart's content. The wee man then shouted in a loud and shrill voice, 'Look now! There is the man who needs to take a rest!' With that Johnny was taken away politely by a group of wee men, who were very strong considering their small stature. He was taken to lovely bedroom, which was a great relief to Johnny for he was sure he was going to be thrown into a dungeon or some class of deep, dark hole in the ground.

There was a fire burning in a big ornate fireplace in this room, and the fuel was neither turf, wood nor coal – Johnny could not tell what it was at all, but there was a mighty heat from it that warmed the whole room like toast and as soon as Johnny hit the bed he was fast asleep like a wee baby.

When Johnny awoke, daylight was streaming in like a rainbow through beautiful stained-glass windows that adorned the great walls of the picture-perfect room. He sat up in the giant four-poster bed and he saw before him a huge wooden table again laden with fabulous food and drink of every kind. He got himself dressed and was about to sit down to his majestic breakfast when, all of a sudden, the great door of his room opened and the wee man arrived, all smiles and 'Good mornings!' He then says to Johnny, 'You will not get away until you have seen all about this place.' So after Johnny had eaten and drank his fill, the wee man took him on a grand tour. It looked like a palace and covered as much as 2 if not 3 acres of land. Johnny had never seen the likes of it in all his days; it was truly breathtaking and beautiful beyond description.

Well it was time for Johnny to go home and he thanked his wee friend ever so much for his kindness, hospitality and saving him from the terrible sheep-stealers. He wanted to show his gratitude by offering the wee man whatever money he had. But the wee man had no interest in such things as money, and he said to Johnny, 'If you stand in need of anything, I will give you what will keep you comfortable all your life.' Johnny said that this was far too much but the wee man waved his hand at Johnny and went away for a bit and then returned with a bag full of sovereigns and gave them to Johnny. He then gave Johnny a beautiful horse with a saddle and bridle and told him to mount the beast. 'Don't worry,' said the wee man, 'this horse will leave you right at your destination.' Johnny asked the wee man why he was so kind to him and the wee man replied, ''Tis a rare thing when your kind respect us enough to trust you and 'tis an even rarer thing that your kind don't help themselves to our gold without permission. You have proved yourself a trustworthy and decent fellow Johnny McKenna.' With that the wee man patted the horse and it bolted off like a bullet. They flew across the land like the wind, clearing every ditch, hedge and bog hole like it was not there at all. The first place they came to was Shane Faddley's Carrick, where the horse rested for a wee bit and then they were off again. The horse then crossed through Derrkinighbeg and Johnny could see neither ditch nor hedge till he landed at the foot of his own garden.

When his feet touched the ground, the horse disappeared and he walked to his front door, both pleased and honoured that he had befriended none other than the King of the Fairies!

Co. Tyrone: From the Irish *Tír Eoghain*, meaning 'Land of Eoghan', after Eógan mac Néill, first king of Tyrone and son of Niall of the Nine Hostages. William Carleton (1794–1869), the famous novelist and folklorist, was born in Clogher, Co. Tyrone; his work has contributed greatly to the world of Irish folk and fairy lore. There are lots of fairy forts in Co. Tyrone; one in particular is on the Loughmacroroy Road: it is a beautiful wedge cairn with three roof stones still in place. In the centre of this cairn there is a beautiful fairy tree. William Forbes (W.F.) Marshall, the poet and Presbyterian Minister (1888–1959), was born in Sixmilecross,

Co. Tyrone. He was known as 'The Bard of Tyrone' and he wrote some beautiful fairy poetry based on his native county, most notably 'The Fairy Hill', which stands majestically just outside his birthplace.

JOSEPH MCPHERSON AND THE FAIRIES (CO. TYRONE)

This is another story given to us by the Co. Down storyteller Doreen McBride. She herself was given the story by Dr Mary Wrack of Washington DC University. Dr Wrack came across this tale while she was in Ireland conducting research for a book about the Irish diet.

Joseph McPherson lived in the townland of Derryork, near Drumbane Fort in Co. Tyrone. He was a farmer who, like many farmers in those far-off times, supplemented his income by working as a weaver. This was long before industrialisation, when weavers had looms in their homes so they could make linen after doing a hard day's work around their farms.

Joseph became very upset because every night fairies who lived in the nearby fort came into his house and annoyed him by playing around his loom. They refused to go away and leave him alone. One night, in 1804, the fairies invited Joseph to visit their fort and join them for dinner. He was frightened and didn't want to go but they were insistent and carried him off against his will. Joseph was treated like royalty inside the fairy fort. He was given all sorts of delicious things to eat and drink before spending the rest of the night enjoying music and mirth. When the entertainment ended, the fairies took him out of their fort, away up high into the air. He was frightened and confused because he'd no idea where he was. He turned to the fairies and asked, 'Are you taking me up into Heaven to the Temple of God?'

Fairies don't like being asked about God because they aren't sure if he is going to grant them eternal life or not. Annoyed by Joseph's question, they dropped him on top of a lime heap beside the fairy thorn on his farm. He was in a terrible state when he managed to stagger back into his house and told his wife and family all that had happened, but he had one consoling thought: perhaps he'd annoyed the fairies to such an extent by mentioning God that they'd leave him alone in future.

That was not to be. Next evening, after he had finished his farm work and started weaving, he found himself surrounded by what seemed like thousands of fairies. The room was so crowded he could hardly move. He was in such a state of desperation he went and asked his clergyman to please come and get the fairies out of his house. The clergyman found Joseph surrounded by fairies. He told Joseph there are two things that frighten fairies: the Bible and iron. He told Joseph to hold his Bible in his right hand and a penknife in his left and to accompany him reading a passage from the Bible aloud. To everyone's great astonishment, Joseph was suddenly whisked out of the door as he read. At first he was bewildered because he didn't know what had happened. Then he remembered that iron may be used as protection against fairies, so he took his knife out of his pocket and formed circular patterns by passing it quickly around his body with the blade pointing outwards. After a few minutes he heard the fairies chattering and stood absolutely still, clutching his knife in one hand and his Bible in the other. He listened carefully and heard the fairies saying they couldn't possibly take him to dinner while he held a knife and the Bible. Joseph breathed a sigh of relief. He thought the fairies would go away for good, but it was not to be. They bothered him every night. They were such a nuisance that he eventually made a bargain with them: he promised to give them his firstborn child if they went away and left him alone. Shortly after that Joseph's wife had a baby boy. The child lived for two years before it was killed in an accident. Poor Joseph was stricken with grief and guilt. He blamed himself for his son's death because he'd promised his firstborn to the fairies. He became terribly depressed and thought he'd never find peace or be successful in Ireland. When he'd buried his son, he decided the best thing he could do was emigrate to America.

He sold all his possessions. He was sure the fairies would leave him alone and get on with their business around Drumbane Fort.

It was not to be. Shortly after he arrived in America, he wrote home saying he'd enjoyed a pleasant peaceful voyage but the moment he arrived in America he found that fairies from Drumbane Fort had crossed the Atlantic Ocean with him.

I would like to give you a happy ending to this story but as the folklore historian Simon Young says: 'Irish fairy stories rarely end well...'

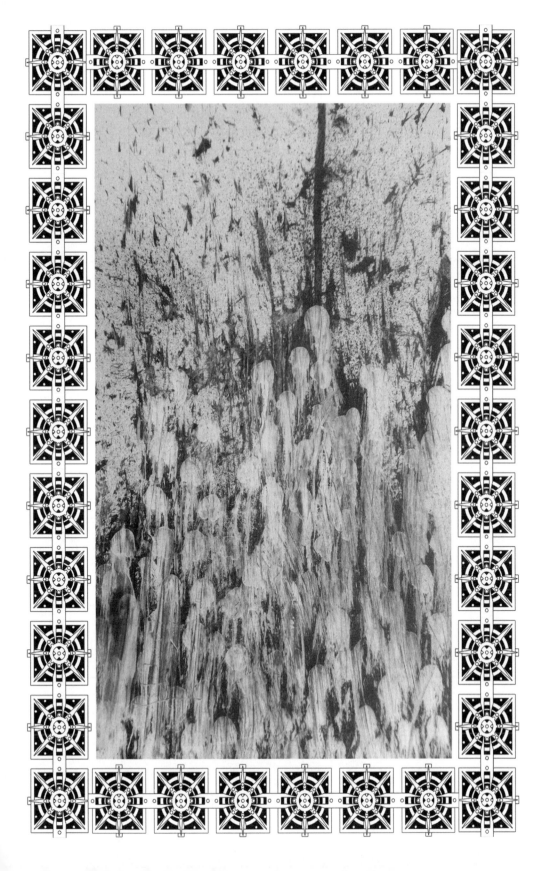

2

THE PROVINCE
OF LEINSTER

Co. Carlow: From the Irish *Ceatharlach*, meaning 'four lakes'. The actual settlement of Co. Carlow is thousands of years old and predates any written Irish history. It was the capital of Ireland in the fourteenth century. Co. Carlow is home to the ancient Browneshill Dolmen, an ancient tomb, which was built between 4000 and 3000 BC. Outside Ballymurphy in Co. Carlow, on top of a remote hill, you will find Rathgeran, which means fort of the rowan trees (rowan trees are said to belong to the fairy folk). The rocks that surround the fort are decorated with spiralling Celtic circles, similar to the carvings outside New Grange in Co. Meath. The last wolf in Ireland was hunted down and killed in Mount Leinster for attacking sheep in 1786. Co. Carlow is also the home of the ancient Celtic King Labhraidh Loingseach, who was believed to have horse's ears.

THE CRYING LADY (CO. CARLOW)

Descriptions of the banshee can be hugely different, and she is called many different things depending on where you are in Ireland and who you are talking to. In some parts of Ireland the banshee is called the *Bough* or the *Boheenka*. Others refer to her as the fairy woman (*Bean Sídhe*), the death messenger, the white lady of sorrow, the woman of peace, and the keening woman.

Some see her as an old hag with flowing white hair and torn clothes, while others see her as a beautiful young woman dressed in a flowing white dress. Don't be fooled if you happen to come across the young lady as opposed to the old lady – run just as fast. Neither sighting ends well.

The banshee can be heard without being seen, but when someone is unfortunate enough to catch a glimpse of her she is usually seen combing her long flowing hair.

Some believe she is directly related to the 'keening women'. Keening is a traditional form of vocal lament for the dead and keening women were hired to cry at wakes and funerals. They would make high-pitched and mournful sounds beside the person laid out. This sound is not unlike the sound we associate with the banshee cry. Keening women were not only responsible for crying beside the corpse but in a lot of cases they helped prepare the body, washing and dressing the deceased and also combing their hair – hence the comb. It is believed in some parts of Ireland that the banshee was once a keening woman who wasn't good at her job and she became a banshee as a means of punishment. In some stories it is said that if you touch her comb you will die. If you see a comb on the ground it is thought to be bad luck to pick it up.

Traditionally the banshee was believed to follow the ancient Gaelic families of Ireland, those being names with 'O' or 'Mac'. There are accounts of some Norman or Norse descendants and also some families 'who came with Cromwell' having their own banshee.

The story we found from Co. Carlow tells a harrowing tale of a banshee. We found this story in the Dúchas archive at University College Dublin. It was collected by a student from Garryhill National School, Co. Carlow, called Patrick Smethers. The story was told to him by John O'Hara from Straduff.

Now everybody is Ireland knows that the banshee is supposed to follow certain families. She appears when a member of that family is going to die. She is seen by people at night sitting in a tree by the roadside combing her hair. It is said that if she throws the comb at someone and hits them with it then they will die soon afterwards. On the night that the person dies she can be heard keening for miles around.

The banshee is supposed to follow a certain family named Bradley, who live in a place named Clonee. One night a man named John O'Hara was coming home to Straduff from Myshall. He had to pass by Clonee on his way home. When he was coming near Bradley's house he saw the banshee in a tree combing her hair. He said 'Good night' but she would not speak. He said 'Good night' again but she would not answer. At last he said, 'Whoever you are I will make you speak,' and he went home for his dog. When he returned the dog would not go near the banshee. So he went home with the dog, got his gun, and loaded it with a bent sixpence. He returned yet again but the banshee was gone.

Less than a week later one of the Bradleys died and that night the keening of the banshee could be heard all over the countryside. People thought that something terrible would surely happen to John O'Hara, but nothing did. He is still 'hale and hearty' and it is some years now since he heard the banshee.

On the Carlow–Kildare border is Duckett's Grove. It is located in Rainstown. This mansion was built between 1818 and 1850 and was home to the Duckett family.

As you drive up to the entrance you will see the family crest and motto. It reads 'Let us be judged by our actions'. Sadly, in 1933 the house was burned down and the cause is unknown.

There are many ghost stories attached to Duckett's Grove and it is well known for its resident banshee.

The banshee is said to be a woman who William Duckett had an affair with; the lady was the daughter of a farmer from the area and sadly she died tragically while out riding her horse. After her death, her mother put the 'widow's curse' on William and thus the Duckett banshee was brought into being.

The property gets a lot of interest and has even had paranormal investigators trying to discover what is going on inside those now ruined walls.

Over the years the banshee has been seen and heard throughout the property. Witnesses even claimed to have heard her wail for two days straight from one of the towers. As a result, a woman walking along a path on the property died suddenly. Former employees claim to have seen her several times. One thing for sure is she is not shy – some former employees became very fearful of the entity and abandoned the property, never to return. Apparently, a man saw and heard the banshee in the walled garden and his mother died the next day.

As mentioned at the beginning of this story, the word banshee means 'fairy woman'. Because of the Victorian portrayal of fairies as delicate, gentle and joyful creatures, which has lived on through their portrayal in Disney films and other children's entertainment, the word 'fairy' has lost its power and has been weakened over the years. We found a wonderful story collected by student Breda Doran from Baile Ui Mhurchadha, Borris, Co. Carlow. This story dates back to around 1898 and was told by the class teacher about a woman named Mary Doyle from the townland of Kyle.

When the Gaels (Celts) first came to Ireland, there was a race of people who ruled the land and they were called the Tuatha Dé Danann, and they claimed to be magicians.

When the Gaels came to the shore the Tuatha Dé Danann were not pleased to see these invaders and told them to go back out to sea and not to return.

So the Gaels sailed out to sea and pretended to go away, but they had every intention of returning. This was an easy manoeuvre for them as they were expert seafarers.

But the Tuatha Dé Danann were wise and knew that the invaders would try to come back. As the Gaels were out at sea they caused a great fog to come around the shore so that they would not be able to come back.

They then caused a great wind, known as a fairy wind (*Sí Gaoithe*), so that many of the ships were dashed to pieces on the rocks and some of the sailors were drowned. But the Gaels were a brave race who never gave in, and in spite of the winds of the magicians they landed in Ireland. When the magicians saw that the Gaels had landed, they knew their day as the monarchs of the land was over. They were very angry for they did not like to be ruled over by the Gaels, nor did they like to leave Ireland for they liked it too well. So they hid themselves in the mountains and hills of Ireland.

These are the Sidhe, or the fairies of whom we have heard so much of.

Co. Dublin: From the Irish *Dubh Linn*, meaning 'Black Pool'; however, its official Irish name is *Baile Átha Cliath*, meaning 'Town of the Hurdled Ford'. Dublin is the capital city of the Republic of Ireland. The dramatist, writer and folklorist James Stephens (1880–1950) was born in Dublin. His book *Irish Fairy Tales* (1920) was illustrated by the great fairy artist Arthur Rackham (1867–1939).

The National Folklore Collection is housed at University College Dublin. Sinéad de Valera (1878–1975), the wife of President Éamon de Valera (1882–1975), was a great collector of Irish fairy stories; she was born in Balbriggan, Co. Dublin. Harry Clarke (1889–1931) was a brilliant stained-glass artist and book illustrator. His style of drawing and use of colour was 'otherworldly'. His depictions of people and fictional characters captured the very essence of the Sidhe. He was born on St Patrick's Day in Dublin.

THE FAIRY PASS (CO. DUBLIN)

The following story is from Lucan in Co. Dublin. It was documented by various sources as part of the National Folklore Collection from 1937 to 1939. It also has a personal connection with Steve Lally, who lived in Beech Park, Lucan, for the first six years of his life and still has fond memories of going to The Grove Cinema with his late father, to see classics such as *Star Wars* and *Superman*.

In Lucan there is also a building called the 'Fairy House' up on a small hill, opposite the entrance to Vesey Park, on your way down to the Hollows. Steve vaguely remembers people talking about it as a child, but it was not somewhere he was ever taken and probably for very good reason – for it was believed that it had been built at the end of a fairy pass.

Now I don't know if you have ever heard of a fairy pass (or path) before, but if not, please allow us to tell you. Long, long ago the old people said that these fairy passes were used by the good folk, better known as the fairy folk, to travel around the country. They were not marked out and could not be seen like a road or a lane; in fact, they are quite invisible. But if you were to build a house upon one or cause an obstruction on one such pass, you would bring an awful lot of bad luck upon yourself.

Even to this day there are still precautions taken before building a house, in order to make sure that you are not obstructing a fairy pass. An old college friend of Steve's, the Wexford artist and folklorist Michael Fortune, explained to us that when he was building his house in Wexford back in 2010 he was advised by his father to place four ash rods (cut branches from the ash tree) in the four corners of the building. The rods were to be left overnight and when they returned in the morning, if any of the rods were knocked over, pulled out of the ground or damaged in any way, then they knew not to build there as it was obstructing a fairy path. Thankfully there were no signs of disgruntled fairy folk and Michael went ahead and built his house.

Parts of the story of the fairy path of Lucan was collected by Mollie Byrne, a student from the Presentation Convent, Lucan, who interviewed a 90-year-old man named only as Mr T. McConnell (*The Schools' Collection*, Vol. 0794, pp. 3–4), while another girl called Maureen Blake, also a student from the Presentation Convent, got her story from a 78-year-old woman named only as Mrs Dignam (*The Schools' Collection*, Vol. 0794, p.10). We have taken it upon ourselves to try and piece them together and get an idea of the full story.

According to Mr T. McConnell there were many historical places in this locality of Lucan. One of these was situated on top of Fairy House Hill – it was a big yellow house. It was formerly the house of Sir John McConnell (maybe an ancestor of the informant) who lived in the fourteenth century. He was a very cruel man. He committed terrible crimes, so awful that no one would ever speak of them. It was said that one night after committing one of these crimes he was punished by the fairies, who were said to have dwelt around the house. It is said that the house was enchanted by the fairies, for it was built at the end of a fairy path.

Some years after Sir John died, a lady was seen on a white horse every night at midnight: She rode as far as Cruck House and then disappeared.

This phantom may well have been a victim of one of Sir John's terrible crimes. Mr T. McConnell went on to say that two men he knew by the names of Mr James Gleeson and Mr Michael Byrne were walking down the avenue leading from this house. At the end of the avenue are the ruins of an old lodge. Just as they were passing, a lady dressed in white stepped out and the men bade her 'Good night'; she did not answer but disappeared through the wall. This was, of course, the phantom lady that haunted this area by night.

There are a great many little hills around this house. They are known as Hollow Hills for they are where the Sidhe dwell.

This house is called Fairy House because it is said to be the end of the fairy pass. It is a cursed place and best to be avoided.

We mentioned earlier about Cruck House, this was a stately home in Lucan and, like Fairy House, it was situated along the fairy pass and had its own fair share of strange happenings. Mrs Dignam, of Lucan, stated that the people of Cruck House used to go to bed at ten o'clock every night – the lights were out, fire was out, all had gone to bed. If anyone was up after that hour it is said that the fairies would chase them.

Mrs Dignam tells a tale that took place along the fairy pass in the year 1868. She states that near Cruck House was a small thatched house where there lived an old man called Mr Dignam (possibly an ancestor of Mrs Dignam) and his wife and children. Outside was a lovely garden full of fruit and vegetables.

One Saturday night Mr Dignam's wife was washing some small items of clothing when she heard whispering coming from the garden, so she went outside to locate its source. The whispering was coming from the garden alright but she could not see a thing. She knew it was not her husband as he was in bed resting after a long day working at the market. Poor Mrs Dignam could not understand why she could hear voices but could see no one. She tried telling herself that it was two of the local children stealing cabbages from her garden.

She even called out, 'Molly Kelly and whoever is with you, be away with ye now, for if I catch ye, there'll be Hell to pay!' After that she went back inside to her husband's room and said to him, 'Molly Kelly and her sister are in our garden taking the cabbages. Come out and we shall catch them.'

The old man replied, 'My good woman, come in and shut the door and go to bed and don't mind them.'

'But,' she said, 'I must go out and put these clothes on the line.' Her husband had fallen asleep as this point and her concerns fell on deaf ears.

So she went outside again to put the things on the line. As she was hanging out the clothes she thought she felt something brush past her, like a small person, a child. She got an awful fright and she called them most awful names and all the robbers as they were. She was both angry and afraid at the same time, and she threatened to go after them with a stick and give them a good thrashing.

This did not seem to frighten her tormentors in any way at all; in fact, the whispering grew louder and louder and still she could see nobody but herself.

She ran inside the house and again went into her husband's room and said, 'If you don't come out we will have no vegetables and then what shall we do and the times are so bad.' But he only nodded his head and said, 'Shut the door and go to bed, it is the best thing to do, for to do otherwise would draw them upon you!'

She had no sooner shut the door when a terrible noise shook the house like thunder. The windows shook, the clothes flew off the bed and the holy statues fell from the mantelpiece but they were not broken. 'Now,' said the old man, 'you see what you have done! The fairies will haunt this place every night.'

The old man knew that his house was built on the fairy pass and he had never said anything about it and he knew the best thing to do was not to interfere or get involved with any of their activities. But his poor wife did not know of this and had upset the wee folk with her shouts and threats. Ironically, it was her that was trespassing on their path and they were not too happy about it at all.

The fairies wanted to see if the humans who were living on their path would encounter them physically, for if they did, it would allow them to cross over into their world. Unfortunately, the poor woman did touch them and as a result the house and its inhabitants were fair game for the fairy folk.

If only Mr Dignam had told his poor wife, they may have been saved the torment. But he was a proud man and would not speak of such things to his wife, for fear that she may see him as foolish. But she was to find out the hard way and their story was passed on as a warning to anyone who dared build their house on a fairy pass.

According to Mrs Dignam, back in those days if you went into a certain field in Lucan known as 'The Fairy Field' near Cruck House after twelve at night you would not be able to leave. Instead you would be carried off to an unknown place and there you would have to stay until morning.

The fairy pass itself extends for about a mile; the entrance is between two trees, which stand on the left-hand side of the fairy field, and passes over the fort and into another field and ends at an avenue where the Fairy House stood. Long ago a lady on a white horse used to be seen galloping across the fairy pass every night at twelve until she came to a certain bush, where she disappeared. This, of course, is the same phantom woman mentioned by Mr T. McConnell.

The fairy pass is still there and I wonder if any houses are built upon it now? Well, if there are we are sure the occupants would know all about it.

Co. Kildare: From the Irish *Cill Dara*, meaning 'Church of the Oak Tree'. Kildare is a county full of magic, mystery and myth. It was at the Curragh of Kildare where St Brigid lay down her cloak and covered the land with it. Maynooth Castle and Kilkea Castle both belonged to Earl Gerald Fitzgerald, better known as 'The Wizard Earl'. In the grounds of Kilkea Castle, outside Castledermot, is a small medieval church with a carving of a mermaid; she has a comb in her right hand and there is a serpent with a cat-like head about to bite off her tail. The High King and Queen of Leinster, King Mesgegra and his wife Queen Buan, are laid to rest in Co. Kildare. 'The Hill of Allen' in Co. Kildare is one of the most famous mythical locations in Ireland, as Fionn mac Cumhaill had an enormous fortress there. It was in Castletown House, Celbridge, where the Devil himself apparently appeared to Tom Conolly. Co. Kildare was also home to Christy Moore, Dónal Lunny and Liam O'Flynn, all members of the legendary Irish folk group Planxty.

THE POOKA HORSE (CO. KILDARE)

Steve first came across the story 'The Kildare Pooka' in William Butler Yeats' 1888 publication *Folk and Fairy Tales of the Irish Peasantry*. In Yeats' collection the story was retold by Patrick Kennedy (1801–1873) from his own book, *Legendry Fictions of the Irish Celts* (1866). Kennedy, from Kilmyshal, Co. Wexford, was well known for his collection of Leinster folk tales. At the age of 21 he enrolled in a teacher training program meat the Kildare Place Society, officially known as the Society for Promoting the Education of the Poor of Ireland, and in 1822 he was appointed as a teacher there. He gave up teaching at some point and opened a lending library and bookshop in Dublin.

What is very strange about Kennedy's story is that he has all the names of places, characters and buildings removed from the text only to be replaced by the first letter of each word followed by a dash, but all of which alluded to Rathcoffey Castle or House. Since then Steve has seen this story in many other folklore collections, all with the same names and titles removed. Growing up in Rathcoffey, Steve was once told by an old-timer that Rathcoffey Castle had its own ghost or pooka in residence.

The pooka is a solitary and sinister fairy who has most likely never appeared in human form. His shape is usually that of a horse, bull, goat, eagle or an ass. As a horse, he takes great delight in throwing an unwary rider from his back, and taking them over ditches, rivers and mountains, shaking them off in the early grey light of morning.

Then, many years later, by sheer chance, Steve came across a collection called *Irish Fairy Tales* by the Irish historian and folklorist Padraic O'Farrell, published in 1997. And there it was, 'The Rathcoffey Pooka'. And the missing names were filled in! This is one of our favourite stories and, like all the stories in this collection, we have put our own twist on the tale. This story is part of Steve's repertoire, and he shares it whenever he travels around storytelling.

In the province of Leinster there lies Co. Kildare and within Kildare lies Rathcoffey in the civil parish of Balraheen, halfway between Maynooth and Clane, and standing on top of Rathcoffey Hill is Rathcoffey Castle. The castle is now in ruins but it was once a magnificent building renowned for its feasts and banquets. Now you see there are two parts to Rathcoffey Castle, one is the original remains of the twelfth-century Norman castle built by the Wogan family. The second and most prominent feature is the shell of Rathcoffey House, built by Archibald Hamilton Rowan in 1784. Rowan was a prominent figure in the 1798 Rebellion. In 1790 he was a founding member of the Dublin Society of United Irish Men, working alongside such famous revolutionaries as William Drennan and Theobald Wolfe Tone. It is more than likely for this reason that Patrick Kennedy was so secretive about the names and places associated with the story.

Archibald was often away a lot on serious business, as it was around the time of the Great Rising of 1798. But the people of the great house still entertained guests and whenever the master of the house returned they always made sure to put on a great spread for him and his comrades.

Now, auld Archibald was in a lot of bother for his involvement in certain political activities around the time. To put it another way, he was what you might call a 'Wanted Man'. On one occasion he was hiding out at Rathcoffey House when he saw a troop of English soldiers riding towards him over the hill. Well, Archibald did not waste any time for he knew these boys were not calling round for a cup of tea and a chat. So he whistled out for his horse, who came galloping out from his stable beside the house. Archibald was standing on the balcony of his house and jumped off it, landing square on the horse's back, and away they rode towards Clongowes Wood, which was known at the time as Castlebrowne. His pursuers were hot on his trail and firing their muskets at him. He rode like the devil towards Castlebrowne and when he got there he burst through the front doors, went straight up the stairs, opened the window in one of the top rooms and threw his hat out of the window. Well, now his posse were close behind and followed him up to the room and saw the open window and his hat lying on the ground below so the figured he had jumped out to escape. They ran back down the stairs and searched everywhere for him but there was neither sight nor sound of him at all.

What his tormentors did not know was that there was a secret chamber in the library on the top floor of Clongowes Wood Castle. Archibald opened a secret door that was disguised as a row of bookshelves and in he went to join his dear friend Wogan Browne for a glass of fine wine and a game of cards and enjoy a good laugh at his pursuers' expense. That secret room has since been sealed up but the door that looks like a row of bookshelves is still there. In June 2018 Steve and Paula

were shown this secret door by Charlie Connor, a Jesuit still living at Clongowes Wood College. It was indeed a great privilege to feel part of such a great story.

Now back to our story…

Archibald Hamilton Rowan was never told about the strange goings-on at night, after all the merriment was over and all the crockery and cooking ware was left in the kitchen to be washed. Oh no! The staff never dared mention how none of them had risked entering the kitchen after midnight as they were all scared out of their wits by the sound of banging and clattering coming from within, and all this cacophony was accompanied by the sound of hysterical laughter and whistling. And every morning to their amazement the kitchen was always found spotless and everything clean and in its place. You could have eaten your dinner off the floor it was so well scrubbed.

Now, there was a young scullery boy who lived and worked at the castle and he was a very lazy boy – he was so lazy that the only time he would lift his hand to do something was when he wished to scratch his head or pick his nose. He was so lazy that he made his Mammy cry. Rathcoffey Castle was a great place for a boy like this to work in as he never had to do a stroke. Sure it was heaven altogether, and why should he do anything when whoever it was coming to the kitchen at night was doing such a fine job, far better than he could ever do himself.

Well, one night out of curiosity and boredom he decided to see who or what was making all the noise and doing all the cleaning. He waited till all the ware was brought into the kitchen and left piled high to the ceiling with the mice eating away at the leftovers. He decided to build himself a nice big fire in the fireplace and he knew that no one would bother him as they were all too frightened to go into the kitchen after dark. He lay down on some cushions before the hearth. Ah! It was a grand fire indeed. He could feel the warmth of the flames against his face, smell the aromatic smoke as it curled up the chimney. The flames threw shadows on the walls like dancing demons and he was eased into a deep sleep by the gentle sound of the wood crackling.

Then, all of a sudden, he was woken by the most terrible howling and shrieking. He could hear the words '**I've got ya now ya boy ya! I've got ya now!**' bellowing into his face. The boy looked up in terror and standing above him was a great black horse with red eyes like burning coals and steam hissing out of its flared nostrils.

'Who-o-o are you?' stammered the boy, his heart pounding with fear. The horse grinned at him, revealing two rows of ivory white teeth, and there was a glint of menace in the creature's eye that sent a shiver down the boy's spine.

The horse pulled over a chair, sat down in it and crossed his legs. He then reached in to his big black mane and produced a large clay pipe. He lit the pipe, took a deep drag on it, exhaled the thick smoke out of his nostrils then cleared his throat and spat onto the fire, causing it to hiss like an angry serpent. And then the horse began...

'I am the Pooka Horse, I dwell amongst the ruins and the hilltops, I have been driven monstrous by much solitude and they say I am of the race of the Nightmare! But I was once a boy like you, a lazy boy just like you!' The pooka horse looked ever so pleased with himself as he went on to tell the poor boy his story. 'I was so lazy, I made my Mammy cry and the fairies were so angry with me they sent a big black pooka horse, who threw me on his back and ran the full length and breadth of Ireland with me holding on for dear life. He ran to the South, where he took me to the top of Mount Carrantuohill in the County Kerry and he howled like wolf, then he took me to the West, where my teeth chattered as his hooves clattered across the mighty Burren in the County Clare, then he took me to the North, where we jumped across Maggie's Leap in the County Down, and finally he brought me to the East, where my heart pounded as he bounded across the plains of the Curragh of Kildare. He came to a sudden halt and I was sent flying into the furze bushes, and when I came to I was no longer a boy but the great black pooka horse that you see before you now.'

The creature went on to explain that there was a curse upon him. 'I would remain a pooka horse and travel the land seeking out lazy people and when I found them, I would have to carry out all their chores and labour. The only way to break the spell is to find a boy or a girl lazier than I was, and catch them sleeping when they should be working.' The pooka grinned menacingly at the boy and took a deep drag from his pipe. 'I found you a long time ago boy, dossing about, skiving off your duties and playing truant. All I had to do was to catch you sleeping. I waited and worked here doing all your chores and now I got ya! Ha!' roared the pooka horse.

'Please!' begged the boy. 'Please give me one last chance, I promise I will never be lazy again and do all that is asked of me and more.' The pooka horse leered down at the boy, his lips curled back in a snarl, and hissed, 'We'll see, we'll see…' With that the pooka put out his pipe, pushed it back into his mane, and turned to the door. The boy heard him galloping across the plain outside, crying, 'We'll see! We'll see!'

The poor lad jumped up and began to scrub, mop and wash everything in the kitchen. He did this every day and night for a brave long while. And there was no sign of the pooka horse. The people of Rathcoffey Castle were very pleased with their scullery boy and they rewarded him well, giving him a day off every week to do as he pleased. And they were no longer full of fear at night with all that strange commotion going on in the kitchen.

As time went on the boy began to think that the pooka horse was a thing of the past; in fact, he started to believe that he imagined the whole experience. And he had been working so hard, far harder than anyone else in the castle, and he deserved a night off. He was due a holiday the following week, but he could not wait.

So one night after the festivities were over and all the dirty dishes were brought into the kitchen, he built himself a large fire. Ah! How lovely it was! He needed a rest and this was well-deserved.

It was not long before he drifted off to sleep, snoring away contentedly…

'Ahhhhhhh! Ha! Ha! I got you now for sure, ya boy ya!' The lad jumped out of his sleep absolutely terrified, his heart beating in his breast.

Standing above him was the pooka horse. The boy gawked in disbelief as the monster turned back into human form and he watched as his own body began to cover with hair and his hands turn to hooves. Standing before him was a young man looking ever so pleased with himself, then he turned and ran from the house singing out 'I'm Free! I'm Free!'

The scullery boy had become a pooka horse and was doomed to search the land for a boy or a girl lazier than himself to lift the terrible curse. But he could not bring himself to punish a child in such a dreadful way. So instead he went about helping the poor, the weak and the sick. He helped wherever he could and never slacked on any job he started. He did all this without anyone knowing who did it or receiving any thanks. Then one day many years later the curse was lifted and he was no longer a boy but a young man. And he then travelled from house to house, school to school, telling young people his story and warning them of what might happen if they were lazy. And somewhere out there roams a pooka horse who is keen to pass the curse on to someone else, so be wary and diligent in your work, for he might come looking for you…

Co. Kilkenny: From the Irish *Chill Chainnigh*. Chainnigh, or Canice, was the saint who founded the town, so it literally means 'Canice's Church'. Kilkenny is a county full of ancient castles, forts, passage graves and round towers. It is also renowned for witches, the most famous being Dame Alice Kyteler (1263–*c*.1325), who was born into a noble family. She was married four times; each husband died and she was accused of their deaths and dealings with the Devil himself. Outside the townland of Owning in Co. Kilkenny you will find Kilmogue Portal Dolmen, known locally as *Leac na Scail*, which means the stone of the shadow or ghost. It is the tallest dolmen in Ireland. Freestone Hill Fort and cairn in the townland of Coolrange is home to a large hillfort that surrounds the hill. In its centre stands a lone fairy tree, which is treated with great respect by the locals, for it is believed to hold great power.

THE BANSHEE WELCOMING PARTY (CO. KILKENNY)

We found this story in the Dúchas archive at University College Dublin. It is part of *The Schools' Collection*, Vol. 0856, pp.112–15. It was written and related by Stephen Dwyer from Greenridge, Co. Kilkenny. The school it was recorded at was Naomh Eoin, Cill Choinnigh on 3 November 1937. This story is about a family banshee and is part of *The Schools' Collection*, Vol. 0856, pp.112–15. It was handed down from Dwyer's great-grandfather, who went by the name Holohan. Dwyer remembered his own father telling him the story when he was a child; he wrote down the words his father told him.

So, settle down and prepare to be enchanted and startled by this magnificent tale of the banshee.

'Everybody has heard of the banshee, a female fairy of Ireland, who makes herself known by wailing and shrieking before a death and usually within a particular family. The banshee is known in Irish as the "Woman of the Fairies" (fairy woman). There is a tradition in our family handed down by my great-grandfather, whose name was Holohan, he lived at a place called Sugarstown near Thomastown, Co. Kilkenny.

'He met the banshee, and the terrifying experience he had on that winter's night long ago is remembered with awe by the family, as if it were only yesterday, and that it actually happened to themselves. It is one of the fireside stories which I have often heard my father relate to us. It is a true story because it is preserved in in our family. Here is the story told to me by my father and handed down to him in the exact words of his own father.'

When Stephen Dwyer's great-grandfather Holohan was a child, times were very hard in Ireland as the Famine was in full swing with death and despair at every turn. His own father had died when he was still a baby and his mother had to work very hard to rear the family. They were desperate times, with starvation and poverty crushing the souls of all those who came in the wake of the Great Hunger. But God was good to them and they survived. As soon as Holohan was old enough to work, he went out to make himself a living whatever way he could to take care of his poor mother and his younger brothers and sisters. But there was no work to be had in Ireland and Holohan was left destitute. So he decided that he would do what so many of his fellow countrymen and women had done, he emigrated to America.

Holohan made it to America and he got on well over there, making plenty of money and sending what he could back to his family in Kilkenny. He spent a long time in the States, but after many years he missed home. This is what he said on the matter: 'After many years I, like other exiles, got a longing to return to the old home. My mother and brothers and sisters were overjoyed at the news, and on the very morning on which I sailed from New York, I received a letter of welcome from my poor mother.'

He went on to say that the notepaper from his mother was be-dewed in tears, but they were tears of joy. His mother was beside herself with delight knowing that her eldest son was arriving home after so many years away from her. She told Holohan in the letter that they had a

great spree in store for him and his brothers and sisters would be there to greet him too.

Shortly afterwards he set sail from New York to take the long voyage home to Ireland. After almost a month at sea he arrived at the harbour of Cork City, and from there he got a mail coach to Kilkenny – this was another long journey of almost 100 miles. Eventually he arrived in Kilkenny town at around 9 p.m. The coach was putting up for the night in an inn there, but Holohan was keen to get home so he set off on foot to Sugarstown, Co. Kilkenny. This was over a 10-mile walk but he did not mind and was determined to see the old homestead. After about 5 miles he arrived at Bennetsbridge, where he met some old friends from his childhood. He spent a few hours with them playing cards and having a sing-a-long. At midnight he bid them farewell and resumed his journey home. In the distance he could hear the sound of music and merrymaking, he knew that this was the spree that his mother had talked about in her letter to him and was excited about seeing them all.

Just as he turned a bend in the road he heard a woman's voice calling out, 'Mother bids thee come, she is waiting too long!'

That particular night the stars were shining bright but the moon was pale in the sky above him. Holohan knew that this was no ordinary mortal woman who was wailing in the night wind, he knew that it was the banshee, the woman of the fairies, and he knew what her keening meant too.

He heard her call out again with a bloodcurdling shriek and wasted no time. He quickly ran across the slope of the hill, passing the grove or the fairy mound that he knew so well from his boyhood days. He was out of breath and full of fear. He glanced around, 'Mother of Mercy!' he yelled as he watched the banshee swirl in circles above in the night sky, her long silver hair flowing and her snow-white dress trailing after her.

Then she descended from the sky and gracefully sat down on a rock before him, her hair was streaming down onto the damp moss and her face was bowed on her bosom. Holohan called out to her, 'Tell me quick, is there anything wrong at home?'

'Mother and brothers and sisters bid thee come!' she answered in a low and mournful moan.

Then she threw her head back, showing her terrible face and burning eyes that turned Holohan's blood to ice, and shrieked so loud that he thought his ears might burst.

She flew away from him crying and shrieking, the sound of her wailing was all around him and it haunted Holohan right up to his death.

He ran as fast as he could over the hills and mounds until at last he was at his own house. He expected to hear the sound of music and laughter and see his family ready to welcome him into their arms.

The cottage was silent and there was no sign or sound of any sort of celebration. Holohan threw open the door and to his horror he saw his brothers and sisters kneeling around his poor mother lying dead in her bed. He fell to his knees and as he kissed the icy cold lips of his mother, he could hear the faint wailing of the banshee being carried on the night wind. She called out over the land, the hills, the trees and the mounds, 'Dying! Dying! Dying! Dying!'

Co. Laois: From the Irish *laoise*, meaning light. It also comes from the word *Laoighsigh*, which was the name of an ancient tribe descended from Conall Cearnach, a mighty warrior and leader of the Red Branch Knights. Co. Laois was formerly known as 'Queen's County' after Queen Mary I, who was better known as Bloody Mary. The Rock of Dunamase lies between Stradbally and Portlaoise, where the ruins of *Dún Másc*, meaning 'Fort of the Mask', stands. It is guarded by a great hound called Bandog, who spews fire from its massive jaws at anyone approaching. The town of Ballyfin, which means 'Finn's Town', is named after the great Celtic hero Fionn or Finn Mac Cumhaill. The Revd John Canon O'Hanlon (1821–1905) was a well-regarded writer and folklorist from Stradbally, Co. Laois.

THE FAIRY GLEN OF MOUNTRATH
(CO. LAOIS)

Steve's late father Patrick Lally was a native of Co. Laois – he grew up in the town of Mountrath, a small town right between Dublin and Limerick. ('Mountrath' comes from the Irish *Moin Ratha*; meaning 'fort of the bog'.) Steve remembers his father telling stories about his childhood in Mountrath, his time in school at Ballyfin, and his own father, who was the local Garda Sergeant. Steve's father went on to study science at University College Dublin (where the National Folklore Collection is housed). He both worked and was highly regarded in the world of science and medicine up until his death in 1993. Although Pat Lally was a man of learning and logic, he was always aware of powers that exist far beyond our basic human understating that not even science itself can explain. He also loved a good story and this one is for him.

The following tale features two accounts from a strange world that lies beyond the ethereal wall between the human and fairy worlds. It was collected by a student called Nora Phelan from Scoil Briscula, Mountrath, Co. Laois, in February 1938. It is part of the National Folklore Collection, UCD. The stories came from Kathleen McCarthy (*The Schools' Collection*, Vol. 0833, pp.77–9) and Denis Keenan (*The Schools' Collection,* Vol. 0833, pp.80–2).

Many stories are told locally about numerous peoples' adventures in the Fairy Glen of Mountrath when they pass by it at night.

Kathleen McCarthy collected this story from her grandmother, Catherine Holland, from the townland of Upper Sconce, Co. Laois. She gave a brief description of the story and we took it upon ourselves to embellish it.

One night long ago when Catherine Holland was a slip of 17, she was coming from a dance in Clonrare, just outside of Mountrath. She was with two of her young male friends from the neighbourhood, one being her cousin.

They were laughing and having great craic altogether as they were coming around by the fairy glen when they suddenly heard the most beautiful music coming out of the darkness. It sounded like a harp being played with exquisite tenderness.

Although it was a fine harvest night, with the moon shining in the sky above them like a big silver dollar, the glen was dark. Even in daylight with the trees growing so thickly on all sides around it, the fairy glen was always a place of shadows and darkness.

The three young people went over to the wall to listen and see where this enchanting music was coming from. Then out of the shadows came a beautiful woman, a shining vision as Catherine described it, and although the night was dark they could see her perfectly. She was tall with golden-brown hair and eyes that shone like pools of blue sapphire. Her dress was green and it rustled in the wind, she had a silver belt around her waist, silver leaves in her golden-brown hair and silver streamers fluttered like wings from her shoulders. She stretched out her slender arms and said to Catherine's cousin with the brightest smile and in the sweetest voice, 'Come and dance with me a *stór*' (*stór* is Irish for my love/my darling).

The poor fella drew back frightened, and Catherine and her friend were frightened too and could not utter a word. Then she turned to the other young man and held out her arms, smiling at him seductively; he was a jolly devil-may-care sort of fellow as Catherine described him in her account of the events. He was the sort of chap who would not like to look afraid or not be up for the craic, as they say.

He straightened himself up and with a sure and confident tone said, 'I will come with all my heart,' and, stretching out his arms to take her, he bounded across the low wall and ran towards the beautiful woman that beckoned him.

They tripped along among the thick trees that surrounded the fairy glen as if skipping along to the music, which now became infinitely sweeter.

Catherine and her cousin waited a very long time for their friend's return, until day was almost breaking, until the music ceased and they could hear the workmen turning in at Ballyfin gates; but there was no tail or tidings of him. Sadly and reluctantly they decided it was time to go home and hope that their friend would show up sooner or later.

A month later he did show up; he had arrived back at his own house wearing the same clothes from the night he had disappeared and amazingly they were not one bit stained or worn. But his face was drawn and pale, the light gone from his eyes and the smile from his lips. He was not the same happy-go-lucky fella that they had known before – he was sombre and quiet, like a young man suffering from a broken heart.

He never spoke of his experience in the fairy glen or the strange woman that he had run away with, and he was so shy and timid that nobody dared ask him, for fear they might make matters worse. He became a changed man, his passion for life was gone and he was a shell of

his former self. Now he never joined in a dance, a song or a story. It was as if he had left the best part of himself in the shadows of the fairy glen. His friends and family were heartbroken themselves to see this young man they had known all their lives become so distant and removed from the world around him.

A year passed by, and on the anniversary of the night he spent in the fairy glen, he became dangerously ill. A terrible sickness had gotten a hold of him and there was a wild look in his eyes, the people round him thought that he must be mad with the fever. The priest and the doctor were sent for, who said nothing could be done for him. The doctor had never seen such an affliction before and was baffled and disturbed by what he saw. The priest believed that the young man was possessed by some demon and he did all he could with the power that God had invested in him to help this poor soul.

But there was nothing he could do for the poor lad, and it became obvious that the young fella was not going to make it. With shaking hands, the priest administered the last sacraments and when the young man was breathing his last, he stretched out his arms as if he were going to grasp someone; he looked happy and content as he smiled his old brilliant smile and said joyfully, 'I will come with all my heart a *stór*'. With that the young man died and he was laid to rest shortly afterwards.

Catherine and her cousin never went to the fairy glen again and never spoke of what had happened. One night many years later as they were walking home from a dance they could hear that sweet and beautiful music carried on the nocturnal wind, and in the midst of it they could hear a woman laughing and then they heard the voice of an old friend that they had not heard in a very long time, he sounded so happy and full of joy as he called out, 'I love you with all my heart, and I promise I will never leave you again a *stór*!'

This next story about the Fairy Glen of Mountrath was told to young Nora Phelan by Denis Keenan from the townland of Knocks, Co. Laois.

He told her that Patrick Geoghan, a gardener in Ballyfin fifty years previous (which would have it the year 1888), was always talking about 'Moll the Fairy'. Moll was a small fairy-like woman who lived beside the fairy glen. Mr Geoghan was constantly asking Moll to take him on a visit to the fairies' palace in the glen, and she always said to him, 'You can come with me whenever it pleases yourself.'

This was really just a bit of flirting and play-making between the two of them and it was not to be of any real significance.

It was a beautiful calm bright summer's evening and the birds were singing melodiously in the high trees and the green hedges around the fairy glen. And it was on this bright and cheerful summers' evening that Pat was returning from his work at Ballyfin. As he walked and whistled along the country road, he passed by Moll's house.

He was in high spirits after paying a visit to John Rafter, the owner of the public house at the bottom of the hill who was also a very generous man and always gave Patrick a pint on the house, for he would keep the hedges in check outside the pub and keep the place looking well.

As usual Patrick shouted to Moll, who was coming in from milking the goats. 'Eh Moll, when are you bringing me to see the fairies?'

'Tonight if you like,' she answered.

'Alright I'll go with you tonight,' he said.

Now he thought that this was just a bit of craic and he had not expected Moll to give such a clear and direct answer. But she stood there and told him to come on in and wait for her while she got ready. So he went in and waited till Moll was ready.

When they left the house together and set off for the fairy glen, Moll warned him cautiously what to do and say when he entered the fairy palace. She made a point of telling him not to take anything from the fairies' hands, for if he did so he would never be let home again. She said there were many souls who made that mistake and never returned and those that did were far worse for it.

It was late – about ten o'clock – when they crossed the low wall at the back of the house surrounding the fairy glen. When they got to it, they were greeted by a large number of strange-looking little men and women, all of them gaily dressed, some of them singing merrily and others playing on musical instruments.

They all led Pat and Moll through a tunnel at the bottom of a huge oak tree. The tunnel was long and dark and Pat was starting to think that this was a very bad idea. He really thought that it was all a bit of craic with Moll but now he realised very quickly that it was quite serious indeed. He looked at Moll with pure amazement for she was not just a fairy by name and appearance, be the hokey she actually was one of the good folk.

The couple were taken to a beautiful palace, the likes of which Pat, a simple gardener, had never seen before. It was breathtaking –

the walls were made of solid gold and the turrets were topped with silver and jewels. Then they were taken to the main gates, these were made of solid gold and were guarded by two sentries dressed in the finest military garb.

On entering, Pat and Moll were greeted by a fairy king and queen dressed beautifully with gold and silver streamers hanging to the floor from their silk and satin robes.

They greeted their guests with great gusto and warmth. The king and queen were quite tall and both were fine-looking creatures. The king was handsome with a mischievous boy-like quality about him and his queen was very beautiful with enchanting eyes of emerald green that sparkled like jewels in the firelight.

The palace itself was so beautifully furnished that Pat could hardly believe his eyes. Never in all his life had he seen such finery and luxurious architecture. The floor of the palace shone like glass, which was made of such finely polished gold that he could see his reflection in it. All he could do was look at it all with his mouth open. Moll scolded him and said he looked like a poltroon.

They were both brought in and seated in two beautiful chairs. Little waiters and waitresses came with trays and dishes with intoxicating drinks of all kinds and although they were very tempting, Pat remembered what Moll had said and refused to take them. Moll, however, was at liberty to take anything she wished. In fact, she tried everything and looked like she was very much enjoying it.

Poor Pat was getting quite upset now as he was hungry and thirsty and he thought that Moll was being very selfish. He looked at Moll and said, 'This is not fair, what am I to do? They keep offering me all this wonderful food and drink and I am so famished and the thirst has me driven mad. Not only that, the wee folk are being insulted by my refusal to take any of it. 'Tis an awful predicament that I am in Moll. And 'tis alright for you to eat away and sup to your heart's content; 'tis very unfair of you Moll. What am I to do at all?'

It was obvious that Moll was intoxicated as she was lit up like a Tilley lamp. She grinned from ear to ear and looked at poor auld Pat and replied, 'Sorry Pat, I lost the run of myself. It must be awful hard for ya alright. I meant to say that if you ask them to put salt on your food, they will not offer you another thing again, and then we will have a dance Pat!'

Pat nodded at Moll and when the wee waiters and waitresses came to him again with platters laden with magnificent food, he piped up, 'Can I have some salt to put on that please? Thank you!'

Well, when they heard that they looked at him as if he had asked them to throw their rotten food in the bin. They were horrified and with that the wee servants tutted at him, turned their noses up in the air, then spun around on their heels and marched away, very affronted indeed.

Moll turned to Pat and asked him how he got on. 'It worked very well indeed,' he replied. Without further ado, Moll took Pat by the hand and they walked over to the magnificent dance hall.

They danced and sang with the fairies till daybreak, which was about five o'clock. When the sun began to rise all that they saw around them began to disappear like a fading image before their eyes and the music and laughter quieted down until all they could hear was the sound of the birds welcoming the dawn and the cock as he crew from his perch.

Holding hands, they both returned home to Moll's house and Pat looked at her in a way that he had never done before and he asked her if she would marry him. Moll was overjoyed and said that she surely would. Well it was announced that Pat the Gardner and Moll the Fairy were to be married. It was a fine wedding indeed with lots of celebrations. Pat could eat and drink his fill without worry and he thought Moll looked so beautiful in her wedding dress and he was never so happy in all his life.

Well after the wedding you will never guess where they went on their honeymoon, yes that's right, off to the fairy glen they went and into the palace at the bottom of the oak tree. There they had another wedding feast, only this time Pat ate and drank away to his heart's content, for he was now part of the fairy family.

Moll and Pat had children and they too had children and some of them may still be about the town of Mounthrath in the county of Laois.

Co. Longford: From the Irish *An Longfoirt*, meaning 'The Port'. Co. Longford has a rich and diverse mythological history. In Co. Longford you will find Ardagh Hill or Bri Leigh, home of the legendary 'Midir', a king of the ancient Tuatha Dé Danann. It is also home to some of the greatest Irish folklorists. Legan was the home of Patrick Greene (Pádraig Mac Gréine) (1900–2007). He died at the age of 106 and was a teacher and folklore collector. He is estimated to have transcribed 10,000 pages of folklore material in the course of his work. Co. Longford was also the birthplace of the world-renowned writer, playwright and folklorist Padraic Colum (1881–1972), who was born in a Co. Longford workhouse.

THE LEGENDS OF LOUGH GOWNA (CO. LONGFORD)

We found these stories about Irish mermaids and monsters in the Dúchas Archive from *The Schools' Collection*, Vol. 0762, pp.310–12. The collector was from St Columba's National School, Cloonagh, Granard, in Co. Longford. Their name was not stated but there are several informants who give fascinating accounts of mermaids and sea monsters from Lough Gowna. Lough Gowna is a freshwater lake located on the border between Co. Longford and Co. Cavan. These accounts were recorded in November 1937.

The Irish equivalent of mermaids are merrows. They have fish's tails like mermaids but also little webs between their fingers. They are said to be gentle creatures who often fall in love with mortal fishermen. According to Katherine Briggs in her beautiful collection *A Dictionary of Fairies: Hobgoblins, Brownies, Bogies and other Supernatural Creatures* (1976), sometimes merrows come ashore in the form of little hornless cattle, but in their proper shape they wear red feather caps, by means of which they go through the water. If these caps are stolen or lost they cannot return to the sea again. Some stories we have come across state that these merrows settle with fishermen and if they happen to find the red feather hat that they once lost they will just up and leave their mortal husband and in some cases their children, because the lure of the sea is so strong.

There are male merrows too and they are said to have little faces like pigs, yet the female merrows are beautiful in comparison.

Our story begins in 1934 with a Miss Ellen Rudden, an old lady from Granard, Co. Longford. She was walking the road along Lough Gowna on a summer's evening when her attention was attracted to the lake by a mournful wail that came from the opposite shore.

She plainly saw a creature that looked like a person with long hair, lying on its back in the water near the shore. What she did not know was that this strange creature was called a merrow or *murdhuacha*. They are something between a banshee and a mermaid and are dreaded, because they appear before storms and drownings.

Two nights after Ellen saw the merrow, a poor woman who was suffering from mental illness escaped from her house in the middle of the night. Those who were in charge of caring for her followed the woman but there was no sign of her at all. She had run towards Lough Gowna, screaming, 'She is calling me! She is calling me!' Her body was found the next evening, floating lifelessly in the lake.

Another informant was Mr Pat Curry, an old man of 75 who said that this same creature always appears before a drowning takes place in the lake. He saw her one evening when he was a young boy working with his father in a field near the lake, and he always remembered that his father said, 'There will be someone drowned before long.' Two or three days after, there was a funeral in the district, and four men came from Columbkille across the lake in a boat to attend the funeral. On the return journey they heard a terrible mournful cry coming from across the lake. They had no idea what it was and then the water started to turn and swell, the boat capsized and the four men were in the water. One of the men could not hold on and the others said that he was pulled below the surface by something. The poor man drowned and his comrades were very distraught by the whole experience.

A Mr Rodgers who died in 1897 (forty years before this story was recorded), said that the merrow was seen near Inch Island, and her mournful cry was distinctly heard before a drowning that took place near the home of the Doffing family, a long time ago.

They were a wealthy family and Ralf Doffing (called locally Rafe) was the owner of the estate at the time. He was the sort of fellow that had plenty of money but did not use it too wisely. He enjoyed showing off his wealth and making it well known that he enjoyed a lavish lifestyle.

On one occasion he had a shooting party, and at night they feasted on an old yacht that he had on Lough Gowna. The yacht was never used for sailing because it was too large for the shallow lake, and it remained in deep water out from the shores, for sleeping in summer, and for entertaining guests.

On this particular night, after enjoying themselves drinking and shooting at the stars, they were about to return to the shore, and three of them got safely onto the small boat that was waiting below the yacht. But the fourth man, who had had too much to drink, tumbled down the ladder from the yacht and overturned the boat, and all four men were drowned.

The old people used to make a joke about these rich libertines after their demise. 'Sure they could not have better luck because they spent part of the time firing at the moon from the deck of the yacht.'

Bizarrely, for an island, Ireland has an amazingly limited number of references to sea monsters in the existing folklore. We sometimes read stories referring to Selkies. We came across a lovely article by Matt Staggs called 'Meet the Selkies: Scotland's Shape-Shifting Seal Fairies' (2018). He states that they are also known as roane and water kelpies, and are shape-shifting fairies that travel about the ocean disguised as seals. He says that while tales of these mysterious creatures have made their way to every corner of the globe, they are native to the Orkney and Shetland Islands of Scotland. We sometimes hear stories of them on the north coast of Ireland and, oddly enough, in inland lakes. They are not described as dangerous; in fact, they are fairly harmless.

These are most common to the north and along the coast of current-day Scotland but, for the most part, the tales portray the creatures as relatively benign (they're certainly not described as fearful or terrifying).

The following story was collected from a Mr Francis Reilly. He was rowing a boat on Lough Gowna one day with two old friends who had gone off to become priests. The two holy men were home on their holidays. Mr Reilly had known them from way back and he was delighted to see the lads after such a long time. The day was beautiful, the sun was shining and the water was calm, so they decided to take a long sail on the lake, and visit the Island of Inch, which was about 5 miles from where they started.

When they were about half an hour out, the two priests saw a strange creature come to the surface. They could not believe their eyes, for they had never seen such a creature before. It had the head of a calf and a very long neck, which appeared above the water, but they could not describe what its body was like, as it was submerged in the darkness of the lake, but it appeared to be very large indeed. The creature made a low moaning noise a bit like a cow and then it disappeared below the surface once again and swam away, its huge shadow dwarfing the boat and its terrified passengers. It seems like they had encountered something similar to the Loch Ness Monster.

They were all very shaken by this experience and they asked Mr Reilly to pull to the nearest shore, and they abandoned the sail. They never thought there was such a creature to be found in an inland lake, or any other waters for that matter.

Lough Gowna is full of strange secrets lurking in its depths; some are wonderful and even friendly and some are to be feared and avoided at all costs …

Co. Louth: From the Irish *Lú*, after the Sun God Lugh. 'Lugh of the Long Arm' was a high-ranking member of the Tuatha Dé Danann. He defeated the dreaded Fomorians, a savage race of demonic creatures and their leader Balor of the Baleful Eye at what is now called the Poisoned Glen in Co. Donegal. When the old Gods lost their power after the people turned to Christianity, Lugh was demoted to a cobbler and became what is now known as 'the leprechaun'. Co. Louth is steeped in myth and folklore. Ireland's greatest hero and mythical character 'Cú Chulainn' hailed from Co. Louth. Knockbridge Stone in Co. Louth is where Cú Chulainn died, overcome by magic and betrayal. He was wounded and bound himself to this stone so he would die on his feet. It is said that when he had died the Morrighan (the shape-shifting Celtic Goddess of War, Fate and Death) took the form of a hooded crow and landed on his shoulders.

THE LEPRECHAUN WHISPERER
(CO. LOUTH)

Kevin Woods of Carlingford in Co. Louth is believed to be the last lep-rechaun whisperer in Ireland. Steve met him back in 2012 and kept in touch with him.

We visited him at his home in Carlingford, where he lives with his wife and family. Carlingford is a special little place with winding medieval streets, rugged landscape and sea views that look over across to the Mournes.

Kevin is a friendly man who kindly showed us around his property. He runs a successful business beside his home and has an underground lep-rechaun and fairy cavern right beside the beautiful Carlingford Lough. He himself gives personal tours and tells the stories of his encounter with leprechauns. You can then visit below the ground, where he believes lep-rechauns and fairies converge in the morning as the sun rises. He showed us two tunnels, one of which links with the fairy glen in Rostrevor, Co. Down, and the other with Foy Mountain, which Kevin believes is the home of Ireland's last remaining leprechauns.

Kevin's story begins twenty-eight years ago when the late P.J. O'Hare, a local publican, heard a terrible scream coming from Foy Mountain. He went up to investigate but he couldn't find anybody. However, the ground around the place (the Slate Rock) was burned and in the middle of the burning he found some bones and near the bones he found what he thought was a leprechaun suit, with four pieces of gold in the pocket of the trousers. He brought the suit down to Kevin Woods to see what he thought. He trusted that Kevin would believe him. P.J. O'Hare believed that there were leprechauns in the mountains and they were very much alive. Kevin told him it was a load of rubbish and he told P.J. that he would prove it to him. So, Kevin hatched a plan. He told P.J. that he would get as many people up on the Cooley Mountains to search it high and low. But he also knew that for people to help search for leprechauns they would want something in return, so Kevin hid IR£4,000 punt all around the mountain – IR£1,000 under four different toy leprechauns. He sold leprechaun hunting licences for IR£10 each. He said that when the big day arrived for the hunt the place was full of people – they came in their thousands with butterfly nets and traps. Kevin ended up making IR£8,000 for his day.

If you go into P.J. O'Hares pub in Carlingford today, you will see the wee suit that he found up on the Cooley Mountains. It is framed in a glass case.

Sadly, eight years after that hunt, P.J. O'Hare passed away.

Kevin had fond memories of the leprechaun hunt but still wasn't convinced that the mountain was inhabited by leprechauns.

About two years after P.J. died, Kevin was out fixing the wall at his house. To his surprise he found four gold coins. Kevin felt the best thing to do was go back up the mountain and return the coins to where P.J. had found them all those years previously. When Kevin reached the spot, to his amazement he admits to seeing three leprechauns sitting on a rock. When they saw him they disappeared. He went home to his wife and retold the story, and she advised him to not tell a soul for fear he would be locked up. But he told everybody and, of course, nobody believed him. So, off Kevin went in search of the leprechauns. He headed up the same path as before and was determined to talk to a leprechaun. This time when he reached the top he saw one leprechaun. The leprechaun did not disappear but instead spoke with Kevin and he told him his name was Carraig (the Irish word for rock). He told Kevin that there had been millions of leprechauns in Ireland at one time but they had all died except for 236 of them. He asked Kevin if he would try and get more people to believe in them and Kevin said he would do what he could. Carraig asked him to get leprechauns protected as a species and he said he would have a go at that too.

He told Kevin the story of their lives and how they were here from the beginning of time. They described themselves as spirits. He said that the Mourne Mountains and the Cooley Mountains were created about fifty million years ago and he went on to say that the lough in Carlingford was created 15,000 years ago. He told Kevin how they looked down and saw the first humans arrive from central Europe. He spoke about the Vikings arriving in 804 and how St Patrick sailed into Carlingford in 428. The Vikings burned the place twice and that was the first time that the leprechaun spirit interacted with the human spirit. They decided to help the human spirit but they soon regretted it. They said they helped the human spirit when the Vikings first arrived and then again when the Normans reached us in 1210. They told Kevin that the Vikings were cruel and so the leprechauns decided to intervene, for the cruelty was too much for them to stand by and watch. He said that the leprechaun spirit grew so close to the human spirit that at one stage you couldn't tell the difference between one and the other. He said that the leprechaun spirit attached itself to the human spirit. Then when the Irish people went off to America to seek their fortune and they became more involved with filthy money and housing and property – that was when the human spirit died, for humans were only interested in what they could buy. Greed took over. And when the human spirit died, so too did the leprechaun spirit.

Apparently, the leprechauns explained to Kevin that there had once been millions of them but they had died out because people stopped believing in them, and they needed someone from humankind to protect them otherwise they would die out altogether.

One legend says that the leprechaun is actually the ancient Irish God Lug. After the Irish people forgot the old gods, the legend goes, Lug became a fairy cobbler named Lugh Chromain, which means 'little stooping Lug'.

Lugh, Lug or Lú, also known as 'Lugh of the Long Arm' and 'The Shining One', was an important god of Irish mythology. He was a high-ranking member of the Tuatha Dé Danann, the fairy people of Ireland. He is portrayed as a great warrior and protector against the dreaded Fomorians, a monstrous race of invading demons. He was the God of skill, crafts and the arts, as well as oaths, truth and the law. He was also seen as a Sun God, Storm God, and a Sky God. The Harvest festival Lughnasa is named after him.

Kevin Woods wrote a book called *The Last Leprechauns in Ireland* and while he was writing it he lobbied the EU for six years and finally got leprechauns protected as a species in 2009 under the European Habitats Directive covering the protection of flora and fauna in the EU. Kevin has worked tirelessly for the recognition of leprechaun rights. He got them added to the EU list because they couldn't prove they *didn't* exist.

Cooley Distillery is nestled in the foothills of the Cooley Mountains in Co. Louth, and in 2011 they conducted a survey to see if the Irish people believed in leprechauns. More than half of those surveyed said that they were creatures that once lived in Ireland, and the rest felt they were still in existence today.

Leprechauns are seen as the bankers of the Sidhe; they apparently know where all the gold is hidden and they are in control of the gold. We often see leprechauns represented as cheerful and merry, who go around with a glint in their eyes and are never too far away from a pot of gold. They are also the shoemakers of the Sidhe and their job is to make and mend shoes for other fairy folk. A lovely book by Skye Alexander called *Fairies: The Myths, Legends and Lore* (2014) has a section on leprechauns that says they are part of the elf clan. They are apparently easy to spot because they have red hair and beards, wear green suits and have shiny buckles on their shoes. They smoke pipes and wear shamrocks in their lapels. They are brilliant musicians and love nothing more than a good time. They are not known to be malicious or devious but instead love to play harmless tricks on humans. It is said that if you catch a leprechaun then they are obliged to tell you where there is hidden treasure. If you see one, be on your guard and make sure to be kind, for they will be sure to reward you. But keep a close eye because they have a habit of disappearing in the blink of an eye.

The Leprechaun
By William Allingham

Little Cowboy, what have you heard,
Up on the lonely rath's green mound?
Only the plaintive yellow bird
Sighing in sultry fields around,
Chary, chary, chary, chee-ee! –
Only the grasshopper and the bee? –
'Tip-tap, rip-rap,
Tick-a-tack-too!
Scarlet leather, sewn together,
This will make a shoe.
Left, right, pull it tight;
Summer days are warm;
Underground in winter,
Laughing at the storm!'
Lay your ear close to the hill.
Do you not catch the tiny clamour,
Busy click of an elfin hammer.
Voice of the Leprachaun singing shrill
As he merrily plies his trade?

He's a span
And a quarter in height.
Get him in sight, hold him tight,
And you're a made Man!

You watch your cattle the summer day,
Sup on potatoes, sleep in the hay;
How would you like to roll in your carriage,
Look for a duchess's daughter in marriage?
Seize the Shoemaker – then you may!
'Big boots a-hunting,
Sandals in the hall,
White for a wedding-feast,
Pink for a ball.
This way, that way,
So we make a shoe;
Getting rich every stitch,
Tick-tack-too!'
Nine-and-ninety treasure-crocks
This keen miser-fairy hath,
Hid in mountains, woods, and rocks,
Ruin and round-tow'r, cave and rath,
And where the cormorants build;
From times of old
Guarded by him;
Each of them fill'd
Full to the brim
With gold!

I caught him at work one day, myself,
In the castle-ditch where foxglove grows, –
A wrinkled, wizen'd, and bearded Elf,
Spectacles stuck on his pointed nose,
Silver buckles to his hose,
Leather apron – shoe in his lap –
'Rip-rap, tip-tap,
Tick-tack-too!

(A grasshopper on my cap!
Away the moth flew!)
Buskins for a fairy prince,
Brogues for his son, –
Pay me well, pay me well,
When the job is done!'

The rogue was mine, beyond a doubt.
I stared at him; he stared at me;
'Servant, Sir!' 'Humph!' says he,
And pull'd a snuff-box out.
He took a long pinch, look'd better pleased,
The queer little Leprachaun;
Offer'd the box with a whimsical grace, –
Pouf! he flung the dust in my face,
And while I sneezed,
Was gone!

Co. Meath: From the Irish *An Mhí*, meaning 'The Middle'. Co. Meath is a prominent county with regards to folklore and mythology; in fact it is known as 'The Royal County'. The Hill of Tara was the seat of the High Kings of Ireland, it was also where Finn Mac Cumhail fought and slew the Monster of Tara. It is the home of *Brú na Bóinne* (Palace of the Boyne); here you will find some of the world's most important prehistoric sites such as Newgrange, Knowth and Dowth. On the Hill of Tara there was a stone known as the *Lia Fáil* – it was thought to have been brought to Ireland by the Tuatha Dé Danann. It was used to inaugurate new kings as the stone would cry out if the king was the rightful heir. In Co. Meath you will also find Loughcrew, an ancient tomb where the Creation Goddess known as 'The Cailleach' once lived. Co. Meath was also home to the war poet Francis Ledwidge (1887–1917), who wrote some beautiful fairy poetry.

THE PÚCA PRÁINE (CO. MEATH)

County Meath is rich in folklore, history and enchantment. From its ancient tombs to its fairy forts, it is brimming with fine tales to tell. This story is no exception; it is based on a bizarre creature called the Púca Práine.

It was inspired by a tale found in the Dúchas Archive at UCD, *The Schools' Collection*, Vol. 0694, pp.401–2. It was told by Andy Rispin, but the name of the collector is unknown. It was recorded at Coolronan National School, Co. Meath.

There is a rath or mound near the Castle of Fraine (which is now in ruins) in the townland of Fraine, Co. Meath. Within this mound lives the Púca Práine. It is said that the Púca dwells amongst the ruins and hilltops and is driven monstrous by much solitude.

The Púca Práine was a holy man who lived in the townland of Fraine long ago. He was a hermit and spent his days and nights alone, dedicating his time and energy to prayer and meditation. One might say that he lived like a snail in his own little shell, alone and content with very little.

So, when he died, he was reincarnated as a snail. As a snail he lived in the stones and rocks of Fraine Rath, just as solitary and content as he had always been.

Now this was no ordinary snail, for it was given great powers and it would utilise them whenever it saw fit to do so. For example, when an old or weak person passed by the townland of Fraine and they wanted to go home, but they did not have the strength or the energy to do it, they would go to the rath (a circular enclosure surrounded by an earthen wall: used as a dwelling and stronghold in former times) and seek out the snail.

They would do this by calling out the name of the holy man. When they did this, the snail would turn into a black pony, but with the head of a snail. What a strange sight this must have been, a creature with the body of a black pony and the head of a snail, it really is the stuff of nightmares.

When this strange creature appeared, the person would get up on the pony's back and it would carry them home. Now the Púca Práine may well have had the head of a gastropod, but its powerful equestrian body could run like the wind and it could clear any hedge, ditch or stream with a single jump. The Púca Práine would have its passenger back to their front door in record time.

But this was not always the case, for sometimes folk would try and take advantage of the kind Púca Práine. An example of this was recorded in 1837. There were three brothers living near Kildalkey or *Cill Dealga* (meaning 'Dealga's Church'), a village and parish in the Barony of Lune, Co. Meath. Their names were Daniel, Paraic and Wat Moran. The Moran boys were said to have the ability to predict the future. They said once that carts and wagons would go without horses and that after that carts and wagons would travel up in the sky. They were, of course, talking about cars and aeroplanes.

But be that as it may, Daniel Moran did not foresee the consequences of trying to take advantage of the Púca Práine.

On a warm day, Daniel was going home to Kildalkey by Fraine Rath. He called out for the Púca Práine to carry him home.

The beast appeared before Daniel and it stared with scrutiny at the one who had summoned him. The Púca Práine could see that Daniel was neither tired nor old. But yet it kneeled down before him and he let Daniel climb upon his back. He then bolted off like the wind and brought Daniel through hedges, bushes and ditches till his feet and legs were torn and bloody.

When they reached home, the Púca Práine threw Daniel off his back and he landed dazed and frightened at his front door with his clothes in tatters. His brothers came out when they heard the commotion and saw Daniel in a heap on the doorstep.

They were shocked to see their brother after such a long time. Daniel was confused about this, as he thought he was only an hour away, but he had been gone for a week.

The brothers took him in and took care of him and he told them the whole strange story. After that Daniel Moran was a great man for the stories and people from miles around would come and listen to him. And, of course, their favourite story was that of the Púca Práine. He said that it was still there and he knew the name of the holy man that you had to call out to summon the beast.

But he never did tell the name to anyone, he took it with him to his grave. But maybe if you are in the townland of Fraine and you happen to come across Fraine Rath, call out the names of as many old holy men that you can think of. And if you guess the right one, you may well summon the Púca Práine. And if you do, make sure you are either very tired, very old, or both!

Co. Offaly: From the Irish *Uíbh Fhailí*, after the Kingdom of Uí Failghe, which was ruled by the Ó Conchobhair Failghe (anglicised as O'Conor Faly), formerly known as 'Kings County'. It is here that the Dowris Hoard (consisting of 200 Bronze Age objects) was found. Co. Offaly is the home of Leap Castle, the most haunted castle in Ireland. It is in Co. Offaly where you will find the early Christian monastery of Clonmacnoise, founded by St Ciaran in AD 544. Croghan Hill in Co. Offaly is mentioned in the epic poem 'The Faerie Queene' by the English Elizabethan poet Edmund Spenser (1552–1599), published in 1590. T.W. (Thomas William Hazen) Rolleston (1857–1920), the wonderful writer, poet and collector of Celtic mythology, was born in Glasshouse, Shinrone, Co. Offaly.

MESSIN' WITH THE WEE FOLK (CO. OFFALY)

The following stories are recorded accounts of folk tampering with the fairy raths or forts of the Slieve Bloom Mountains. They were passed on to us by Co. Offaly storyteller Frank Bergin. Steve worked with Frank at the Slieve Bloom Storytelling Festival in 2015. Frank was born and raised in the Slieve Bloom Mountains in the townland of Roscomroe, in the parish of Kinnity. The mighty Slieve Bloom mountain range straddles both Co. Offaly and Co. Laois. They are steeped in folklore and legend – even their name comes from ancient Celtic mythology, for Slieve Bloom means 'The Mountain of Bladma or Blod' – Blod was the son of Cú (the Hound).

The first of these stories involves a family consisting of an old woman and her three sons living in the Slieve Bloom Mountains. One day when the mother was wandering about the mountains looking for nuts and berries, she came across a magnificent group of hazel trees growing on a fairy fort or rath. Now there are fairy raths all over the Slieve Bloom Mountains and it was and still is a well-known fact that one should never interfere with them or the system of fairy paths that link them together. But this woman paid no heed to such *piseogs* (superstitions). She was delighted, for she was in great need of a big strong basket to put the spuds into and the hazel rods and saplings would provide the perfect materials to create such a basket.

She rushed back to the homestead and told her eldest son where the fort was and to go and cut as many rods and saplings as he could and bring them back to her at once. The poor fellow knew better than to question his mother and off he went with his sharp knife and axe to find the fairy fort. It was not long before he found the mystical fort and lo and behold there certainly was a wonderful collection of hazel trees growing upon it. He climbed up onto the fort and began to cut and chop his way through the trees. As he did, he got an awful strange feeling, like he was being watched. He then felt something brush past him and it was at this point that he decided to call it a night; it was starting to get dark anyway.

When he got home he handed over the rods to his mother, who told him to get a bite to eat and then go to bed. She began weaving the rods into a basket with great eagerness. Her son went to bed complaining of a sore back, which he put down to the work with the rods. The next morning when the poor fellow woke up he could hardly move at all. He managed to pull himself out of the bed and when he did, he could not stand up straight at all. His mother shouted over at him, 'Would ye stand up straight, you're like a fellow looking for money he dropped!' The old woman never had much sympathy for her sons, especially after her living through the Great Hunger. This dark time in Ireland's history left many people hard and even cruel in their ways and dealings with other folk. 'Well I need more rods to finish this basket!' she cried out and she called for her second son to go to the fort and cut her a good lump of rods and bring them back to her straight away.

The poor lad headed off and he was not too happy about it at all. He had heard what his brother had said the night before about being watched and something brushing past him. But he reasoned with him-self that his brother was merely spooked as it was getting dark, but it was early in the day now and he had plenty of light. When he got to the fort, he climbed up and began to cut and chop with the axe and knife he had taken with him. But he too got a funny feeling that he was being watched, and as he worked away he was sure that something had hit against him. He worked on, trying to convince himself that it was all in his imagination, until he felt like something had bitten his leg. He let out a shout of both fear and pain. Well that was it, there was no way he was going to spend any more time in this terrible place. He gathered up what he had cut and made his way swiftly back home. When he got back his mother took the rods from him excitedly and began to weave her basket. As she worked she told the son to get something to eat and finish off his chores about the house, for that useless older brother of his could do nothing as he was bent over like a horseshoe. It was not long though before he too felt a terrible pain in his back and took to his bed.

The old woman ran out of rods and was not too pleased about this as two of her sons were now bent over like auld fellas. She called in her youngest son who was outside (and let the truth be known was avoiding his mother for he was afraid of being sent to the fort). But nevertheless he was called in and his tough auld mother instructed him to go to the fort and get enough rods for her to finish her basket. Only this time she told him to take it easy and look after his back so that he would not end up like his two older brothers. Reluctantly he went to the fort and just like his brothers before him he climbed up and began working away at the rods. Now whatever it was in the fort that had scared away his two older siblings was starting to get very agitated with these strangers coming and stealing their rods. As the young lad worked away he too felt like he was being watched and he even heard voices whispering all around him. They sounded angry and although he could not understand what they were saying, he knew that it was not friendly or well-meaning.

The voices got louder and the lad felt little hands grabbing at his legs and then he felt something sink its teeth into him. He screamed in terror and agony as he ran back to the house, grasping the bundle of precious hazel rods. When he got back he threw the rods down at his mother's feet and swore he would never go back to the fort again. The poor boy was beside himself with fear and he showed his mother where he had been bitten on his leg. 'Tis only a scratch, you probably caught your leg on some thorns,' she scoffed, with no sign of compassion for her child. She told the boy to get something to eat and go to his bed.

The old woman worked away at the basket and it was not long before she had it all finished. She was very proud of her handiwork and was keen to try it out and see how strong it was. Now there was a big pile of spuds in the corner of the room and it was for this reason that she wanted a basket, for it was unseemly and no good to have the lovely spuds piled up on the floor. Oh what a lovely sight it was to see the spuds neatly gathered in the fine big basket. She decided that in the morning she would treat herself and her sons to a fine breakfast of boxty (potato bread) and butter, she even felt a wee bit bad for not being nice to her sons and showing them more attention.

She went to bed herself and the next morning she was up bright and early to make the lovely breakfast. But when she got to the basket she let out a terrible scream, for all the spuds were rotten with blight and the smell would have knocked you over. She called her sons but none of them came as they were all stooped and twisted.

This was a terrible situation altogether. There was only one thing for it and that was to go to see the wise woman, or fairy doctor, who lived up on the Slieve Bloom Mountains and find out what was going on. As she made her way up the mountain she could see a wee curl of smoke on the horizon that was coming from the wise woman's hovel.

When she got to the wee shack she heard the old woman calling her inside by her name, as if she could see her through the walls. She opened the door and went inside, and there was the wise woman sitting by the fire, as if she was waiting for her. She told the fairy doctor all about her three sons and how they were all made cripples after cutting the hazel rods and how when the basket was finished it had rotted all the spuds. The mother was beside herself as she proclaimed that they would all starve with her sons unable to work and not a bite to eat in the house. The fairy doctor remained calm and composed and asked the old woman where they got the rods from. She explained that she had seen them on one of the forts up the mountain. The wise woman laughed when she heard this.

''Tis no laughin' matter!' said the old woman angrily.

'Ye got them from a fairy fort, sure 'tis no wonder at all that ye are havin' bad luck!' replied the fairy doctor. She explained to the old woman that these rods belonged to the good folk, who did not take kindly at all to folk stealing their property.

'What am I to do?' asked the old woman and the fairy doctor explained that she was to take all her three sons back to the fairy fort and return

the basket. If they were to do this then they would make their peace with the fairy folk and all should be well. The old woman thanked the fairy doctor and promised she would pray for her in return for her services.

As soon as she got back she told her sons to come with her to the fort and for one of them to take the basket with him.

Oh! 'Twas a sorrowful sight indeed to see the old woman and her three sons stooped over as they made their weary way shuffling up the mountain to the fort. They looked like ancient beasts of burden that had been broken down by years of hard, thankless labour. After a long and arduous journey they finally reached the fort and as soon as they did the three sons threw the basket into the fort, where it landed with a soft crunching of grass.

As soon as this was done the three sons all stood up straight and the auld mother cried with joy and relief. When they got home all the spuds were piled nicely in the corner and they were as fresh as the day they were picked. After that the old woman never asked her sons to interfere with the good folk, nor were they ever in any rush to do so either.

Another story that Frank told us about the Slieve Bloom Mountains also involved the hazel tree, although this time it was concerning its fruit, the hazelnut.

According to the old people, a long time ago the hazelnut was a lot bigger than it is today and it had no hard shell but was made of a soft flesh like a tomato and was simply delicious. Now a group of young lads were going about the Slieve Bloom Mountains looking for their favourite nuts and berries. Their favourite beyond any shadow of a doubt was the hazelnut with its beautiful soft flesh that was so sweet and juicy. They thought that they had struck gold when they found a whole heap of them growing on a fairy fort up the mountain. The boys gathered as many as they could and ate a right amount too. Then they brought the rest of them back to their homes. But that night, to their great dismay, all their teeth started to fall out. Their parents were very concerned and decided the best thing to do was to take them all up to see the fairy doctor and find out what was going on. They all arrived at the wise woman's hovel and when they did, there she was waiting for them. They explained to her what had happened and she asked them where they found the nuts. The children told her that they had picked them off a fort on the mountain. Well, as you can imagine she found this awful amusing indeed and enlightened them by telling them all that they had stolen from the fairy folk and this was their punishment. But she went on to explain that if they were to return whatever nuts they had left then it should all be resolved. They then left the old woman a few bob and they headed home.

When everyone got back to their homes they made sure to collect all the hazelnuts and bring them back to the fairy fort. When they did, they threw them all back and as if by magic all their teeth grew back and they were very happy indeed. Now, although some of the nuts were returned, the fairy folk were still very annoyed with random strangers coming along and helping themselves to their precious fruit. So they decided to teach them all a lesson by making the nuts much smaller and giving them a hard shell, so that you could never take a bite out of one unless you wanted to lose a few teeth.

The final story that Frank told us was based around the fairy paths of the Slieve Bloom Mountains. As we now know, there are many fairy forts in this mountain range and they are all interlinked with a system of hidden pathways known as fairy paths. It is considered to be both foolish and dangerous to build any structure or create any form of obstruction on these paths. It is also strongly advised that if you are going to build something where there are fairy forts or trees in the area, you need to put four ash rods or pegs from an ash tree in the four corners of the foundations. Some folk leave them overnight, others leave them for a couple of days and then they come back to check them. If the pegs or rods are damaged or missing, then it is considered to be solid proof that the foundations are obstructing a fairy path. The builder is then strongly advised to build elsewhere.

This particular story deals with a certain character who had more money than sense and wanted to build a house for himself on the Slieve Bloom Mountains. He was advised that where he was building was right upon a fairy path, but he paid no heed to such 'auld nonsense', as he called it. So off he went and from the very get-go he was having trouble. The scaffolding kept falling down, the mortar would not mix properly for him, when he hit a stone with a hammer it would turn to dust and the whitewash would not dry. This fellow was losing a power of money over all this. He spent enough money on materials and hired help that would have easily paid for another five or six houses. But he was determined that he would not let *piseogery* (superstitions) get the better of him so he persevered and eventually his house was built and he moved in. Well now that was not the end of it at all for at night he would hear knocking at the front and back doors and the sound of running and voices outside. He never caught anyone or anything but he had no peace. Then he decided to light a fire, that's when it all got a lot worse, for every time he did so the whole house would fill with thick black smoke. He would have to run outside to avoid suffocation. The poor man tried everything in his power to fix it – he had chimneysweeps galore and he even had the chimney itself widened, but it was no good. No matter what he did the smoke just kept billowing out of the fireplace and destroying the house and all its contents. In the end this man had no choice but to give up. He finally moved out of the house and built a new one far away from anything remotely attached to the good folk.

That old house on the fairy path was never lived in again and has over the years turned to a ruin, but the ruins are still there, somewhere up on the Slieve Bloom Mountains in Co. Offaly.

To finish up Frank Bergin told us that although we can't see these fairy paths, there is a road in Co. Offaly between Rosbeg and Kinnity called *Bothar an Phúca*, which means the 'The Pooka's Road'. I wonder if anyone has dared build their house on this road and, if so, what sort of stories would they have to tell.

Co. Westmeath: From the Irish *Na Hiarmhí*, meaning 'West-Middle'. The county is situated right in the centre of Ireland, which is more commonly known as 'The Midlands'. It is a very historical county with many ancient castles and forts. Túathal Techtmar, a high king of Ireland, was based in Co. Westmeath; his grandson was Conn Cétchathach, a mighty warrior better known as 'Conn of the Hundred Battles'. The Hill of Uisneach stands right in the centre of Ireland where, on a clear day, it is said that you can see twenty of the thirty-two counties. This is where 'Lugh of the Long Arm', hero and God of the Tuatha Dé Danann, is said to have come and saved his mother's people from the Formorians. The townland of Nure, near Mullingar, is better known as 'Lilliput' after Johnathon Swift (1667–1745) was inspired to write his classic *Gulliver's Travels* (1726) after visiting there. The world-renowned tenor Count John McCormack (1884–1945) was born in Athlone, Co. Westmeath. One of his most famous songs was 'The Fairy Tree of Clogheen', written by Temple Lane.

THE SLUAGH SIDHE (CO. WESTMEATH)

This is a story we found in the Schools Collection in Duchas. Imelda Dunican collected it from Mrs Caffret in Kilbeggan, Co. Westmeath, the date is unknown but thought to be *c.*1938. Vol. 0732, pp.490–4. We adapted the story and made it our own.

Long ago, old people had a positive belief in fairies, goblins, elves, leprechauns, banshees and Clurichauns (a mischievous fairy in Irish folklore known for his great love of drinking and a tendency to haunt wine cellars). But mothers above all guarded their babies (and still do in some cases) just in case they were taken away by the fairies. They put a pinch of salt under the pillow in the pram as a means of protection. When people praised babies they often forgot to add the little prayer 'God Bless it', so mothers would offer up the little prayer themselves in silent thought – just in case!

Some years ago, a young mother who already had two little girls was made wonderfully happy by the gift of a beautiful baby boy. There was great rejoicing and the father thought this was the most wonderful baby in the parish. The father was a farmer and to his delight the baby thrived and he was the proudest father for miles. When the boy was almost a year old, it happened that the hay season was not such a fine one as usual, so every fine hour that came the farmer and his wife spent in trying to save it. The mother generally took the children with her to the fields, and while the parents worked the children tumbled in the hay and sure the children loved getting out in the fresh air, and would tumble down the hills and play hide-and-seek. As this family had a wee baby, they usually left it in its little cradle asleep in the shade under a tree.

It was August, a calm evening, and the parents were at work, trying to make use of the last of the sun for that day. The girls were sitting over by the tree beside the baby in his cradle and were beginning to feel a little tired. It was near six in the evening when suddenly a rustling, whistling sound passed by, causing the hay to rise in swirls all over the field. Both parents made the sign of the cross, for well they knew it was the Sluagh Sidhe (In Irish and Scottish folklore the Sluagh were the spirits of the restless dead. Some believe they were some ill-begotten form of fairy folk. The Sluagh are known to steal the souls of the dying. They usually wait till the sun has gone down and then they strike. Dark shadows and sometimes a flock of ravens and a ferocious wind comes out of nowhere. The Sluagh Sidhe is also referred to as the Under Folk, the Wild Hunt, or the Host of Unforgiven Dead).

The parents were scared because the mood took a darker turn and they feared for their *choldre*. Not to cause too much panic, they decided to work on when the wind died down. When they came over to where the two little girls were they found them fast asleep but the wee baby boy was crying in his cradle. The parents thought it unusual because the baby was usually nice and quiet. From that day onwards, the baby wasn't the same. It didn't seem to thrive one bit, night and day he cried. The years passed by and the little girls grew up strong and healthy but the wee boy never walked or talked – he just lay in his cradle whining.

There was an old man who lived nearby, and he was a genius on the bagpipes. When he visited the house he would play a tune for the family, which they loved. It was quickly noticed that the wee boy in the cradle would stay quiet whenever the old man played the tune. It seemed to be the only thing that would keep him happy. One evening the man came and as it turned out it lashed from the heavens and the old man couldn't carry his bagpipes home so he decided to leave them behind. The next day the farmer and his wife went to a fair and left the two girls to housekeep and look after the boy. Something during the day attracted their attention outside and the girls left the house. The younger girl returned and, to her surprise, she saw that the wee boy was up on the rafters and playing the bagpipes. She ran out to tell her sister and when they both returned the wee boy was fast asleep in his cradle. When their parents came home the girls ran to the door and told them what had happened and they wouldn't believe them. They said the girl must have

been dreaming. Yet they kept a close eye on the boy after that.

The incident was soon forgotten and one day a travelling woman happened to call and was made very welcome indeed. During the conversation, the mother confided in the woman and told her the story about her son, how the wind came in the field that calm August evening. She felt so comfortable with the woman that she even told her about the day her and her husband where at the fair and her daughter saw her wee brother up on the rafters playing the bagpipes.

The woman was in shock, her mouth was open and her eyes wide listening to the story. The travelling woman advised her to get thirteen eggs and boil them.

'What good would that do?' the mother asked but the woman just said, 'When they are boiled take them out of the pot one by one. Put a special mark on the last egg, but keep the shell of the marked egg. When it is empty fill it with water and put it on a live coal to boil. Have the wee lad on your knee and see how he reacts.'

When the travelling woman left the mother got to work boiling the eggs. When all was ready she took the wee boy on her knee. When he saw the water boiling in the eggshell he let out a roar of laughter and said, 'Be Gad, I'm as old as the hills around but it's the first time I ever saw water boiled in an eggshell!'

Up jumped the wee fella and ran out the door and when the mother turned around again there standing beside the fire was a beautiful looking youth the living image of his father. The mother often wondered if the changing wind on that August evening all those years ago had something to do with it? Was her baby taken and replaced with something else? She tried not to think too much about it and held her son in her arms and offered up a little prayer to herself in silent thought.

Co. Wexford: In Irish it is known as Loch Garman, meaning 'Garman's Lake', but the English translation comes from the Old Norse *Waesfjord*, meaning 'Fjord of the Mud Flats'. This is a county with no shortage of folklore and fairy stories. A language known as 'Yola' was spoken in Co. Wexford until it became extinct in the mid-nineteenth century. During the Viking period (800–1169), Co. Wexford was one of the most important harbours and settlements in Ireland. One of Ireland's most celebrated and important folklorists, Patrick Kennedy (1801–1873), was born in Kilmyshall, Bunclody, Co. Wexford; he collected many fairy stories from his home county. The poet and folklorist Jane Francesca Agnes, Lady Wilde (Speranza) (1821–1896), mother of the great writer and playwright Oscar Wilde (1854–1900), was born in Co. Wexford.

JEMMY DOYLE AND THE FAIRY FEAST (CO. WEXFORD)

We found this story in Patrick Kennedy's *Legendary Fictions of the Irish Celts*, published in 1866. It was originally called 'Jemmy Doyle in the Fairy Palace', p.116. This is our twist on the same tale.

One late evening Jemmy Doyle was coming down Scollagh Gap – a hollow between the Blackstairs Mountains, between Ballymurphy and Kiltealy. It was starting to get dark and it was that strange sliver of time between the last of the daylight and the beginning of the night time, when the thin veil between the living world and what lies beyond seems to evaporate for just a little while.

It was a long and lonely road that Jemmy walked upon that night in late summer. He knew the road well and was not afraid of the shadows coming from the half-light, nor the strange sounds that seemed to emerge from those same shadows.

It was more than likely that he had had a few wee half-ones in a local tavern along the way, for Jemmy loved the craic and the ceoil. He was always the heart and soul of every get-together and he loved to sing and listen to music, and if there was a bottle of poteen, sure all the better! So, he was more than likely in good spirits and a few shadows and hoots from the dark were not going to scare him, and he swore when he told the story in later years that on that particular night he was sober as a judge.

But the strangest thing happened when he walked around a bend in the road – he saw a magnificent house a bit away from the road surrounded by trees. In all his days Jemmy had never seen this house before and he had walked this road many times. He was dumbfounded and could not understand why he had never noticed such a fine building before. It was the sort of house that would have belonged to a rich landlord, the sort of house that the likes of Jemmy Doyle would never be welcomed into. He noticed that the front doors of the manor were flung open and light was streaming out into the darkness like an explosion of radiance and illumination. Not only that, but the sound of wonderful music and joyous laughter poured from the house too. Oh! The tunes were all so sweet, just like the ones Jemmy had remembered as a boy. He loved music and he recognised many of the jigs and reels and he found himself dancing on the road, humming to the tunes that flooded from the house.

His curiosity could take it no more, he had to look and see what was going on inside. So over he went to the open doors and he looked in. He could not believe his eyes for he saw a large grand hall with people dressed like royalty. They were all eating and drinking and when they were not doing that they were all laughing and dancing. The hall was lined with tables full of every type of food and drink that you could think of and from the walls hung exquisite tapestries depicting scenes the likes of he had never seen or thought of in all his days.

At the far end of the hall was an orchestra composed of every type of musical instrument that you can think of, and a few fellas were even playing the bones.

The tunes they were playing were just out of this world, and come to think of it that is exactly what they were. The hall was lit up with chandeliers, Tilley lamps and candles; the room was filled with a warm glowing light and the atmosphere was electric. Then, all of a sudden, Jemmy was spotted by a well-dressed man sitting at the top of one of the tables. He stood up and approached Jemmy.

'Ah, Mr Doyle! So very good of you to join us, we were expecting you and you are not a moment too late. Please take a seat and help yourself to all the food and drink that your heart desires.'

The man was ever so polite and courteous to Jemmy, who was being treated like a lord himself. This was not what Jemmy was used to but by God he could get used to it all right!

All the ladies were looking at him like he was some handsome prince and they made cow eyes at him as they rustled their fans and giggled like schoolgirls.

Jemmy did not know what to think but he was happy and apprehensive at the same time, and even felt himself blush. It all seemed far too good to be true.

The well-dressed man kept ushering him to a seat and when he was eventually sat down his host offered him a plate of delicious-looking food and a glass of poteen. Jemmy politely refused and said that he was full after a big meal but he was more than happy to sit and enjoy the lovely music. Now Jemmy remembered how the old people would talk of the good folk or the fairy folk and he knew fine rightly that this was no mortal affair but a gathering of the Sidhe – the fairies themselves.

The man asked Jemmy if he was impressed with what he saw and Jemmy was quick to reply that he had never seen the likes of it in all his days. He then offered him a glass of wine, thinking that he might prefer something lighter, but Jemmy refused as polite as you like and told his host that he was fine for refreshments as the atmosphere was quite enough to lift his spirits.

Well as the night went on Jemmy could see that everyone was having a lovely time and there seemed like there was no malice or trickery about the place and let the truth be known he was more than ready for a sup of liquor or a bite to eat. When his host eventually approached him again with a glass of poteen, he took it gratefully and he saw that his host's face beamed with delight. Just as he was about to drink from the glass he looked up along the table; he had not taken much notice of those sitting next to him as he was so transfixed by all the revelry. He now saw that sitting beside him was his neighbour, who had died over twenty years previous. Poor Jemmy got the shock of his life and then the dead man raised a hand and pointed at Jemmy in a manner that was nothing short of a warning and he said to him, 'For your life, don't touch a bite nor sup, for if you do you shall remain here forever and they will have absolute power over you to do to you as they wish, that is the way of the good folk.' Then the dead neighbour looked back down at his plate as if nothing had been said. Jemmy was very disturbed by this and he noticed that when he looked about him, the fine-looking folk were actually quite ghastly-looking creatures, like ugly monsters.

The corpse spoke with such a low voice that Jemmy could barely hear him and just as well, for his fairy host was in earshot and stood up from the table and raised his glass, then he spoke.

'I wish to propose a toast to Jemmy Doyle, that he may spend a good time with us here and we welcome him with open arms as our eternal guest!'

With that Jemmy stood up and raised his glass to the congregation. 'Your Lordship,' he began, 'I am a poor man with very little in this world and very little to show for my time upon it.' His fairy host looked at him hungrily, almost willing him to drink from the glass, but then Jemmy spoke again. 'Yes, 'tis very little that I have in this world, but by God himself I will not be tricked into losing the one thing that I do possess, my very own soul! Damn the lot of yez! I will not be fooled by yer trickery!'

His fairy host and the entire congregation gasped at this unexpected declaration of defiance. Then Jemmy lifted the glass above his head and threw it to the ground, where it exploded in a hail of sparks and smoke. There was absolute chaos about the place, with the fairy folk screaming and shouting, and the look of pure rage in the fairy host's eyes would turn your blood to ice.

Then a *Si Gaoithe* (a fairy wind) blew through the place and whisked Jemmy off his feet. He spun around in the air like a leaf caught in a storm, then everything went into darkness.

When he came to he found himself back on the side of the road. He was lying beneath a fairy tree but there was no sign of the grand house that he had spent the night in amongst the fairy folk. It was very early in the morning for he heard the sound of a cock crowing and he was wet with the morning dew. His whole body ached and throbbed, as though he had fallen from a great height.

Jemmy used all his strength to pick himself up off the ground; his feet nearly went from under him but he managed to compose himself. When he got to his feet he did his best to get home, he was full of fear and anxiety for there was a faint taste of poteen in the back of his throat and he thought that the fairies may well have taken his soul.

On his way back, he called in to the local priest and begged him to absolve him of his sins and he made a full confession of his dealings with the good folk. The priest was well aware of the good folk and did not take such matters lightly. After Jemmy's confession he splashed him with holy water and said a few prayers that Jemmy had never heard before, it was serious stuff alright!

The priest scolded Jemmy for his loose ways and fondness of the drink, and said that he knew it would only be a matter of time before he landed himself in some class of trouble and by the holy book he had indeed this time.

Jemmy thanked the priest and even swore off the drink with the man of the cloth as his witness. He stayed sober and clean for a long time afterwards but as the years went by he fell back into auld habits, but he never walked a road alone at night nor accepted a drink from a stranger again.

Co. Wicklow: In Irish it is known as *Chill Mhantáin*, meaning 'Church of the Mantan', but the English translation comes from the Old Norse *Víkingaló*, meaning 'Vikings' Meadow'. It is a beautiful county, commonly known as 'The Garden of Ireland'. One could easily imagine the Sidhe frequenting such places as Glendalough and the Wicklow Mountains. Due to its magical scenery, Co. Wicklow was one of the prime locations for John Boorman's 1981 film *Excalibur*, based on the story of King Arthur. At the magnificent Blessington Lakes there is a place called Poulaphouca, from the Irish *Poll an Phúca*, which means 'the Pooka's Hole'. Here a small village was submerged for a hydroelectric plant; the remains of roads can still be seen leading down into the lake. In Wicklow town there is a death messenger known as 'The White Lady of High Street'. She appears on that particular street to any person about to die.

WE HAD ONE IN THE HOUSE FOR A WHILE (CO. WICKLOW)

This story was collected from a Mr and Mrs Kelleher in 1920 by Lady Gregory. Together with William Butler Yeats and Edward Martyn, Lady Gregory co-founded the Irish Literary Theatre and the Abbey Theatre, and wrote several short works for both companies. Lady Gregory produced many books of retellings of stories taken from Irish mythology.

This is a conversation about the fairies between an old married couple. We can almost imagine them both sitting beside the open fire in the cottage, the dog stretched out at their feet, as they converse and try to remember the actual event that happened in their youth. Their memories are a little hazy because they are much older, but they still manage to tell their tale well and with great zeal. It is apparent that they are still very much in love. Then, like older minds often do, they wander off somewhere else and the next thing we know they have taken us to a place called Peacock Well, where there is a big grey bird with a head like a man. I can almost see Lady Gregory sitting near them taking notes, her ears pricked up, leaning in, making sure to catch every word.

Mr Kelleher: I often saw them when I had my eyesight. One time they came about me, shouting and laughing and there were spouts of water all around me. And I thought that I was coming home, but I was not on the right path and couldn't find it and went wandering about, but at last one of them said 'Good evening Kelleher,' and then they went away, and then in a moment I saw where I was by the stile. They were very small, like little boys and girls, and had red caps.

I always saw them like that, but they were bigger at the butt of the river; they go along the course of the rivers. Another time they came about me playing music and I didn't know where I was going, and at last one of them said the same way, 'Good evening, Mr Kelleher,' and I knew that I was at the gate of the college; it is the sweetest music and the best that can be heard, like melodeons and fifes and whistles and every sort.

Mrs Kelleher: I often heard that music too, I heard them playing drums.

Mr Kelleher: We had one of them in the house for a while, it was when I was living up at Ticknok, and it was just after I married that woman there that was a nice slip of a girl at the time. It was in the winter and there was snow on the ground, and I saw one of them outside, and I

brought him in and I put him on the dresser, and he stopped in the house for a while, for about a week.

Mrs Kelleher: It was more than that, it was two or three weeks.

Mr Kelleher: Ah! Maybe it was – I'm not sure. He was about fifteen inches high. He was very friendly. It is likely he slept on the dresser at night. When the boys at the public house were full of porter, they used to come to the house to look at him, and they would laugh to see him, but I wouldn't ever let them hurt him. They said I would be made up, that he would bring me some riches, but I never got them. We had a cage here, I wish I had put him in it, I might have kept him till I was made up.

Mrs Kelleher: It was a cage we had for a thrush. We thought of putting him into it, but he would not have been able to stand in it.

Mr Kelleher: I'm sorry I didn't keep him – I thought sometimes to bring him to Dublin to sell him.

Mrs Kelleher: You wouldn't have got him there.

Mr Kelleher: One day I saw another of the kind not far from the house, but more like a girl, and the clothes greyer than his clothes, that were red. And that evening when I was sitting beside the fire with the missus I told her about it, and the little lad that was sitting on the dresser called out, 'That's Geoffrey-a-wee that's coming for me,' and he jumped down and went out the door and I never saw him again. I thought it was a girl I saw but Geoffrey wouldn't be the name of a girl, would it? He had never spoken before that time. Somehow I think he liked me better than the Missus. I used to feed him with bread and milk.

Mrs Kelleher: I was afraid of him, I was afraid to go near him, I thought he might scratch my eyes out – I used to leave bread and milk for him but I would go away while he was eating it.

Mr Kelleher: I used to feed him with a spoon, I would put the spoon to his mouth.

Mrs Kelleher: He was fresh-looking at first, but after a while he got an old look, a sort of wrinkled look.

Mr Kelleher: He was fresh-looking enough, he had a hardy look.

Mrs Kelleher: He was wearing a red cap and a little red cloth skirt.

Mr Kelleher: Just for the world like a highlander.

Mrs Kelleher: He had a little short coat above that; it was checked and trousers under the skirt and long stockings all red. And as for his shoes, they were tanned, and you could hardly see the soles of them, the sole of his foot was like a baby's.

Mr Kelleher: The time I lost my sight, it was a Thursday evening, and I was walking through the fields. I went to bed that night, and when I rose up in the morning, the sight was gone. The boys said it was likely I had walked on one of their paths. Those small little paths you see through the fields are made by them. They are very often in the quarries; they have great fun up there, and about Peacock Well. Peacock Well was blessed by a saint, and another well near, that cures the headache.

I saw one time a big grey bird about the cow house, and I went to a comrade-boy and asked him to come and help me to catch it, but when we came back it was gone. It was very strange-looking and I thought that it had a head like a man.

We feel that maybe the type of fairy that the couple had captured was a redcap – the wickedest type of fairies. Redcaps are known to live in old ruined castles and towers, and like to live alone. They are often described as old broad-shouldered men.

According to Katharine Briggs, redcaps are not always bad; she tells of one who lived in Grantully Castle in Perthshire, he had a little room of his own at the top of the castle, and she said people felt lucky to have him around the place.

In the interaction between the old man and woman it is clear that the man was fond of the fairy man despite regretting not keeping a hold of him, for he felt he could have brought him a windfall of some kind. The old woman was less trusting of him and was almost happy that he moved on. But they lived to tell the tale and nothing bad ever came of the couple and so they had that to be thankful for, for riches come in many packages and they were blessed to be sitting beside a warm open fire still talking and still sharing the stories of times gone by.

3

THE PROVINCE OF MUNSTER

Co. Clare: From the Irish *An Chláir*, meaning 'Plank Bridge'. Co. Clare is a place full of wonder and myth. It holds the oldest known evidence of human existence in all of Ireland after the bones of a bear butchered with prehistoric tools dating back to 10,500 BC was found in the Alice and Gwendoline Cave. Biddy Early (1798–1874), Ireland's most famous (or infamous) fairy doctor, was born on Faha Ridge. Co. Clare is also the home of Brian Merriman (*c.*1747–1805), whose fairy masterpiece *The Midnight Court* is based in the county. The storyteller, author and collector of Irish fairy stories Eddie (Edmund) Lenihan is originally from Brosna, Co. Kerry, but now lives in Crushenn, Co. Clare.

THE PALACE BELOW THE LAKE (CO. CLARE)

We found the bones of this story in The School's Collection in Duchas. Vol. 0589, p.105. The story was collected by Thomas J. Reidy, and it was told to him by a Michael Reidy from Tulla, Co. Clare.

Long ago in the mountains of Snaiti (Snaty or Inis Snáite), about two miles outside Kilkishen, there lived a man named Pat O'Leary. Pat did not have very much in the line of possessions and wealth, in fact all he had to his name was a dairy cow. She was a good beast and produced plenty of fresh creamy milk, and Pat was very fond of her indeed.

Pat hadn't much to his name but his heart was full and he was a kind and gentle man. He had fallen deeply in love with a beautiful local girl who was known to the locals as 'Dark-Haired Mary of the Mountain'. She had raven black hair and eyes as green as the sea, her skin was snow white, and whenever Pat thought of her his heart skipped a beat and he wondered of how lucky he was that such a creature could love a fella like him.

He had proposed to Dark-Haired Mary of the Mountain, and she had accepted his proposal with much delight.

But as we know, poor Pat had not much in the line of a dowry and he did not want to look poor and unworthy in front of Mary's people. So there was only one thing for it, he would have to sell his only valuable possession, his fine dairy cow, and that was that. He decided to bring her to the Fair of Tulla and sell the animal to the highest bidder.

He started off for Tulla early in the night or late in the day, whichever way you want to look at it, 'tis all the same.

When he arrived at Cullane Lake it was midnight and the moon was shining in the sky like a big silver dollar. He decided to take a rest for both himself and the cow. As he was resting, a strange wee man came out of the shadows and he spoke to him kindly and gently. He said, 'Pat, isn't it early for you to be going to the fair?'

Poor Pat was already shocked that this wee crathur had appeared out of nowhere in front of him, but now he had addressed him by his own name as if he knew him. He was a strange-looking little man, he looked both wise and youthful all at once, and he wore a jacket of velvet so green it shone, fine yellow britches, well-polished black boots and a red cap upon his head.

'Don't be afraid Pat, shure I am only here to help you. Come with me for I have a great many things to show you.'

With that the wee man produced a hazel rod from under his jacket and he waved it before Pat. As soon as he did this, a magnificent palace rose up out of Cullane Lake.

'Where did that come from?' asked Pat, bewildered by what he saw.

'Shure it was always there!' said the wee man and laughed at the look of amazement on Pat's face.

The wee man then asked Pat to go into the palace and leave the cow outside. Pat had never seen the likes of this magnificent building, which shone and sparkled in the moonlight like a great diamond. It was like something from a dream and Pat pinched himself to make sure that he was not dreaming. The gates of the castle were made of pure gold and the steps up to it were carved from beautiful marble. When they entered the palace, they were greeted by hundreds of little footmen and servants all lined up and bowing to the strange wee man and his guest form the mortal world.

Down the long hallway they went, until they came to a set of huge ornate doors. The doors swung open before them and Pat could not believe his eyes, for before him was the most beautiful hall he had ever seen, it must have been the size of three football fields. In this great hall were hundreds of dancers, musicians, singers and storytellers, all having the time of their lives. They all greeted the strange wee man and they were all very polite and courteous to Pat.

There was music, dancing, and entertainment of all kinds there – Pat thought that he had died and gone to Heaven. But he knew fine rightly that he was not in Heaven, but the heart of a fairy kingdom and this wee man that he was with must be the king himself.

He wished his true love Mary was there to share this wonderful experience with him and that she deserved all the magnificence and beauty that place had to offer.

In the middle of the hall there was a huge table laden down with every sort and type of food and drink that you could imagine.

Then he saw there was another table covered in buns, it reminded him of a story that he had heard from a farmer called Patsy McDermott from Killinkere in County Cavan. In his story he described a table with every type of bun that you could imagine: there was sticky buns, dry buns, sugary buns, sweet buns, hard buns, soft buns, short buns, long buns, big buns, little buns, flat buns, round buns, half buns, full buns, cream

buns, iced buns, hot buns, cold buns, honey buns, big buns, little buns, jam buns, jelly buns, currant buns, cherry buns, apple buns, pear buns, banana buns, plum buns, custard buns, coffee buns, chocolate buns, buttered buns, burnt buns, frosted buns, nutty buns, chewy buns, triangle buns, square buns, fun buns, and, of course, fairy buns!

Pat was invited to eat, but, knowing that he was in a fairy palace, he refused. It was said that if a person should eat with the fairies he or she could not leave them and Pat knew that. There was a big part of Pat that would have loved to have lived amongst the good folk, but he would be heartbroken if he was never to see his beautiful Mary again.

At that point the strange wee man who Pat now recognised as the King of the Fairies told him it was time to leave and that they should go to the fair.

They left the wonderful palace together and made their way to the fair. As soon as they did the King of the Fairies stopped in his tracks and spoke to Pat, and this is what he said: 'Pat, I have been watching you for a long time now, and I have seen that you are a good man with a good heart. You were willing to part with the only thing that was of any valve to you so that you might marry your one true love. I wish to buy this fine cow that has been reared and cared for with love and kindness. Its milk is the sweetest in all of Ireland and we the fairy folk like nothing more than a cup of sweet fresh milk.'

With that the wee man produced a leather bag and gave it to Pat. He looked inside and it was full of pure, solid gold coins. Pat thanked the wee man, who disappeared with the cow. He knew not to tell a soul that it was fairy gold, for if he did it would turn to ashes or worse.

When Pat got back to Snaiti the locals looked at him like they had seen a ghost. One woman fainted and another one blessed herself as he passed her. He thought that this was most peculiar. Shure he was only away for a few hours and no one was expecting him till the following day anyway. He called into his parents' cottage and he was alarmed to see his mother cry out in horror and his father fall to his knees in prayer. What in Heaven's name was going on? Had everybody gone mad?

He went to his parents and reassured them that he was alright and asked them what all the drama was about. They told him that he had been gone for over a year and the last they heard of him was from a local farmer who saw him walk into Cullane Lake. They were sure that he had lost his mind and had taken his own life in the lake.

This was a great shock to Pat, who believed that he had been away for only a few hours, half a day at most. But then time in the fairy world is a very different thing indeed. But sadly, he could not tell that he was taken by the fairies for folk would surely believe that he had gone insane.

He told them that he had been captured by thieves but he had managed to escape with their gold and was keen to get home and see his dear parents and his one true love Mary.

He asked where Mary was and he was told that she had gone into mourning and had hardly spoken a word to a soul since he had gone.

When Pat heard this he ran as fast as his legs would carry him all the way up the mountain to where Mary lived with her parents. Her mother and father reacted in a similar fashion as those before and thought that he may be a phantom, cursed to roam the world as punishment for taking his own life. He reassured them as before that he was not a ghost or the living dead and he told him the tale of the robbers and how he had escaped.

He went inside the house and sitting down by the unlit fire was Mary with a great black shawl draped over her head and shoulders. She sat crouched over like a very old woman.

Pat called out to her and when she looked up she could not believe her eyes. Mary screamed and was about to fall to the floor with the shock of it all, when Pat caught her just in time.

When she had settled herself, he looked into her eyes and said, 'Dark Haired Mary of the Mountain, I have been away a long time and I have seen many things, beyond your wildest dreams.' He told her that although he had seen so many magnificent things, nothing could compare to her beauty and his undying love for her. They kissed and that evening a wedding was set in progress and a great tent was erected – people came from all over to celebrate this wonderful occasion. And there was no concern about a dowry or comfort for the newlywed couple, for Pat had more wealth now than he could have ever imagined.

After they were married Pat and Mary emigrated to America, where they lived long and happy lives together. Mary bore many children and their children's children still live there and come over to visit Co. Clare once in a while to see where it all began with the love of a simple man and woman, and a wee bit of help from the fairy folk.

Co. Cork: From the Irish *Corcaigh* from Corcach, meaning 'Marsh'. The City of Cork was originally a monastic settlement set up by St Finbar in the sixth century and became a town between AD 915 and 922, when the Viking invaders built a port and trading post there. Co. Cork was also the home of the wise woman or fairy doctor Máire Ní Mhurchú. Its coastlines are well-known haunts for merrows (or mermaids). Along the south coast of Cork, just before Ross Carbery, is a wedge cairn and the locals call it *Callaheenacladdig*, which means 'Hag of the Sea' or 'The Old Witch of the Shore'. East of Kilcatherine Point in Co. Cork you will find a stone that is meant to be the fossilised Cailleach Beara turned to stone. She is said to be waiting for her companion, the God of the Sea, Manannán mac Lir. The world-renowned folklorist Eileen O'Faolain (1902–1988), wife of the famous Irish writer Seán Ó Faoláin (1900–1991), was born in Co. Cork. The revered folklorist and poet Thomas Crofton Croker (1798–1854) was also born in Co. Cork.

A FAR SPIN FOR TOBACCO (CO. CORK)

We found this lovely story in a book called *Folktales of Ireland* (edited by Sean O'Sullivan, 1966). It's called 'Sean Palmer's Voyage to America with the Fairies'. We have decided to call our version 'A Far Spin for Tobacco'.

Sean Palmer lived in Rineen Ban, Co. Cork. He had a small farm and owned a fishing boat. He didn't have a big pile of money but had enough to get by. He lived a simple sort of life, he fished during the summer season, and enjoyed nothing more than a plate full of spuds and a puff of his pipe. He was married to Mary and they had three children. Sean was very fond of tobacco, and he loved his clay pipe. But where Sean and his family lived was remote and the nearest shop was miles away so tobacco was hard to come by, so Sean cherished every drag of that clay pipe.

Have you ever heard of an egg woman? These were women who travelled around the countryside from house to house with goods that they sold in exchange for eggs. They had all the essentials that every household could not do without – soap, needles and pins and that all-important tobacco. They had what they called a 'finger of tobacco'. They would measure the tobacco with the middle finger of their right hand from the tip to the knuckle. But on this particular occasion the egg woman didn't show up. As you can imagine, Sean was getting really annoyed and was starting to take his anger out on his family because he needed his fix so badly.

He decided to take matters into his own hands and headed off for the nearest shop. He had waited three days for the egg woman and was growing more restless and could see he was beginning to cause his family a lot of bother. He looked at his wife and said, 'Mary, I can't stand this any longer, I need tobacco.' She agreed and so he headed off for Sean The Locks'. Sean The Locks' was the nearest shop. Mary said to him, 'Have your dinner before you go, and it will help you on your way,' but Sean wasn't hanging around any longer. He said, 'This house won't be worth living in if I stay here another minute.' So off he went in search of his beloved smoke.

He picked up his blackthorn stick and headed up the lane away from the cottage. Mary watched him go with a sense of both worry and relief. He had no shoes or socks on his feet and it was near dark and he had an angry head on him like he was on the warpath. You may think it strange that he had no shoes or socks upon his feet but back in those days shoes were kept for special occasions, like mass or fair days.

As Sean approached the quay, he could see all the fishing boats and he saw two men. As he walked nearer he could hear his name being spoke. 'That's Sean Palmer, I know where he is headed,' they said. His ears cocked up. 'He has no tobacco.' He waved at them and they both waved back. One of the men said to him, 'We take it you don't have any tobacco?' Sean thought to himself, I must look desperate for a smoke and it must be written all over my troubled face. The other man went on to say, 'Do you see those men down there in that wee boat? Go down to them and you will be sure to get your fill of tobacco.'

Sean thought he was dreaming, sure it could never be that easy? Although he never had to go in search of tobacco before because the egg woman always supplied it. He saw that it was getting late and maybe he wouldn't make Sean The Locks' anyway so he thought to himself, if I get a pipe-full to tide me over sure that will do me grand. He was beginning to feel a little guilty for refusing to eat the dinner Mary had made for him, so he thought at least he could get enough for a few smokes and be home before the spuds went cold. He went down to the boat, smiled at the two men in the boat and said to them, 'I would be grateful if you could give me a smoke of tobacco, it's been three days since I got a drag and I can't stand it any longer.'

'Of course,' they said. 'That you shall get, and plenty, and to spare'. They went on, 'Step into the boat and take a seat.' Sean couldn't believe how decent the men were and so he took them up on the offer. He thought the least he could do was have a chat with them if they were giving him some tobacco. One of the men handed him his own pipe and said, 'Here you are Sean, smoke that to your satisfaction.' Sean couldn't believe his luck. The pipe was lit up and glowing like a hot fire and Sean felt he had died and gone to heaven. Mary and her pot of spuds couldn't have been further from his mind. Sean thanked them and puffed away until he was surrounded by a cloud of thick grey smoke. He thought to himself, this is the best pipe of tobacco I have ever smoked in my life. The two men that Sean first met at the quay where still standing on the pier and so the two men in the boat asked them to join them and so they did. So the boat soon had the five men inside and no sooner had their backsides hit the seats when the sails were up and ready for sail.

'To the sea with you boys!' shouted one of the men and they were off. Sean had no idea what was happening but sure he still had the pipe in his mouth so he went along with it, sure the men seemed to be friendly and they seemed to know what they were doing and they were generous so he tried not to worry too much. No one spoke for a while and it didn't seem long before Sean saw lights in the near distance. He said to one of the men, 'Are those the lights of the Lohar houses?' The man had a smirk on his face. 'Wait a while Sean and you will see much nicer houses than those of Lohar.'

Sean was baffled. We have to remember that Sean had a boat of his own and he knew those waters better than the next fisherman. But for once he felt a little confused. He thought it was the amount of smoking that maybe had him all mixed up. He looked around him and said to the men, 'There is Rineen Ban to the west'. The four men laughed in unison. 'Och! God help you,' said one of the men. 'You are at New York Quay.'

Sean couldn't believe his eyes, he had only seen New York on post-cards his siblings sent home. Sean got off the boat and was in total shock.

He had never seen so many people in all his life. It was like fair day times a hundred. All the faces were of strangers and he didn't know a soul. He felt everyone was looking at him. Sure all he had on him were rags and not a thing on his feet. A man walked up to him and said, 'You look like a man I know called Sean Palmer from Rineen Ban.' Sean recognised the man as Andy Pickett from the same road as him back home. Sure Sean remembered the young Pickett fella going to America to find work and if Andy was in America then Sean knew he was too. Andy walked on. Sean was pinching himself, half hoping to wake up but also enjoying the adventure. One of the men who took him over in the boat said, 'Sean, you really are in America, you have a brother here in New York, have you not?'

'I sure have,' said Sean, 'but New York is a big place, and how on earth could I find him, I don't even know his address off by heart?'

'Never mind,' said the man. 'Come along and we will find him.'

Two of the men went with Sean and the other two stayed behind to guard the boat. They walked the streets of New York together. Sean couldn't believe the height of the buildings. He felt like a little mouse. He said hello to passing strangers and thought how rude of them not to even answer. Sure this place wasn't at all like Rineen Ban. Rineen Ban may be small and less busy but by God he thought it smelled a lot better and was a hell of a lot quieter and at least the people had the decency to say hello. He was beginning to wonder what took his brother and sister and half the lads and ladies he went to school with over the sea to such an unfriendly place with a million streets that made no sense – with numbers on signs – sure how would a man like him not get lost? Sure he couldn't see a field or a blade of grass in sight. Finally, the two men stopped at a tenement. 'Your brother Paddy lives in that house Sean, knock on the door and ask for him.'

Sean knocked on the door and a stranger answered. 'Does Paddy Palmer from Rineen Ban live here?' Sean asked.

'Yes he does, I will show you to his room.' When Paddy saw him he went as white as a sheet. He thought that Sean had died and his ghost was visiting him from beyond. Stood before him was his brother whom he hadn't seen in years. Sure Sean had no shoes or socks on his dirty feet and his clothes were in tatters, but he seemed real to Paddy all the same. 'Sean are you dead?'

Sean smiled and said, 'No Paddy I am very much alive.'

'How and when did you get to America'? Paddy asked, excited that his brother was alive and well and standing in front of him.

'I landed about a quarter of an hour ago,' Sean replied.

'And when did you leave home?'

'I left about half an hour ago,' Sean said.

Paddy was beginning to get worried, maybe his brother was not of sane mind. 'Take a seat Sean and tell me what happened?'

So Sean took a seat on the end of his brother's bed. The room was small and overlooked grey buildings and rooftops with grass growing on top of some of them. Sean was relieved to see some green at last. He began to tell Paddy how he was dying for a smoke and how the egg woman didn't show up, and he was getting on the wife's nerves and so he decided to head for Sean The Locks' shop and get himself some tobacco before he went astray in the head. 'It was after nightfall and I didn't even get the spuds into me because I was so hungry for a smoke.' He then told him that when he reached Rineen Ban Quay he met two men at the pier who pointed him towards two other men who were in a boat. He said the men were fierce generous and gave him as much tobacco as he could handle. 'Sure, I was in my element Paddy. I was in a haze of smoke and the next thing I knew the sails were up and there was lights in the distance.' He told him how he thought it was the lights of the harbour near home when the four men began to laugh at him and told him they had reached New York. 'Sure I couldn't believe my ears Paddy, not half an hour ago I was sitting at the fire in the cottage and here I am standing in America.'

Paddy couldn't believe his own ears. Sean told him how he met Andy Pickett at the harbour and then he told him how two of the men from the boat led him to Paddy's door. 'I will tell you what Sean, you sit there and I will fix you some supper and I will run in next door to the store and get you some tobacco and when I get back you can put my good suit on and I will give you my best brogues.'

Sean was overwhelmed and said, 'Paddy, don't be daft, I am grand as I am.'

'No Sean, I insist – you look like a down-and-out and I can't let you leave my house looking like that – what sort of a brother would I be if I done that?'

Sean sat down and ate a big feed fit for a king; as they say in the countryside, it was enough to choke a donkey. Just as he was finishing, Paddy came back through the door with a large parcel of tobacco. Paddy said to him, 'Now, Sean, here is half a year's supply of tobacco.' He then reached into his coat pocket and took out a fistful of dollars and handed them to him along with the parcel of tobacco.

'I will not take all this from you Paddy,' Sean said, embarrassed.

'I insist,' said Paddy with a smile. 'I was going to send you money for Christmas anyway, and seeing as you are right in front of me sure it saves me the bother.'

'Thank you, Paddy, that is real decent of you and I appreciate everything.' He changed into the suit and thanked his brother once again. Paddy looked at him and said, 'It was so lovely to see you Sean, and goodbye for now and God speed you.'

Sean walked out onto the street and joined the two men who were waiting on him. 'My Goodness Sean, you did well out of that visit: tobacco, a few pound and a brand new suit,' said one of the men with a smile. 'Give me the parcel and the cash and I will put it on the boat for you.' Sean trusted the man and did as he was asked. Then the other man pipes up, 'Sure, don't you have a sister in Boston?'

'I have, to be sure, I know she is somewhere in Boston but I have no clue where.'

'I know where she lives,' said the man. He told Sean how he would take him to see her while the other man took the goods his brother gave him to the boat. Next thing he knew he was in a different city. It wasn't long before they reached a big blue door. It was clean and shiny with a gold knocker and flowers out the front. He remembered how his sister always loved tending to the garden back at the home place when she was a child.

'Knock on the door Sean, your sister Cait will answer.'

Sean took a deep breath and composed himself and gave the door a good confident knock. A middle-aged woman peeped through the door and asked who he was looking for. 'I am here to see Cait Palmer.'

The woman opened the door a little wider. 'I am Cait Palmer.'

'Do you not recognise your own brother?' His sister reacted much the same as his brother Paddy had in New York City. She thought that Sean had died and was coming to say one last goodbye before he went to Heaven.

'My God and all the saints! Sean Palmer why would you appear to me? Sure I am liable to drop dead along with you.'

'No Cait, I am very much alive, sure I have been up with Paddy in New York – sure where do you think I got such a fancy get-up? Sure you know fine rightly that poor Sean Palmer wouldn't have a suit as good as this or a pair of shoes like these.' He waved his shoes towards her, proud he had a pair at all. Cait couldn't believe what she was seeing. 'Sure ask Paddy when you see him next.'

Cait asked Sean how he got there and when and Sean retold the whole story about running out of tobacco and the next thing seeing the bright lights of New York City. Sure she had to take a seat on the steps to hear the rest. He told her how Paddy gave him money and tobacco as well as the suit and shoes. She opened her purse and took out a $20 note and handed it to him. 'Take that home with you and I will send you some more at Christmas time.' Sean didn't want anything from her but thanked her all the same. He hugged her and told her to take good care of herself and that he hoped to see her again soon. She went back in through the big shiny blue door with the gold knocker, still shaking from what she had just experienced.

By this stage the second man had caught up with them and they were headed back for New York, and as they were approaching the city Sean realised he didn't have the pipe. 'I have lost the pipe,' he said to the men in sheer panic. The men reassured him it was OK, sure they could replace it. One of the men then said to Sean, 'Did you know a Cait "Strockaire" O'Shea from the top of Lohar?'

'I did indeed,' says Sean with a broad smile, remembering what a beauty she was. He once had a notion to marry her and next thing he knew she moved to America. He told them the story and then said with a giggle, 'The luck of the Irish.'

'Would you like to see her now?' said the other man. 'She lives here on this very lane.' Sean said he would very much like to see her, so the two men led him to the door of her house. It was a bit more run-down compared to his sister's place but it was nice all the same and he was excited for he was going to see Cait after all these years. As he heard footsteps approaching the big black door with number 33 etched onto the top of it with faded yellow paint he wondered how much had she changed and if the years had been kind to her? Cait opened the door and was so surprised to see her old neighbour she threw her arms around him and it was like they never parted. She asked him what he was doing in America and how he got there. He decided to pretend he had been there a few months and was on his way home again and decided to look her up before he went back. He didn't want to have to explain to anyone else that he left his house only an hour ago. He didn't mind telling his brother and sister the truth, sure they always thought Sean was a bit touched, but he couldn't let Cait 'Strockaire' O'Shea think his head had gone astray, or, even worse, think he was a ghost. He told her he was sailing back that very night. Cait was delighted to see him but sad he was leaving and for a few moments they talked about old times. She opened her purse and gave him a $20 note and asked him to give $15 to her brother Con, who still lived in the home place in Lohar, and she told Sean to keep $5 for himself. She said, 'Have a drink for my health on your crossing home.' Sean thanked her and said he would deliver the money to Con as soon as he got back on Irish soil. He was about to leave when Cait called him back. 'By the way Sean, did you ever marry?' He didn't give her a straight answer and so she was left wondering. She said back to him, 'Sure maybe we may both splice it up yet?' 'You could never tell,' replied Sean, as he waved goodbye, 'stranger things have happened.'

Sean met up with the two men outside and they were eager to find out how he got on. Sean told them that they had a nice chat and that she had given him money to give to her brother and some money for him to drink to her health on the way home. The two men seemed happy for Sean but told him they would need to hurry back as time was running out. This worried Sean because he didn't think there was a clock ticking and he wondered what would happen if time ran out. They got back to the boat and met with the other two men. They told Sean to hop on board. They spread the sails and they were off. They were hardly out to sea when Sean felt the pipe between his teeth. He said to the men, 'This is the pipe I thought I lost.' They told him if it was still red to puff away till his heart was content. Sean didn't need much encouragement.

'Ah,' he exclaimed, 'it is a true saying that.'

'What?' asked the men.

'That a lucky man only needs to be born.'

The men looked a bit puzzled but smiled all the same. In what seemed like only a few minutes Sean saw lights in the distance and this time he was sure it was the houses of Lohar. He was so confident he said it to the men.

'Yes, they are,' said one of the men, 'this time you are correct.'

Sean was baffled and said, 'Well, that's awful strange, one minute I am in New York and then Boston and then I am back at Rineen Ban Quay. Sure, you'd be slower in a dream.'

Before long he had stepped out of the boat and onto dry land. He had his parcel in his hand and he was in great form and when he turned around to thank the men for such a pleasant trip they were gone. They had vanished – it was as if the sea swallowed them whole. He looked around him, the sky was dark and he could neither see nor hear a thing except a few candles lit in the windows of the houses up on the hill and a few birds chatting before they turned in for the night.

He made his way home and knocked on the door. He could hear his wife shouting at their eldest daughter to open it; he could hear her say, 'I presume it's that father of yours who forgot to come home – I bet he was up all night playing cards and smoking his pipe at Sean The Locks' shop.'

When his daughter opened the door, she didn't recognise her father, for the man before her was dressed in a new suit and shiny shoes and he held a parcel under his arm. She ran back in and her mother came out. She did recognise Sean straight away. She had seen him dressed like that once upon a time on their wedding day – that was a while ago, she thought to herself, but by God he looked every bit as handsome.

'Where have you been Sean, and where in God's name did you get that lovely suit?'

'I have been in New York and my brother Paddy was kind enough to give me his suit and shoes – he didn't like to see me in rags and shoeless walking the streets of New York. You know it's not as clean as Rineen Ban.'

Mary was beginning to worry at this stage. 'Sit down Sean and I will get you a cup of tea. Did you fall on your head, or worse still did someone give you too much to drink?'

'No Mary, I am grand and I had a great time without a drop of drink.' He told her the whole story and how Paddy had given him tobacco and money and how his sister Cait in Boston had given him money and then he met with their old neighbour Cait 'Strockaire' O'Shea, and how she had given him money to take home to her brother Con and told him to keep some for himself to not forget to have a drink for her. Mary was listening and soaking it all up and then she took a hold of the tobacco box and was able to read the label of the box and the date. She saw that it did indeed come from New York City. She couldn't believe her eyes. She sat down and this time Sean made *her* a cup of tea, because to Sean and Mary tea fixed a lot of life's problems, and this was no exception. She asked him how he managed to get there and back in such a short time. Sure he had no clue. They sat up half the night talking and trying to figure out what had actually happened.

The next morning Sean awoke more tired than usual and was both relieved and surprised to see the suit his brother gave him draped over the chair at the foot of the bed. He got up and put it on in fear of it disappearing. He ate his breakfast while his daughter looked at him with a puzzled look upon her face. Sean then went out for a walk around his small farm. The sun was in the sky and he had a smoke of his pipe. He walked around in that suit for many years and decided that shoes would not be kept for special occasions. Sure to Sean Palmer *life* was a special occasion. He counted his blessings. He didn't give old Cait 'Strockaire' O'Shea another thought because he saw before him the faithful and beautiful wife he did end up marrying. The neighbours began to talk and sure letters were coming home from America from the likes of Andy Pickett and Cait 'Strockaire' O'Shea, saying how they met with Sean Palmer in New York. Sure the neighbours just thought Sean went for a short visit to see his siblings but in actual fact he went with the fairies and was there and back in a few hours. He never did tell them the truth and his siblings made sure not to tell anyone. He never did forget his journey to America and was forever grateful to the 'good folk' for they sure were good to Sean Palmer from Rineen Ban.

Co. Kerry: From the Irish *Ciarraí*, which comes from 'The Ciarraighe', an ancient race of people who settled in the region. They were also known as the people of Ciar (ciar-raighe), Ciar being the son of Fergus mac Róich, who gave his name to Co. Kerry. Co. Kerry is also known as 'The Kingdom'. It is a beautiful county with breathtaking views and landscapes. Off its coast are the two Skellig Islands, Skellig Michael and Little Skellig. Early Christian monks once lived on Skellig Michael, and recently it became home to the Jedi Master Luke Skywalker of *Star Wars* fame. A couple of miles outside Killarney you can find Lissyviggeen Stone Circle. This is a small circle with seven uprights surrounded by a bank and two large stones outside the bank. They are known locally as 'The Seven Sisters'. There are two stories connected with it, one being that the two outside stones are the parents and the seven stones inside the circle are the children. The second claims that the seven stones are sisters and the two larger stones are pipers. But the shared theme is that they were all turned to stone for dancing. Co. Kerry is also home to one of Ireland's greatest seanchaí's (storyteller), Eamon Kelly (1914–2001).

THE FAIRY SPANCEL (CO. KERRY)

We were given a book called *Legends of Killarney* (a reprint of Donal O'Cahill's edited collection of 1956) by Steve's aunt and uncle, Maureen and Donal O'Donoghue from Killarney, Co. Kerry. Maureen was a school teacher and music teacher and Donal was the headmaster of Faha National School in Co. Kerry. Donal was a great lover of literature, poetry and stories, and sadly he passed away in March 2017.

Long ago in a time that was not now but existed when we did not, there was once a man called Terry Casey, a decent sort of a man who had inherited a bit of land that was left to him in some class of a will. The land stood at the foot of Mangerton Mountain in Co. Kerry.

He was only 5 foot tall but it was big enough for him as you are big enough for yourself. He had the heart of a lion and no man in all of Kerry worked as hard as Terry Casey. But he had to, as the land was so full of stones that the birds did not dare catch a worm from it for fear that they might break their beaks and there were so many furze bushes the whole place looked like a wild head of hair.

But auld Terry persevered and he burnt the furze and made walls with the stones. He built a lovely little house on the hill so that no one would be looking down their noses at him. Well the time came when Terry decided he was in a good place to find himself a wife and not long after this noble decision he met Judy O'Donoghue, who had for a dowry a canopy settle bed, four rush-bottomed chairs, a collop of sheep, five pigs and a maol cow.

Everything was going very well for a good while, until Terry noticed although his family were growing in size his livestock were decreasing gradually, with one misfortune after another.

His horse had died of the 'grip', his sheep of the 'gid' and now his pigs had succumbed to the 'measles'. But despite all this misfortune Terry tried to make the best of what he had. He figured that there was nothing he could do about the animals dying and he was thankful that they had been spared their cow and they would keep in plentiful supply of milk, cheese and butter.

But it was not long after this that the poor auld cow took a fall and that was the end of it.

'Were ruined for sure,' says Terry. 'Shur the children themselves will starve and die without the sup of milk and Judy will have me killed with her scolding for putting the cow in such a high and rocky place in The Horse's Glen.' Well with a heavy heart he decided to skin the cow and maybe make something from its hide. 'Shur 'tis better to have somethin' other than nothin' and the meat won't go to waste neither.' Poor auld Terry was an optimistic soul and always tried to see the positive in everything. But when he went to get the cow he found it in a mangled heap at the foot of the hill. 'Oh be the Tear O' War!' he cried. It seemed as though the poor man's world was falling apart before his very eyes. He wondered why on earth was such misfortune being bestowed upon him?

Well he did his best to skin the hide, what was left of it anyway. As he worked he never noticed how quickly the time passed and he was surprised by the terrible darkness around him. To make things worse, a great and powerful wind came howling over the glen from the lake below. Terry realised that this was no ordinary wind but a *Si Gaoithe*, a fairy wind.

He remembered all the tales he was told as a child about the fairies, the banshee and the pooka. He was full of fear and his heart was in his mouth. He threw the hide over his shoulder and pulled a tuft of grass to clean his knife. And with the fear and confusion of it all, he shoved the grass along with the knife into his pocket and ran for home.

Now anyone who knows anything will know that a four-leafed shamrock allows people to see all sorts of enchantments and one happened to be in the tuft of grass. So when Terry turned to look at the carcass of the cow he was shocked and horrified to see not the remains of the beast but a fairy sitting bolt upright and he looked as if he had been flayed alive.

And if this was not terrifying enough, poor Terry was ready to drop dead with the fright when he heard the wee crathur speak to him.

'Terry Casey, you *spalpeen* (poor farmer or hired worker),' he cried. 'You'd better come back with my skin. 'Tis a queer pass when a gentleman can't have a sleep without an *omadhaun* (fool) like you taking the hide off of him. Bring it back or 'twill be worse for ya!'

Although Terry was very scared, he began to muster up a bit of courage. It was clear now that the Good People or fairy folk had taken his cow and he hoped he might be able to get her back. And if the worst came to the worst, he thought he could defend himself with his black-handled knife, for whoever has come into contact with the fairies will always tell you that iron or steel will always break their enchantments. So he gripped the knife in his pocket and addressed the fairy.

'Well sir,' he said, trying to look and sound as brave as he could. 'If this is what you want,' he held up the hide, 'then you must know that 'tis the skin of me auld maol cow that died up on hill there yonder, and better a beast never walked on four legs. I'll never see the likes of her again, but there's no use in talking, so there's no use in talkin'; good luck now your honour!' and with that Terry turned on his heel and began to depart.

'Well now, do you think you can just saunter off like that?' roared the fairy, who was most annoyed by Terry's insolence. The wee man jumped up before him with the speed and agility of a greyhound. 'Drop my skin, or you will sup sorrow!' shouted the fairy.

'I'll do no such thing ya little ferret!' exclaimed Terry, producing his black-handled knife.

'You'll never put a hand on it till ya give me back my maol cow.'

'Take it easy now sir,' said the fairy, who was starting to get a bit worried now when he saw the knife. 'Shur maybe I'll befriend you Terry Casey, for I've taken a fierce liking to ya; give me the skin now and I will be able to get the cow back to ya.'

'Well thank you kindly sir,' says Terry, with a sly wink. 'But you must give me my cow back first.'

'Well there she is now for you!' cried the fairy. Hearing a cow lowing, Terry wheeled about and lo and behold there was his maol cow running towards him with a *spancel* (tether) hanging from one of her legs.

So Terry threw the hide to the fairy and was about to head away with his cow when all of a sudden the fairy jumped with fierce agility right before him.

'Have the good manners to leave back me my *spancel*!' he ordered angrily.

'I'll do nothing of the sort,' shouted Terry, as he drove the cow along, holding the knife firmly in his grip.

'Give me the tuft of grass in your pocket so!' pleaded the fairy, and only then did Terry remember that he had it at all. 'Be Jeepers you may have that and you're welcome to it,' replied Terry. But no sooner had he handed the wee man the tuft of grass than the enchanted creature disappeared before his eyes. Terry got such a fright, he fell to the ground. It was midnight before Terry came to his senses, and he found that he was back on his farm with his cow grazing away happily next to him, the *spancel* still hanging from her leg. And it turned out to be a powerful lucky charm, for that day onward his cow gave more milk than any six cows in the parish and his good fortune increased.

For he became a wealthy and respected man, through selling the sweet milk, butter and cheese that his cow produced. But even with all his wealth and prosperity, Terry Casey never dared go near The Horse's Glen again...

Co. Limerick: From the Irish *Luimneach*, meaning 'The flat area or barren spot of land'. Limerick is a great county rich in history, culture and stories; it has some of the finest fairy folklore in the country. *Cnoc Áine*, or the Hill of Áine in Co. Limerick, is the home of Áine the Queen of the Munster Fairies. To the Celts the cairn on the summit was her palace and the entrance to the Otherworld. *Cnoc Fírinne* is traditionally known the 'Hill of Truth'. It is said to personify Donn Fírinne: in Celtic mythology he is the God of Death and Fertility. In folklore he is seen as a Giant or the King of the Munster Fairies. He is said to live at the bottom of a deep hole in the hillside and it is said that anyone who dares come near this entrance will never be seen again. It was believed that thunderstorms were caused by Donn Fírinne riding his horse through the sky, and if clouds were over the hill it meant that he was gathering them together to make rain. Kevin Danaher (1913–2002), the prominent Irish folklorist, was born in Athea, Co. Limerick.

DANNO AND THE DEVIL (CO. LIMERICK)

By James Patrick Ryan

My Nana Browne (*née* Welsh) was born in the very early 1920s in a place called Killalee in Garryowen in Limerick City. Killalee was populated by people who worked all kinds of jobs in Limerick city. Killalee was a very old estate of houses that had been built in the 1900s. My Nana always spoke so lovingly of the place and the great people who lived there.

Nana had once told me that her mother often met the dead neighbours late at night in Killalee as she hung out her washing. These dead were praying so they could leave purgatory and enter heaven. They never did anything but walk up and down the small streets whispering prayers to themselves.

Nana was from a large family and in those days when you could read and write you were sent out into the world to find work. She got her first job at the age of 11 in Spillanes Tabacco factory in what is now Sarsfield Street. She stayed in that job well into her teens and made many lifetime friends there.

One night in her middle teens she was walking home from work with a friend of hers called Frannie Doyle on a dreary wintry evening. It was past 11 o'clock and it was pitch dark. As usual they were joking and gossiping about the day when they passed a small field not far from Killalee. 'Hello Maggie Browne and Frannie Doyle,' said a voice out of the darkness.

The two young women were startled and looked around to find where the voice was coming from. 'I'm here' said the voice. The two of them looked into the field and saw a very old woman sitting on a tree stump. That tree stump had always been avoided by the locals as it was a bad luck place, they said. Her hair was undone and fell down her shoulders. She had a winter coat on for the night was cold. They both recognised the woman immediately.

'Mammy Delahunty! What are you doing inside in that field?' the girls asked the woman. Mammy Delahunty was the oldest woman in Killalee; in fact, both girls thought she was the oldest woman in the world. Though her age was great, Mammy Delahunty was a very active woman well into her nineties. She was a caring woman who considered every child in Killalee her own. She was still looking after grandchildren and great-grandchildren at that time. Mammy also had what locals said was the 'cure'. Instead of finding a doctor for various ailments, Mammy was consulted and advised the best course of action. She was known to be able to cure anything, from the gout to whooping cough. Her advice was given freely but come Christmas every year all the locals would drop off something to Mammy's house by way of a thank you. Those presents never stayed long in her house and were distributed wherever they were needed.

'I got up this morning and no one was talking to me,' said the old woman. 'I shouted at the lot of them but they all ignored me so I put on my winter coat and walked out the door.' The woman explained she walked the streets of Limerick all day but was ignored by everyone she knew. Even in the shops no one said hello or bid her good morning. This really upset the woman and she said she believed she must have done wrong to someone so now everyone had decided to ignore her.

The two young women were very sympathetic to the old woman's plight and wanted to help her. They decided they would bring the woman home and confront her family who had so cruelly ignored her. 'C'mon,' my Nana said, taking the woman by the arm and her friend took the other.

'Oh no no no no,' said a voice from behind the woman. This was a voice they had never heard before. It was loud and sharp and it frightened both the girls so much they let go of the woman, who sat back down on the tree stump. A very tall boney man in a shirt and waistcoat emerged from the darkness.

'This is Danno,' said the old woman. 'He is the only person who has spoken to me all day long.'

'Yes,' said Danno. 'I am looking after Mrs Delahunty now.'

My grandmother was very nervous of this man. There was something about him that was just a little peculiar but she had to be brave. 'I think Mammy Delahunty needs to come home to Killalee with us.'

'Danno says he will look after me,' said the old woman.

'YES I WILL LOOK AFTER THE OLD WOMAN. HER FAMILY DO NOT WANT HER,' Danno said very loudly.

The old woman told the girls that Danno was going to take her to a nice place where everyone would know her and they would all look after her.

'What's the name of that place?' asked Frannie to the boney man.

'It's not for girls like ye to know,' said the man.

'Ya Danno said it's a very nice place for me to rest, isn't that right Danno?' said the old woman to Danno.

'It's a fine place Mrs Delahunty, great weather, great people not a soul could deny it's a great place to live,' said Danno, sounding very nice to the old woman.

'Soul' thought my grandmother to herself. 'He wants her soul,' said Nana to her friend.

'Are you the Devil?' asked my grandmother to Danno.

'The Devil she calls me,' said Danno to the old woman.

'You are not the Devil are you?' Mrs Delahunty asked Danno.

'Ha ha ha I am not the Devil, I am one of the Good People and I need a new recruit – and a woman as smart as Mrs Delahunty is the best candidate I have found in ages. Now be on yer way because come 12 midnight she will join the ranks of the women of the Good People.'

All three women knew exactly what Danno was speaking of. Mrs Delahunty would be a banshee by 12 midnight. Frannie looked at her watch and whispered, 'fifteen minutes away from 12.'

'Please don't take this old woman,' said my Nana to Danno.

'Ye never understand our kind do ye?' said Danno. 'I have to take a soul of a human, I need to pay tribute.' Danno explained that he had to take an old woman every so often to keep the Devil happy. 'We never mess with the Devil and when he needs a new banshee then one is delivered to him,' said Danno. 'Don't worry,' he continued, 'she won't be in hell with the Devil, she will only be working for him.' Danno put his large hands on Mrs Delahunty's shoulders to stop her leaving as the old woman began to cry quietly. 'Just stay sitting there now Mrs. It will all be over very soon.'

That was when my Nana realised that if Mammy stayed sitting on that stump she would pass into the employ of the Devil within a few minutes. Nana looked at her young friend and they both agreed without speaking that they would fight for the soul of Mammy Delahunty. Both girls lunged at the arms of Danno and tried to pry him loose of the old lady. His arms were like concrete and would not budge. They switched to try to move his hands and fingers but there was no movement either. 'Pinch him,' said Frannie to my Nana and this finally made Danno screech with pain as the girls gave him the worst pinches visited on anyone. Danno let go of the old woman with the pain in his hands but grabbed my Nana and her friend by their throats with each of his big hands. 'You will all come with me tonight!' shouted Danno.

The bells of St Johns cathedral began to chime 12 o'clock and my Nana and her friend knew they were too late. They would be taken to hell to please the Devil along with Mrs Delahunty. All of a sudden, the grip on their throats was gone and Danno had his hands at his sides. From behind them a sweet voice spoke.

'Danno unhand those children and that old lady.'

The girls turned around to see a small beautiful woman wearing summery clothes of a light green colour surrounded by a bright light.

'The Devil needs his due,' shouted Danno at the bright lady.

'He will get his due,' said the woman but he won't take the soul of sweet Mrs Delahunty or two harmless young girls,' she told him firmly. 'Children, Danno would like to apologise for his actions,' she said softly. The very tall man had his face firmly fixed on the ground as he whispered his apologies. With that Danno was gone.

My Nana and her friend helped the old woman to her feet. 'We are taking you home,' Frannie told the old woman. Both girls took her by the arm and Mrs Delahunty smiled a very wide smile. 'I'm going home,' said Mammy Delahunty and she disappeared from their arms.

'Oh no!' shouted my Nana, 'They have taken her after all.'

'No,' said the young woman to the girls. 'She has gone to a better place. You won't find Mrs Delahunty walking the streets of Killalee at night either. She was pure goodness and there is only one place for her. Run home now girls as the hour is late.'

My Nana and her friend waved goodbye to the woman who had rescued them and ran all the way to Killalee. When they arrived, there were lots of people on the streets. My Nana saw her mother and asked her what the commotion was for.

'Mrs Delahunty passed away this morning,' her mother told her. 'She is laid out in her house – go in and pay your respects'.

Both girls walked up to the door of Mammy's house and pushed their way through the crowds. There were many sad faces in the hallway but the people around her coffin didn't seem as sad. My Nana nudged her way to the open coffin and looked in. Mrs Delahunty, though very old, was radiant in her funeral garb and had a big wide smile on her face. A happier corpse was never seen before or since.

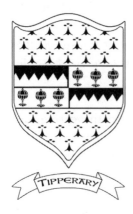

Co. Tipperary: From the Irish *Thiobraid Árán*, meaning 'The Well of the Arra'. Co. Tipperary has a wealth of folklore and mythology, as it is home to 'The Rock of Cashel', the seat to the Kings of Munster. Bridget Cleary (1869–1895) from Ballyvadlea, Co. Tipperary was burned to death by her husband Michael Cleary because he believed she was in fact a changeling left behind by the fairies. Slievenamon, from the Irish *Sliabh na mBan*, meaning 'Mountain of the Women', is a mountain in Co. Tipperary where Fionn Mac Cumhail was seduced by many women, but he could only take one partner. The mountain also appears in the folktale 'The Horned Women', which can be found in Joseph Jacobs' 1892 collection *Celtic Fairy Tales*. Tipperary is also where the famous folktale 'The Legend of Knockgrafton' took place, the story of the lovable Hunchback 'Lusmore' who meets the fairies.

SHAMAN OR CHARLATAN
(CO. TIPPERARY)

We were delighted to get these wonderful and frightening stories from Simon Young, the folklore historian and the man currently behind The Fairy Investigation Society (www.fairyist.com). This society was founded in Britain in 1927 by Captain Sir Quentin C.A. Craufurd, MBE and the artist Bernard Sleigh to collect information on fairy sightings. Young says the only credential required to join the society is a genuine belief in fairies.

Fairy doctors were believed to be the direct link between the Fairy World and the World of Mortals. They were also known as wise men and women, also fairy or herb men and women. It was said that to become a fairy doctor, one would need to spend a minimum of seven years living amongst the Sidhe, learning their ways and customs. According to Simon Young:

> If you had a problem with your fairy neighbours and you needed advice, you would talk to your local fairy doctor. Fairy doctors also dealt with non-fairy illnesses and tracked down stolen objects. They worked too against witches and stood in as veterinarians.

Like any resource, whether it be spiritual, natural, financial or medical, history has proven that human beings will exploit it for their own ends. Thankfully there are some people who use these resources in a positive manner and are genuine. The fairy world is not exempt from such exploitation by humans, and while so many of the fairy doctors were genuine some were not'.

In an article by Simon Young entitled 'True Fairy Stories? Nineteenth Century Irish Fairy Folklore', (Tradition Today, 2018) he also describes a terrible case involving a fairy doctor. In 1834 a young girl called Brown from Co. Kilkenny fell ill in the fields with brain fever. She was given over to the care of a doctor, but the physician could not help the poor child with his limited and rudimentary methods. At this point the family called in a fairy doctor, Edward Daly, who doubled as a house painter and was famous for having lived many years with the fairies (fourteen to be exact). Daly entered the sickroom drunk (fairy doctors are often described as being tipsy on the job) and announced to the girl (or, as he claimed, the fairy): 'Ha, my old boy, it's well I know you, and so I may for I was long enough with you and you know that well too, and many's the time I whistled a jig tune for you when I was with you.' He spoke as if he had recognised the fairy lurking within the young girl.

Daly treated his patient on several occasions. He dragged the half-naked girl out of the bed by her hair, flogged her with a wet towel, punched her and stamped upon her. The girl died, possibly because of Daly's ministrations, and a court case resulted. One of the fascinating things to come out of this case is the support given by the family to Daly throughout, while they were furious with the physician who had bled their girl: fairies hate blood.

The mother had physically interposed herself between her son and Daly when the boy wanted to rescue his sister from a beating. Then, even after the girl's death, the family was reluctant to testify in court against Daly, partly, one suspects, from belief in his methods, and partly from fear: though Daly had sensibly decamped before the trial began. One witness left the courtroom saying: 'I did not tell the whole of it to the jury nor I wouldn't for fear I'd be made a fairy of myself.'

It is said that many of these fairy doctors were more conmen and women than wise men and women. It was easy for these charlatans to prey on the poor and uneducated; many of them could read and write, which added to their authority. They used the concept of a changeling (a child left behind by the fairies in the place of a stolen human child) to both explain away and diagnose conditions such as mental illness, deformity and physical disability. This is not so different to the methods of Matthew Hopkins – the Witchfinder General (c.1620–1647); he is believed to have been responsible for the deaths and torture of over 300 men and women between the years 1644 and 1646. Hopkins was immortalised by the great Vincent Price in the Michael Reeves' 1968 classic film *Witchfinder General*. A far cry from *Darby O'Gill and the Little People*.

The following story is the harrowing account of a child at the mercy of a fairy doctor. It is a true story from 1850, told in all its gruesome detail from the actual time of the occurrence. It was taken from The Fairy Investigation Society's website.

This extraordinary instance of Irish superstition has just occurred in the town of Roscrea. The facts are as follows: a poor little girl, aged 6 years, named Mary Anne Kelly, daughter of Thomas Kelly, a resident of Roscrea, has been for six months past in a dying state, under care of the dispensary physician. An old hag who professed to be one of those rare characters, a 'fairy woman', persuaded the parents of the child that she was 'fairy struck' and offered to cure her if they would comply with her directions. To those terms they agreed.

The child was to be placed on a shovel at night, in the open air, in the name of the Devil, after having a prayer or invocation in the same name said over her. In the course of the night the mother was to say to her, 'Mary Anne, if you are able to come in, do so.' This was done for three nights in succession, on the last of which the child died, a victim to the credulity of her father and mother. While enduring the cold of the nights, the cries of the little sufferer were the most piteous; and who can but wonder that a woman – and that woman a mother – should not be softened by the

distressing cries of the child of her bosom, who had been born blind, and although 6 years of age, had never walked?

On Sunday last, Mr O'Meagher, the coroner, held an inquest on the body of the child. The following persons were sworn on the jury, viz., John Delaney (foreman), William Corcoran, Michael Doherty, Patrick Cahill, Richard Quin, Thomas Healey, John Corcoran, Jeremiah Maher, Wm. Saunders, Joseph Glennon, James Phelan, jun. and Solomon B. Matthews. Bridget Peters, the 'fairy doctress' and Mary Kelly, the mother of the deceased, were present in the custody of the police.

The first witness produced was Mary Maher, who stated that the 'fairy woman' administered herbs in milk to the child and said that it did not belong to Mary Kelly, as it was a fairy. Mary Kelly's own child she represented as having been taken away by the 'Good People'; she also stated that she would either 'kill or cure' the child. She blistered the child, and steeped it in water, after which she put the child out on the shovel in the air for three nights.

The 'fairy woman' used to say to the child, 'Mary Anne, get up and come in.' The mother and she helped the child in. The 'doctress' said that on the last night the child would be very black, as there would be some fairies beating it; and that she would either live or die after it. The witness also added that the 'witch' had been in the house of the mother of the child for several weeks for the purpose, and that she heard Mary Kelly, the mother, say to the doctress, 'Why don't you do it quick?'

On the third night, the witness, who was a servant in the house, was ordered to put out the child on a shovel, and having refused to do so, she was discharged. Another woman named Mary Whitford deposed that she heard Bridget Peters, the 'fairy woman', say that she had stuped the child three times and had given her 'verbena and foxglove'. Surgeon Powell deposed that he knew the deceased child, who had an affection of the brain and was very delicate. He was of the opinion that death was caused by the treatment of Bridget Peters and Mary Kelly. The coroner charged the jury, who returned a verdict of Manslaughter against both prisoners, who were then committed to gaol to abide their trial at the next assizes of Nenagh.

Tipperary Assizes (North Riding) Nenagh, Friday, March 21. A Fairy Doctress – Superstition. Bridget Peters, a decent-looking woman, was indicted for having caused the death of Mary Anne Kelly, by administering large quantities of foxglove. Messrs Scott, QC, and Sausse, QC, prosecuted.

It appeared that the deceased was a child about 6 years of age, and had been delicate almost from its birth, being affected with a softening of the brain, and partial paralysis. The father of the child was a pensioner from the army, living in Roscrea, and in comfortable circumstances, and Dr Powell, a medical gentleman of experience, had been in the habit of attending the deceased, but had no hopes of her ever recovering. The prisoner is what is called a 'fairy doctor', and the mother of Mary Anne Kelly having consulted her, she promised to recover her, or not charge anything unless her skill was successful.

The consequence was that this unlicensed general practitioner made up some mysterious preparations in a cauldron, putting in a variety of herbs, including foxglove, which acts very peculiarly on the nervous system, and Vervain, which is regarded as a very wonderful medicine by those who are superstitious.

But the prisoner, after examining the child, very significantly nodded her head, and told Mrs Kelly that is not her child, but a changeling, and that something must be done to recover the missing girl, who was with the fairies; accordingly, after every dose of the doctress, she had the deceased stripped by Mary Maher, the servant in the family, and carried out naked on a shovel and laid on a dunghill, the poor patient calling out mamma, and in a state of great alarm.

The shock of such exposure, and this while under the depressing influence of foxglove, caused a great shock to the system, and on the morning of the 4th of September, another dose having been administered, the poor victim of this superstition died, although the prisoner concealed the fact until evening, pretending that she was in a sound sleep and getting on well. A book called *Culpepper's Manual*, with a statement of how the planets acted on each drug, was found on the prisoner, and had evidently been often consulted by this 'knowing woman'. The jury found the prisoner guilty of witchcraft on the 13th of September 1850.

Co. Waterford: In Irish it is known as *Phort Láirge*, meaning, 'Larag's Port'. The English translation comes from the Old Norse *Vedrarfjord*. Co. Waterford is colloquially known as 'The Déise', after an ancient Gaelic tribe of the same name who settled in Munster between the fourth and eighth centuries. This county has an ancient past full of Megalithic tombs and Ogham Stones. The remains of its Viking heritage still exists with Reginald's Tower (the first building in Ireland to be built from bricks and mortar). St Declán converted 'The Déise' to Christiany in the fifth century and built a monastery in Ardmore, Co. Waterford. It is believed there was a fort, which was a stronghold for the *Fir Bolg* (the Men of the Spear), in the centre of Waterford town. This race of powerful warriors were eventually defeated and wiped out by the Tuatha Dé Danann.

THE FAIRY TEACUPS (CO. WATERFORD)

This terrific story was collected by Philomena Walsh and was told to her by Joseph Walsh. We found it in the *The Schools' Collection*, Vol. 0652, p.247 in the National Folklore Collection, University College Dublin. It is from Passage East, Co. Waterford. The school it was collected from was An Pasaiste Thoir, Port Lairge. The details available in the archive inspired us to write a version of our own. We elaborated a little to benefit the story, but names and places remain the same.

Maurice Power was an old man who lived beside Crooke Church near Passage East in Co. Waterford. This is a story about an experience he had when he was a much younger man.

One evening he was coming home from a fair a little bit worse for wear, but in great form. He decided to stay back for a few drinks and so on his return home he was a little merry, swaying a little from left to right, but causing no trouble – just happy in himself and minding his own business. He finally reached Kill St Nicholas crossroads and just as he was passing by the Lis (a field) he heard music.

At first, he thought his mind was playing tricks and maybe it was just wishful thinking on his part because he sure wasn't ready to turn in for the night. He was mad for a bit more craic and sure hearing music was only a true delight for him. So, Maurice did what many a person would do on the way home from having a few drinks – he followed the music... he followed the craic! As far as he was concerned the night was hardly over.

Lis was a field that was familiar to Maurice, and so he felt safe when entering it and he was curious to know who the musicians were. Were they locals or travelling through the area and stopped off for a tune? Well Maurice nearly died when he saw who it was. Right before him were the 'Good People'. He had heard stories growing up but he had never met a fairy in the flesh. They were nice to Maurice and invited him to join their gathering. Maurice felt comfortable enough to take them up on their offer and so he sat with them and enjoyed the beautiful music. They were dancing and laughing, and Maurice was quickly swept along by the whole feeling. He soon noticed that the fairies were drinking from little teacups and Maurice had never seen anything as small and dainty in his whole life, and when he saw them he thought how his young daughters would love to play with little teacups like those.

When the fairies' backs were turned Maurice took a few of the teacups and slipped them into his pocket and carried on partying with the fairies. The fairies were still in great form and dancing away so Maurice felt he got away with stealing their teacups. This is usually unheard of because there isn't much that passes a fairy. So he thought he was clever and was probably the only man alive who managed to outwit the fairies. They are usually careful and watchful and not many manage to fool a fairy.

Maurice was beginning to sober up and started to realise what was actually happening – he was in a field at a fairy gathering and he was the only one who wasn't one of them, and he began to feel a little fearful and also he remembered that he had stolen something from them and even if he had wanted to return the teacups he knew it would have been a bad idea because the wee folk could turn on him, and Maurice had heard stories growing up about the fairies. Good stories, of course, but bad stories too and he didn't want his experience to end up a bad one. So, Maurice was polite and thanked the fairies for having him and he made his excuses and left.

This time he walked a little faster back out the gate and went towards home. He knew his wife and kids would be getting up soon – that's if they weren't up already. When he returned home his wife was waiting. She was both angry and worried about where he was all night. He told her the story and out of a mix of inbuilt fear and respect for the fairies she gave him the benefit of the doubt and his story was so convincing and so intriguing she had little choice but to believe him. His story had such detail and as he was telling it she could almost see the little folk – their little feet dancing and their green and red soft velvet jackets and their table with all sorts of food and drink and the music, well she could almost hear the music as Maurice described it. His wife was convinced he was with the fairies and when the children got up he told them the very same story and their little eyes lit up and they too were taken to somewhere else. Then he got to the part about the teacups – he said the fairies had given him a few teacups to take home with him for his little girls.

At this point the girls were giddy with excitement. These little girls wouldn't have had many toys and certainly didn't have china teacups to play with. Maurice was in his element – he had the full attention of his little girls, they were holding onto his every word and behind them stood his wife, who was also impressed by the way he was with their little girls. For that moment he felt like the most wonderful father and husband in all of the world. So, he reached into his pocket and out he took his treasure and to his horror all that he found were cockleshells. The girls began to cry and the mother was disgusted and felt he had made the whole story up. He went from being the king of the castle to being no one. They were so annoyed at him.

Maurice was upset and angry with the fairies and himself so he went for a lie down. When he awoke he had a strange pain in his head, a pain like he had never had before. He put his hand to his head to rub his scalp when to his horror he found that his beautiful, thick, black glossy hair was gone. He was completely bald. His hair never grew back. He felt the fairies obviously punished him for stealing from them. Maurice never betrayed the fairies again and he never, ever followed the sound of fiddles again. He came straight home to his wife and children and every day when he looked in the mirror it was a reminder to always respect the 'good folk' for they are always watching. Never forget you cannot fool a fairy.

4

THE PROVINCE
OF CONNACHT

Co. Galway: The county was named after the River Gaillimh, which means 'Stony'. Co. Galway is a favourite and well-known stomping ground for the Sidhe. The Fairy Hill of Knockma in north Galway is meant to be the home of Maebh, Queen of Connacht and old world goddess of the Tuatha Dé Danann. Here you will also find Finvarra's Castle. In folklore Finvarra was the King of the Connacht Fairies. It is said that the Connacht Fairies fought here with the Ulster Fairies over who would be blessed with the best crops.

From its mainland to the Arran Islands, Galway is a place of song, music and stories. It is the home of the Claddagh Ring and off the coast of Galway is the strange and mythical island called Hy Brasil, which is cloaked in mist except for one day every seven years. Even when the mist has gone it is still almost impossible to reach its shores. Lady (Isabella Augusta) Gregory, the founder of The Abbey Theatre and great collector of Irish mythology and folklore, was born in Roxborough, Co. Galway.

FAIRY FARMERS (CO. GALWAY)

As part of our research for this book, we interviewed various people regarding stories about the fairies. One of these people was the farmer Pat Noone from Curragh Kilconnell, Ballinasloe, Co. Galway.

Steve's own grandmother, who was from Galway, was a great story-teller herself and as a child he loved to go and visit her with his parents. She passed away a long time ago when he was still a child, but her stories stayed with him to this day.

We were delighted to get in touch with Pat Noone, who was very forthcoming and helpful in giving us a wonderful story about his own encounter with the good folk. The conversation started off with Pat explaining to Steve that there were seven Celtic bronze ceremonial swords found on his land in 1840; his grandfather had spoken of them for he had been told of their existence by the old people. The swords were eventually found by the English at the turn of the last century, when they were putting down the railwayaw. So it was already estab-lished the land that his farm was on was considered sacred. Pat's family have farmed this land for generations and they have a great love and respect for the land, nature and indeed the fairy folk.

Pat explained that he has had many experiences and encounters with the fairies from as far back as his early childhood. They are as normal and common to him as the sky above us; he also believes that the fairies will revive Ireland. By this he means that the fairies are unhappy with the way that the land is being destroyed with modern development and excessive and unnecessary farming.

In this book you will read stories about people who built houses on fairy paths, cut down fairy trees and farmed over fairy forts. There is always one common denominator to these stories and that is that none of them have a happy ending. When the land is abused, the fairy folk will retaliate and the consequences can be quite severe indeed.

Pat and his family will always make sure to leave out gifts for the fairy folk – apples, wheat, bread, honey, whiskey and even a footing of turf will be left in the bog for them. Depending on what the season is, the produce for that period will be left for the fairies as gifts. He believes that this keeps the balance, as they are guardians of the land and will work with you if you show them due respect.

Pat has a 17-acre fairy field on his land and he once got lost in it, as many do. Luckily he was eventually able to get out of this field. He was asked if he used the old trick of turning his coat inside out and putting it on again in order to escape (apparently the fairies fear madness and if they saw someone doing this they would leave them well alone) but Pat claimed he did not try anything as he was very confused and could not get his bearings.

In this same field there is a fairy fort, a 3,500-year-old cairn (Celtic grave) and a banshee stone – this is a stone where the banshee sits and combs her hair.

Pat said that he himself has seen the banshee, but she was not the old silver-haired hag that popular fiction would have us believe; in fact she was young, around twenty years of age, with straight golden hair and quite beautiful. But Pat did not attempt to converse with her, as he had heard many cautionary tales about this wailing woman and what might happen if you attempt any kind of communication with her. This was a wise decision as Pat is still here in one piece to tell the story.

And one could say that Pat is a 'wise man' in the traditional sense of the word, for like the wise men and women of long ago he is a healer and has his own cure, which he calls fairy water. Now this is not to be confused with poteen, which has many names, such as 'Rare Old Mountain Dew' and holy water. This is made from real water, very similar to the holy water that a priest would use. But Pat has words given to him from the fairies and he uses these words to create the fairy water inside a special stone with a round hole carved into it. Pat uses this fairy water to help cure various ailments and as a land cleanser. Even in the modern age of science and medicine, the old cures can still be the best.

After hearing about Pat beeing given secret information from the fairies, we asked him what the fairies looked like and how would you go about spotting one? He explained that they look just like you and I, only there is something in their eyes that tells you they are not quite the same. He also explained that they are able to emulate us, so if you are tall, short, big or small they shall be the same too. They have an earthiness to them too, like people of long ago who lived off the land and were self-sufficient, not dependent on any of our modern appliances or amenities. They are the guardians of the land and are particularly fond of the colour green – it is frowned upon to have a green shed as it is the chosen colour of the good folk.

It is also very bad luck to build on a fairy path, ley line, or ley-land as Pat calls it, for they will make it known that they are not happy with you. Pat is a water-diviner and he will check the land beforehand to see if there are any fairy paths; if there are then he will suggest you build elsewhere. This was very common practice before the 1970s. As a result, houses were saved from flooding and sinking and worse... but modern houses do not get the same care and attention to detail; the land is checked by academics who would have no interest in such things and more than often the houses are damaged in some way from the land that they are built on.

Michael Fortune, the folklorist from Wexford, said the same thing about building his house. They put four hazel rods in the ground and left them overnight before they started building. The next morning if any of the rods were dislodged or damaged in any way then they would not build.

We asked Pat if he had any experiences with the fairies and he said that he had many encounters with them; in fact, they were as normal to him as the road. Pat stated that he would often meet the fairies. He said that the 1st of May was the biggest day for the fairy folk and he and his family would leave out a May bush (a small tree or branch, typically hawthorn, rowan or sycamore, decorated with seasonal flowers, ribbons, painted eggshells and thickets) in the front lawn for the good folk. Another time of the year that is very traditional with the good folk is Halloween, the 31st of October.

So, on he went with his story of how he met the good folk... It was that time when the world is lying between the dusk of the evening and the dawn of the morning and Pat was out lambing ewes in the fairy field. He met the fairy folk and they were very friendly and courteous towards him. Now Pat had been warned by many people never to accept anything in the line of food or drink from the fairies, as you may never return to your own world if you do. But Pat is not the type to be told what to do and he heartily accepted a drink of whiskey from them. Now as he said himself, he both lived and returned to tell the tale.

He explained that he had a wonderful time and he drank, sang and danced with them in a celebration before they all went away hunting on horseback; in fact, Pat said there were mornings when all the horses were exhausted after running all night on a fairy hunt. In his father's time when the horses were used for most of the heavy work around the farm, his father would have to take the horses out of the fairy field for they would be all exhausted by the fairies the night before. They love the fox-hunting and they were blowing horns and playing music in a great festival celebrating the hunt. He explained that they had a great bonfire going and they sang and told stories about themselves and their adventures.

The main stories they told were about how their world under the ground is being torn apart by modern agricultural growth and they were losing their grip on the land as their fairy paths, forts and trees are being dug up and destroyed. They are very concerned that the land is being destroyed by modern chemicals and pesticides. We should let the rain water the land and the sun warm the soil and the earth keep us safe and let the wind carry us, for if we lose sight of this then we will lose the very essence of existence as humans on this magnificent earth.

They asked Pat if he could help them by telling more people about this and what it is doing to the land, and maybe some of them will listen.

We asked Pat what sort of clothes they wore and he told us that they wear good woollen clothes in the colours of the land, green and brown. He told us that there was a distinct smell from them too, a smell of freshly cut hay and the turned soil from a plough, an invigorating and natural sweet smell of the land. They were very friendly and kind to him, and they were more than happy to let him go back home as he had agreed to tell the world about their plight and the plight of the land through modern farming techniques. His night with them seemed to last a short enough time, but it turned out that Pat had been away for up to fourteen hours.

Now this being said, although Pat could return to his home and family, he made sure never to ask any favours or make any requests of the good folk, for the price may well be too high. They have great power and they can do many things with this power, but they will always look for something in return. And it has been known that people have been taken by the good folk and this is far too high a risk to take for any personal gain. So, although Pat had a great love of the good folk, he is also very respectful and aware that they have been here a very long time and will be here long after he is gone.

Pat said that since then he has seen the fairy folk many times, at the dusk of the evening and the dawn of the morning. He lets them get on with what they are at and he does the same, as they share and work the land together.

He also told us to keep writing the stories of the fairies of Ireland as they wish for their tales to be told so that people may have more respect for the land and the environment around them.

Since we started writing this book and collecting these stories we have found ourselves become more aware of the land and the beauty of nature around us, and how precious it is and the wonderful secrets that dwell within it. We allow the wild foxgloves to grow in the garden for they remind us of the presence of the good folk.

Co. Leitrim: From the Irish *Liatroma*, meaning 'The Grey Ridge'. Co. Leitrim is home to the Book of Fenagh, the finest medieval manuscript of its time. Sí Beag or Sheebeg in Co. Leitrim means 'The Little Fairy Mound', and when you stand on top of this grassy mound, Sí Mór, which means 'The Big Fairy Mound', is visible away to the south. This is meant to be the grave mound of Diarmuid and Gráinne. The mound was excavated and two skeletons were found lying side by side. The poet William Butler Yeats loved Leitrim and spent much time by Lough Allen. Glencar Waterfall in Co. Leitrim inspired him to write his magical poem about a child taken by the fairies entitled 'The Stolen Child' (1886). Glencar Waterfall has a verse dedicated to it in the poem.

Excerpt from W.B. Yeats' 'The Stolen Child'

Where the wandering water gushes
From the hills above Glen-Car,
In pools among the rushes
That scarce could bathe a star.

FAIRY MONEY (CO. LEITRIM)

This story was inspired by a lovely little Co. Leitrim tale that we found in the UCD Schools' Collection, Vol. 0191, pp.264–6. It was recorded at Ros Inbhir National School, Rossinver, Co. Leitrim by Michael G. Hughes. He was given the story by Anthony V. Farrell from Gubanummera, Buckode Kinlough, Co. Sligo. It is a nice example of what to do if you are ever tricked by the fairies.

Have you ever heard of a cash cow? It is a metaphor for a dairy cow that produces milk over the course of its life and requires little maintenance. About seventy years ago a man living near the shores of Lough Melvin had a cow that could produce the same amount of milk as four cows.

Now this was the case for a very long time and the man and his wife were very content and doing well from the profits they made from selling the milk and the butter.

But then a day came that the yield of her milk was very poor, and the farmer and his wife could not make any more profit. They were running very short on cash and they could not maintain the standard of living to which they had become accustomed.

They may well have managed, and hopefully the cow would produce more milk in the near future, but the farmer and his wife didn't have the patience to wait. They felt that there was only one thing to do. For as much as it pained the old couple, they both agreed to sell the cow, as butter was their only source of steady income in those days. Although the cow had had a bad yield of milk, she showed the appearance of a fine milch cow (dairy cow) and was very healthy in appearance, so they felt she would sell at a good price.

So the old farmer headed off to a fair at Kinlough, a village in Co. Leitrim that borders both Co. Donegal and Co. Fermanagh.

When he got there, almost as soon as he arrived he found a ready buyer who offered him a very good price for the cow. The farmer told the buyer that although the cow was a great milker, she had had a bad yield that year. But the buyer did not seem to mind at all and said that it would not matter as he supplied a large institution in Co. Tyrone with milk, and added that the farmer was too honest. The farmer was embarrassed by this and explained that the cow was with them for years and he had not been at a fair or market in a long time and was not used to such

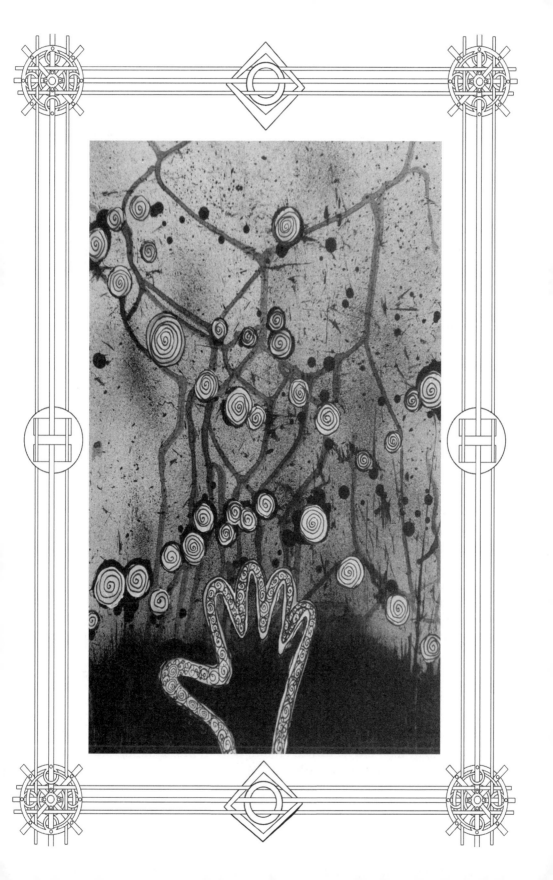

dealings, and if the truth be known it was hard for the farmer to part with the cow, for she brought much joy to their lives.

But the buyer was pleased and admired the farmer's honesty, and when the farmer had finished his business he set out on the road home. As he was leaving, the buyer called to the farmer: 'Watch out for the wee folk, for this cow was one of their own – they may well want their money!'

The farmer laughed at this statement and thought it was just a bit of tomfoolery from the buyer.

As he walked home, night had fallen, but the farmer was in good enough spirits with plenty of silver coins in his pocket. He had not gone far on the road when his money flew out of his pocket and was flung against the road before him.

He looked in vain for his money; he was on his hands and knees going about the place trying to find it, but he had no joy. At last he gave it up saying, 'Can't be helped.' About a mile further on he placed his hand in his pocket and found the last penny of his money safe there.

After going on a bit further, his last penny was hurled against the road again. He looked for it everywhere, but there was no sign of it at all. After looking around for the money, he said to himself, 'Many a man has met with a worse loss.' But he thought it odd that this should happen a second time.

Then, as he went a short way, he put his hands in his pockets and found his money – there it was! Most peculiar indeed, he thought.

Then he realised that the buyer's warning must have been true and it was the fairy folk up to their old tricks, trying to get their money back for the cow.

As a child he had heard the tales that old folk used to tell about tricks and mischief played on them by the good folk. He held onto the money in his hand as he walked on, knowing in his heart of hearts that this was not the end of the trickery and mischief from the wee folk. Sure enough, about 3 miles from his home his money was snatched from his hand and thrown against the road for the third time.

There was no doubt in his mind now that the fairies were working their magic.

He took the only precaution that he knew when dealing with the fairies – he took off his coat and put it on inside out, he then put his left shoe on his right foot and he turned around three times, shouting out loud, 'Ah let all my bad luck be with you!'

With that, the farmer found his money safe again in his pocket. 'Funny money!' he thought to himself and he smiled as he reached home with his money all safe and sound. He was glad too that he had listened to the old folk and their stories, for you never know when you may well have an encounter with the Good People and it is very wise indeed to be prepared. And the next time he got a cow that would yield the milk of four more, he would look after it well and not sell it on for any price. For a cash cow is something that you hold on tight to and never give up for any amount of money!

Co. Mayo: From the Irish *Mhaigh Eo*, meaning 'Plain of the Yew Trees'. Mayo has a long history going back to around 4500 BC with its ancient tombs and forts. It is home to one of the greatest Irish fairy folk tales, 'Guleesh', the story of a young boy who goes on an adventure with the fairies to capture the Princess of France.

Carrowcrum Wedge Cairn outside Ballina is known as 'Diarmuid and Gráinne's Bed'. It is a mysterious structure of ancient stone that stands below a hanging fairy tree.

Co. Mayo has many terrifying tales about the Great Famine (1845–1849), one of them being the *Fear Gorta* (The Hungry Man), a phantom who roamed the famine villages of West Mayo looking for food and alms. William Butler Yeats talks of him in his book *Fairy and Folk Tales of the Irish Peasantry* (1888).

THE BLACK-HANDLED KNIFE (CO. MAYO)

This is a lovely story from Co. Mayo. It is a sorrowful tale and it explores the fairy world beneath the ocean, where the sea fairies dwell. It is inspired by a story we found in the Dúchas archive that was recommended to us by Dr Críostóir Mac Cárthaigh, Director of the National

Folklore Collection at University College Dublin. It was collected by Mary McHale, a student from Scoil Beann-Chorr, Banagher, Co. Mayo. The tale was told to her by a John McHale of Carrowtrasna, Co. Mayo. (*The Schools' Collection*, Vol. 0141, pp.215–16.)

Long ago off Lacken Strand in the harbour of Kilcummin in Killala Bay, Co. Mayo, there lived a fisherman. He was a brave and fearless seafarer. Nothing would ever rattle him when he was out at sea and he was always ready for action, armed with a large black-handled knife, which he took with him all the time. He used this knife for every purpose thinkable in the work of a fisherman, from cutting lines to gutting fish.

One day he and his comrades were out fishing off Lacken Strand, when a terrible storm brewed up. The wind howled and the sea was in total chaos. The men were afraid, apart from the man with the black-handled knife. He stood firm and did not panic like his fellow fishermen. But then they saw something coming towards them that made them all stare with their mouths open and one of the men screamed, '*Sí Tonn ag teacht!*' ('A fairy wave is coming!'). They had never seen the likes of it, they had only heard of these fairy waves in old stories by the fire at night. The wave was as high as a mountain and inside the wave they could see the form of a woman with her arms outstretched. The wave was coming right at them and it was obvious that if they were hit by it they would all be doomed. The man with the black-handled knife drew his weapon and fired it at the wave, for he knew from his grandmother that the fairies cannot work their powers if iron or steel is about them at all.

As soon as the knife hit the wave there was the sound of a terrible scream and the wave subsided immediately and the storm went calm all of a sudden. It was as if it had never happened. The other fishermen thanked their comrade and said that they would get him a new knife, even better than the one he had lost to the sea.

As they rowed back to shore, the man looked overboard to see if he might catch a glimpse of his precious knife. There was no sign of it, but he was sure he could make out the form of a man on horseback riding along the seabed, then the sea went black and he saw no more.

When they got back to shore they all went their separate ways and that night there was a knock on the door of the brave fisherman. He answered the door and there was a finely dressed man, with long black hair and piercing eyes, with a great horse standing at his side. Both man

and beast were soaked to the skin, but it had not been raining outside at all. Most peculiar.

He was sure that this was the figure on horseback that he had seen riding below the ocean. The stranger looked at him with those piercing eyes and said, 'Are you the man who threw that knife at the wave today?'

'I am indeed, have you got it for me?' replied the fisherman, showing no signs of fear.

The stranger was not amused by the seafarer's attitude and he demanded that he come with him.

'I will not!' replied the fisherman and bid the stranger good night. But just before he had a chance to close the door, the stranger changed his tone and sounded sad and mournful. He said, 'Please come with me and I give you my word that I will return you safely once the matter is taken care of.'

'What class of matter would this be?' asked the fisherman.

'The woman you hit with the knife is dying and the only way for her to survive is to have the owner of the knife remove it from her himself.'

The fisherman could see that the stranger was full of grief and he also figured he could get his trusty knife back. 'Alright, I will come with you,' he said and grabbed his big coat.

He climbed onto the back of the mighty horse and the rider commanded the beast to run, which it did like the wind.

When they came to the shoreline the fisherman was wondering if a boat would come and collect them. With that the horse reared up on its hind legs and let out a terrible whinny like a pooka horse and charged straight into the ocean. The fisherman did not have a chance to say a single word as they galloped down below the sea and along the seabed. He could not understand how he was not drowning and he could see clearly all about in this magical underwater world. He saw fish, plants and sea creatures the likes of which he never knew existed, he was truly amazed at this great wonder that was all around him.

As they rode along the seabed he could see a great palace in the distance, it was truly magnificent; its walls and turrets were decorated with shells, corals and stones of every colour, size and shape.

When they got to the palace, two great golden doors opened up before them. They then trotted into the courtyard where they were greeted by strange-looking mermen with green faces and bodies, red pointy noses, flipper arms and wee piggy eyes. Then he saw the beautiful merrows with their long flowing hair and perfect features. They all gathered round the riders and their steed and helped them down from the horse; when this was done they all bowed to the stranger with the piercing eyes, like one might when in the company of royalty.

They were then escorted into the palace, where they were taken up a long decorated hallway to a huge room with a magnificent bed in the centre of it, and on this bed lay a young woman. She was the same woman that the fisherman had seen inside the wave that day. She looked very weak. Then he saw the black handle of the knife protruding from the young woman's chest. It was his knife for sure and he looked at the stranger with a quizzical expression on his face.

The stranger then spoke. 'She is my daughter, she wanted to go upon the land for she had never seen it before and I forbade it, for I knew of the dangers. But she was angered and stormed off in a rage, which caused the terrible storm and waves that you were caught up in. I went riding after her but the last thing I saw was this terrible knife plunging into her chest. I took her back here and then I went looking for the owner of the knife. For only they can remove it without her dying. It is your knife, is it not?'

He stared at the fisherman with a look of both anger and anticipation. 'Tis mine alright,' said the fisherman. He walked closer to the bed and reached for the knife. 'Careful, please be careful,' said the stranger as he watched the man take hold of the handle. When he caught a good hold of it he took a deep breath and pulled the blade from the woman's chest. As soon as he did so, she shot up in the bed and lunged at him with her arms outstretched.

'No, you cannot have him, I promised to take him back!' shouted her father.

The fisherman could see a sadness in her eyes as she lay back down and then he watched as she wept ever so gently. For the first time in his life the seafarer felt a terrible sorrow come over him. The stranger approached him and led him back down the hall to where the horse waited with two ghoulish mermen at either side of it. Quietly the two men mounted the horse and off they rode into the depths of the great ocean.

When they emerged from the sea it was dark all around them and the moon was shining brightly in the sky, sending flickering slivers of silver light across the sea.

They rode in silence back to the fisherman's house and when they arrived he climbed down from the horse and looked up at the rider. 'I do hope she will be alright,' he said.

'She will be fine as long as she stays amongst her own kind – this has been a valuable lesson for her,' replied the stranger. With that the rider turned on his horse and rode away, back to the vast depths of the ocean.

The fisherman stood silently and alone in the moonlight and all he could hear was the sound of the soft wind and the sound of the sea as is rolled in and out upon the shore. He looked down at his knife inside his belt; he pulled it out and in the moonlight he could see specks of green blood on the blade and it sent a shiver down his back.

From that day onwards when the fisherman went out to sea he never took his black-handled-knife with him. For if he ever came across a fairy wave again and saw the beautiful young woman inside its billowing breakers, he would gladly throw himself into her arms and join her in the magical world beneath the sea.

Co. Roscommon: From the Irish *Ros Comáin*, meaning 'Coman's Wood', named after St Coman. Co. Roscommon is where Rathcroghan (*Ráth Cruachan*, meaning 'Fort of Cruachan') can be found. It was the royal seat of Queen Maebh, Connacht's warrior queen. Her mother, Crochen Croderg, was born of the sun goddess Étaín and dropped from her apron as she passed over the western lands on her daily journey to the heavens. When she fell she went into the ground through an opening called an *Owenynagat* (a Celtic otherworld). Rathcroghan was built by Maebh's father, Eochaid Feidlech. Rathcroghan is also the home of The Morrigan, the queen of phantoms/ nightmares. Co. Roscommon is where Douglas Hyde (1860–1949) was born. He was a folklorist, a leading figure in the Gaelic Revival, and Ireland's first President.

THE CASTLE'S TREASURE
(CO. ROSCOMMON)

Sir William Wilde collected this story back in 1852 from a man called Paddy Welsh. It is written here as it would have been told all those years ago. We found this great little story in Henry Glassie's book *Irish Folktales*, published in 1985. The language needs a little getting used to but it's a fun task trying to guess the meaning of the old words!

In some stories we have found that the fairies interfere, and sometimes take a liking to a human and give them access to their treasure. In most cases we have discovered that it is rarely straightforward and comes at a price. We hear of people who have dreams about hidden treasure or maybe just a feeling about a place. But more times than none they will be under some strict instructions as to how they will obtain the treasure. For instance, they will need to look for the treasure at a certain time of day, and they must tell no one about the search.

Here is an example of such a story. Now settle down and enjoy the tale of the Castle's Treasure...

I dreamed one night that I was walking about in the bawn [old castle], when I looked into the old tower that's in the left-hand corner, after you pass the gate, and there I saw, sure enough, a little crock, about the bigness of a pitcher, and it full up of all kinds of money, gold, silver and brass.

When I woke next morning, I said nothing about it, but in a few nights after I had the same dream over again, only I thought I was looking down from the top of the tower, and that all the floors were taken away. Peggy knew be me that I had a dream, for I wasn't quite easy in myself. So I ups and tells her the whole of it, when the childer had gone out.

'Well, Paddy,' says she, 'who knows but it would come true, and be the making of us yet. But you must wait till the dream comes afore you the third time, and then, sure, it can do no harm to try, anyways.'

It wasn't long until I had the third dream, and as the moon was in the last quarter, and the night's mighty dark, Peggy put down the grisset [wrought-iron pan], and made a lock of candles. And so, throwing the loy [an early Irish spade with a long heavy handle made of ash] over my shoulder, and giving my son Michauleen the shovel, we set out about

199

twelve o'clock, and when we got to the castle, it was so dark that you wouldn't see your hand before you. And there wasn't a stir in the old place, barring the owls that where snoring in the chimney.

To work we went just in the middle of the floor, and cleared away the stones and the rubbish, for nearly the course of an hour, with the candles stuck in potatoes, resting on some of the big stones on one side of us. Of course, not a word we said all the while, but dug and shovelled away as hard as hatters, and a mighty tough job it was to lift the floor of the same building.

Well, at last the loy struck on a big flag, and my heart riz within me, for I often heard tell of the crock of gold covered with a flag, and so I pulled away for the bare life, and at last I got it cleared, and was just lifting the edge of it, when—

Oh, what's the use in telling you anything about it. Sure, I know by your eye you don't believe a word I am saying. The dickens a goat was sitting on the flag. But when both of us was trying to lift the stone, my foot slipped, and the clay and rubbish began to give way under us. 'Lord between us and harm,' says the gossoon. And then, in the clapping of your hand, there was a wonderful wind (*Si Gaoithe* or fairy wind) rushed in through the doorway, and out went the lights, and pitched us both down into the hole. And of all the noises you ever heard, was about us in a minute! But I thought it was all over for us… But I made out as fast as I could, and the gossoon after me, and we never stopped running till we stumped over the wall of the big entrance, and it was well we didn't go clean into the moat. Troth, you wouldn't give three ha'pence for me when I was standing on the road – the bouchal itself was stouter – with the weakens that came over me. Och, millia murdher! I wasn't the same man for many a long day. But that was nothing to the tormenting I got from everybody about finding the gold, for the shovel that we left after us was discovered, and there used to be dealers and gentlemen from Dublin – antiquarians, I think they call them – coming to the house continually, and asking Peggy for some of the coins we found in the old castle.

But what these academics from Dublin did not realise was the fact that if Paddy had taken the treasure, it was fairy gold. If he was to say that he had it or even saw it, the gold would automatically turn into múnlach [foul manure]. So from that day to this, no one ever knew if Paddy Welsh found the fairy gold.

SLIGO

Co. Sligo: From the Irish *Shligigh*, meaning 'Shelly Place'. Sligo is known as 'the Kingdom of the Fairies', which lies deep within the majestic rock formation of Benbulben. It was also one of the main hunting grounds for Finn Mac Cumhail and his army of warriors, the Fianna. The brave warrior Diarmuid was pierced through the heart and killed whilst fighting an enchanted boar on Benbulben. Keshcorran Mountain is capped by a large un-opened cairn, known locally as 'the Pinnacle', which can be seen from many parts of Co. Sligo. The Caves of Kesh, are a series of limestone caves. A famous Celtic King, Cormac MacArt was believed to have been born and raised in the caves by a she wolf. Maebh, the Warrior Queen of Connacht, is buried in a cairn in Knocknarea. She has still not forgiven Ulster for denying her the Brown Bull of Cooley. She is not at rest but instead is standing in the cairn with a spear in her hand facing Ulster ready for battle. The poet William Butler Yeats (1865–1939) is buried in Drumcliff, North Co. Sligo.

PINKEEN AND THE FAIRY TREE OF DOOROS (CO. SLIGO)

Our final story in this collection comes from Co. Sligo, better known as the Kingdom of the Fairies. The Kingdom of the Sidhe lies deep in the heart of the mighty Ben Bulben, a magnificent rock formation of limestone in Sligo.

> In the side of Ben Bulben is a white square in the limestone. It is said to be the door of fairyland. There is no more inaccessible place in existence than this white square door; no human foot has ever gone near it, not even

the mountain goats can browse the saxifrage beside its mysterious white-ness. Tradition says that it swings open at nightfall and lets pour through an unearthly troop of hurrying spirits. (*Handbook of the Irish Revival: An Anthology of Irish Cultural and Political Writings 1891–1922*, edited by Declan Kiberd and P.J. Mathews and published by Abbey Theatre Press)

County Sligo is the resting place of the great poet and collector of fairy lore, William Butler Yeats (1865–1939). It also happens to be where Steve Lally was born before his family moved to Lucan in Co. Dublin. Paula Flynn Lally shares the same birthday with Yeats: 13th of June.

We found this magnificent 'Wonder Tale', which captures the magic, tragedy, and epic adventure of a great fairy story, in Edmund Leamy's book *Irish Fairy Tales*, which was first published in 1889 and republished in 1906 by M.A. Gill & Son Ltd, Dublin to honour Leamy after his death.

The Forest of Dooros was in the district of Hy Fiera of the Moy (now the Barony of Tireragh, in Sligo). On a certain occasion the Dé Dannans (the Tuatha Dé Danann – the fairy folk), returning from a hurling match with the Feni, passed through the forest, carrying with them for food during the journey crimson nuts, arbutus-apples and scarlet quicken-berries, which they had brought from the Land of Promise. One of the quicken-berries dropped to the earth and the Dé Dannans passed on, not heeding. From this berry a great quicken-tree sprang up, which had the virtues of the quicken-trees that grow in Fairyland. Its berries have the taste of honey and those who ate of them felt a cheerful glow, as if they had drunk wine or old mead. If a man were even 100 years old, he returned to the age of 30 as soon as he had eaten three of the quicken-berries.

The Dé Dannans heard of this tree, and not wishing that anyone should eat of the berries but themselves, sent a giant of their own people to guard it, namely Sharvan the Surley of Lochlann.

(From *Old Celtic Romances* by P.W. Joyce (1827–1914), p.313, 'The Pursuit of Diarmuid and Grania', Chapter VII: 'Sharvan the Surley Giant, and the Fairy Quicken Tree of Dooros'. Published by Kegan Paul & Co. 1 Paternoster Square, London 1879.)

Once upon a time the fairies of the west, going home from a hurling match with the fairies of the lakes, rested in Dooros Wood for three days and three nights. They spent the days feasting and the nights dancing in the light of the moon, and they danced so hard that they wore the shoes off their feet, and for a whole week after the leprechauns (the fairies' shoemakers), were working night and day making new ones, and the rip, rap, tap, tap of their little hammers were heard in all the hedgerows.

The food on which the fairies feasted were little red berries, and were so like those that grow on the rowan tree that if you only looked at them you might mistake one for the other; but the fairy berries grow only in Fairyland, and are sweeter than any fruit that grows here in this world, and if an old man, bent and grey, ate one of them, he became young and active and strong again; and if an old woman, withered and wrinkled, ate one of them, she became young and bright and fair; and if a little maiden who was not handsome ate of them, she became lovelier than the flower of beauty.

The fairies guarded the berries as carefully as a miser guards his gold, and whenever they were about to leave fairyland they had to promise in the presence of the king and queen that they would not give a single berry to mortal man, nor allow one to fall upon the earth; for if a single berry fell upon the earth a slender tree of many branches, bearing clusters of berries, would at once spring up, and mortal men might eat of them.

But it chanced that this time they were in Dooros Wood they kept up the feasting and dancing so long, and were so full of joy because of their victory over the lake fairies, that one little, weeny fairy, not much bigger than my finger, lost his head, and dropped a berry in the wood.

When the feast was ended the fairies went back to fairyland, and were at home for more than a week before they knew of the little fellow's fault, and this is how they came to know of it.

A great wedding was about to come off, and the Queen of the Fairies sent six of her pages to Dooros Wood to catch fifty butterflies with golden spots on their purple wings, and fifty white without speck or spot, and fifty golden, yellow as the cowslip, to make a dress for herself, and a hundred white, without speck or spot, to make dresses for the bride and bridesmaids.

When the pages came near the wood they heard the most wonderful music, and the sky above them became quite dark, as if a cloud had shut out the sun. They looked up and saw that the cloud was formed of bees, who in a great swarm were flying towards the wood and humming as they flew. Seeing this they were sore afraid until they saw the bees settling on a single tree, and on looking closely at the tree they saw it was covered with fairy berries.

The bees took no notice of the fairies, and so they were no longer afraid, and they hunted the butterflies until they had captured the full number of various colours. Then they returned to Fairyland, and they told the queen about the bees and the berries, and the queen told the king.

The king was very angry, and he sent his heralds to the four corners of Fairyland to summon all his subjects to his presence that he might find out without delay who was the culprit.

They all came except the little weeny fellow who dropped the berry, and of course every one said that it was fear that kept him away, and that he must be guilty.

The heralds were at once sent in search of him, and after a while they found him hiding in a cluster of ferns, and brought him before the king.

The poor little fellow was so frightened that at first he could scarcely speak a word, but after a time he told how he never missed the berry until he had returned to Fairyland, and that he was afraid to say anything to anyone about it.

The king, who would hear of no excuse, sentenced the little culprit to be banished into the land of giants beyond the mountains, to stay there forever and a day unless he could find a giant willing to go to Dooros Wood and guard the fairy tree. When the king had pronounced sentence everyone was very sorry, because the little fellow was a favourite with them all. No fairy harper upon his harp, or piper upon his pipe, or fiddler upon his fiddle, could play half so sweetly as he could play upon an ivy leaf; and when they remembered all the pleasant moonlit nights on which they had danced to his music, and thought that they should never hear or dance to it any more, their little hearts were filled with sorrow. The queen was as sad as any of her subjects, but the king's word should be obeyed.

When the time came for the little fellow to set out into exile, the queen sent her head page to him with a handful of berries. These the queen said he was to offer to the giants, and say at the same time that the giant who was willing to guard the tree could feast on berries just as sweet from morn till night.

As the little fellow went on his way nearly all the fairies followed him to the borders of the land, and when they saw him go up the mountain towards the land of the giants, they all took off their little red caps and waved them until he was out of sight.

On he went walking all day and night, and when the sun rose on the morrow he was on the top of the mountain, and he could see the land of the giants in the valley stretched far below him. Before beginning his descent, he turned around for a last glimpse of Fairyland; but he could see nothing, for a thick, dark cloud shut it out from view. He was very sad, and tired, and footsore, and as he struggled down the rough mountainside, he could not help thinking of the soft, green woods and mossy pathways of the pleasant land he had left behind him.

When he awoke the ground was trembling, and a noise that sounded like thunder fell on his ears. He looked up and saw coming towards him a terrible giant, with one eye that burned like a live coal in the middle of his forehead, his mouth stretched from ear to ear, his teeth were long and crooked, the skin of his face was as black as night, and his arms and chest were all covered with black, shaggy hair; round his body was an iron band, and hanging from this by a chain was a great club with iron spikes. With one blow of this club he could break a rock into splinters, and fire could not burn him, and water could not drown him, and weapons could not wound him, and there was no way to kill him but by giving him three blows of his own club. And he was so bad-tempered that the other giants called him Sharvan the Surly. When the giant spied the red cap of the little fairy he gave the shout that sounded like thunder. The poor fairy was shaking from head to foot.

'What brought you here?' said the giant.

'Please, Mr Giant,' said the fairy, 'the king of the fairies banished me here, and here I must stay forever and a day, unless you come and guard the fairy tree in Dooros Wood.'

'Unless what?' roared the giant, and he gave the fairy a touch of his foot that sent the little fellow rolling down head over heels.

The poor fairy lay as if he were dead, and then the giant, feeling sorry for what he had done, took him up gently between his finger and thumb.

'Don't be frightened, little man,' said he, 'and now, tell me all about the tree.'

'It is the tree of the fairy berry that grows in the Wood of Dooros,' said the fairy, 'and I have some of the berries with me.'

'Oh, you have, have you?' said the giant. 'Let me see them.'

The fairy took three berries from the pocket of his little green coat, and gave them to the giant.

The giant looked at them for a second. He then swallowed the three together, and when he had done so, he felt so happy that he began to shout and dance for joy.

'More, you little thief!' said he. 'More, you little... what's your name?' said the giant.

'Pinkeen, please, Mr Giant,' said the fairy, as he gave up all the berries.

The giant shouted louder than before, and his shouts were heard by all the other giants, who came running towards him.

When Sharvan saw them coming, he caught up Pinkeen and put him in his pocket, that they shouldn't see him.

'What were you shouting for?' said the giants.

'Because,' said Sharvan, 'that rock there fell down on my big toe.'

'You did not shout like a man that was hurt,' said they.

'What is it to you what way I shouted?' said he.

'You might give a civil answer to a civil question,' said they, 'but sure you were always Sharvan the Surly,' and they went away.

When the giants were out of sight, Sharvan took Pinkeen out of his wallet.

'Some more berries, you little thief – I mean little Pinkeen,' said he.

'I have not anymore,' said Pinkeen; 'but if you will guard the tree in Dooros Wood you can feast on them from morn till night.'

'I'll guard every tree in the wood, if I may do that,' said the giant.

'You'll have to guard only one,' said Pinkeen.

'How am I to get to it?' said Sharvan.

'You must first come with me towards Fairyland,' said the fairy.

'Very well,' said Sharvan, 'let us go.' And he took up the fairy and put him into his wallet, and before very long they were on the top of the mountain. Then the giant looked around towards the giant's land; but a black cloud shut it out from view, while the sun was shining on the valley that lay before him, and he could see away in the distance the green woods and shining waters of Fairyland.

It was not long until he reached its borders, but when he tried to cross them his feet stuck to the ground and he could not move a step. Sharvan gave three loud shouts that were heard all over Fairyland, and made the trees in the woods tremble, as if the wind of a storm was sweeping over them.

'Oh, please, Mr Giant, let me out,' said Pinkeen. Sharvan took out the little fellow, who, as soon as he saw he was on the borders of Fairyland, ran as fast as his legs could carry him, and before he had gone very far he

met all the little fairies who, hearing the shouts of the giant, came trooping out from the ferns to see what was the matter. Pinkeen told them it
was the giant who was to guard the tree, shouting because he was stuck
fast on the borders, and they need have no fear of him. The fairies were
so delighted to have Pinkeen back again, that they took him up on their
shoulders and carried him to the king's palace, and all the harpers and
pipers and fiddlers marched before him playing the most incredible music
that was ever heard. The king and queen were on the lawn in front of the
palace when the procession came up and halted before them. The queen's
eyes glistened with pleasure when she saw the little favourite, and the king
was also glad at heart, but he looked very grave as he said:

'Why have you returned?'

Then Pinkeen told His Majesty that he had brought with him a giant
who was willing to guard the fairy tree.

'And who is he and where is he?' asked the king.

'The other giants called him Sharvan the Surly,' said Pinkeen, 'and he
is stuck fast outside the borders of Fairyland.'

'It is well,' said the king, 'you are pardoned.'

When the fairies heard this they tossed their little red caps in the air,
and cheered so loudly that a bee who was clinging to a rosebud fell sense-
less to the ground.

Then the king ordered one of his pages to take a handful of berries,
and to go to Sharvan and show him the way to Dooros Wood. The page,
taking the berries with him, went off to Sharvan, whose roaring nearly
frightened the poor little fellow to death. But as soon as the giant tasted
the berries he got into good humour, and he asked the page if he could
remove the spell of enchantment from him.

'I can,' said the page, 'and I will if you promise me that you will not
try to cross the borders of Fairyland.'

'I promise that, with all my heart,' said the giant. 'But hurry on, my
little man, for there are pins and needles in my legs.'

The page plucked a cowslip, and picking out the five little crimson
spots in the cup of it, he flung one to the north, and one to the south,
and one to the east, and one to the west, and one up into the sky, and the
spell was broken, and the giant's limbs were free. Then Sharvan and the
fairy page set off for Dooros Wood, and it was not long until they came
within view of the fairy tree. When Sharvan saw the berries glistening in
the sun, he gave a shout so loud and strong that the wind of it blew the

little fairy back to Fairyland. But he had to return to the wood to tell the giant that he was to stay all day at the foot of the tree ready to do battle with anyone who might come to steal the berries, and that during the night he was to sleep amongst the branches.

'All right,' said the giant, who could barely speak, as his mouth was full of berries.

Well, the fame of the fairy tree spread far and wide, and every day some adventurer came to try to see if he could carry away some of the berries; but the giant, true to his word, was always on the watch, and not a single day passed on which he did not fight and slay a daring champion, and the giant never received a wound, for fire could not burn him, nor water drown him, nor weapon wound him.

Now, at this time, when Sharvan was keeping watch and ward over the tree, a cruel king was reigning over the lands that looked towards the rising sun. He had slain the rightful king by foul means, and his subjects, loving their murdered sovereign, hated the usurper; but much as they hated him they feared him more, for he was brave and masterful, and he was armed with a helmet and shield which no weapon made by mortal hands could pierce, and he carried always with him two javelins that never missed their mark, and were so fatal that they were called 'the shafts of death.' The murdered king had two children – a boy, whose name was Niall, and a girl, who was called Rosaleen – that is, little Rose; but no rose that ever bloomed was half as sweet or fresh or fair as she. The new king was cruel and mean. He sent the boy adrift on the sea in an open boat, hoping the waves would swallow it; and he got an old witch to cast the spell of deformity over Rosaleen, and under the spell her beauty faded, until at last she became so ugly and wasted that scarcely anyone would speak to her. And, shunned by everyone, she spent her days in the out-houses with the cattle, and every night she cried herself to sleep.

One day, when she was very lonely, a little robin came to pick the crumbs that had fallen about her feet. He appeared so tame that she offered him the bread from her hand, and when he took it she cried with joy at finding that there was one living thing that did not shun her. After this the robin came every day, and he sang so sweetly for her that she almost forgot her loneliness and misery. But once while the robin was with her the tyrant king's daughter, who was very beautiful, passed by with her maids of honour, and seeing Rosaleen the princess said, 'Oh, there is that horrid ugly thing.'

The maids laughed and giggled, and said they had never seen such a fright. Poor Rosaleen felt as if her heart would break, and when the princess and her maids were out of sight she almost cried her eyes out. When the robin saw her crying, he perched on her shoulder and rubbed his little head against her neck and chirruped softly in her ear, and Rosaleen was comforted, for she felt she had at least one friend in the world, although it was only a little robin. But the robin could do more for her than she could dream of. He heard the remark made by the princess, and he saw Rosaleen's tears, and he knew now why she was shunned by everybody, and why she was so unhappy. And that very evening he flew off to Dooros Wood, and called on a cousin of his and told him all about Rosaleen.

'And you want some of the fairy berries, I suppose,' said his cousin, Robin of the Wood.

'I do,' said Rosaleen's little friend.

'Ah,' said Robin of the Wood, 'times have changed since you were here last. The tree is guarded now all the day long by a surly giant. He sleeps in the branches during the night, and he breathes upon them and around them every morning, and his breath is poison to bird and bee. There is only one chance open, and if you try that it may cost you your life.'

'Then tell me what it is, for I would give a hundred lives for Rosaleen,' said her own little robin.

'Well,' said Robin of the Wood, 'every day a champion comes to battle with the giant, and the giant, before he begins the fight, puts a branch of berries in the iron belt that's around his waist, so that when he feels tired or thirsty he can refresh himself, and there is just a bare chance, while he is fighting, of picking one of the berries from the branch; but if his breath falls on you it is certain death.'

'I will take the chance,' said Rosaleen's robin.

'Very well,' said the other. And the two birds flew through the wood until they came within sight of the fairy tree. The giant was lying stretched at the foot of it, eating the berries; but it was not long until a warrior came, who challenged him to battle. The giant jumped up, and plucking a branch from the tree stuck it in his belt, and swinging his iron club above his head strode towards the warrior, and the fight began. The robin perched on a tree behind the giant, and watched and waited for his chance; but it was a long time coming, for the berries were in front of the giant's belt. At last the giant, with one great blow, struck the warrior down, but as he did so he stumbled and fell upon him, and before he had time to recover himself the little robin darted towards him like a flash and picked off one of the berries, and then, as fast as his wings could carry him, he flew towards home, and on his way he passed over a troop of warriors on snow-white steeds. All the horsemen except one wore silver helmets and shining mantles of green silk, fastened by brooches of red gold, but the chief, who rode at the head of the troop, wore a golden helmet, and his mantle was of yellow silk, and he looked by far the noblest of them all. When the robin had left the horsemen far behind him he spied Rosaleen sitting outside the palace gates bemoaning her fate. The robin perched upon her shoulder, and almost before she knew he was there he put the berry between her lips, and the taste was so delicious that Rosaleen ate it at once, and that very moment the witch's withering spell passed away from her, and she became as lovely as the flower of beauty. Just then the warriors on the snow-white steeds came up, and the chief with the mantle of yellow silk and the golden helmet leaped from his horse, and bending his knee before her, said:

'Fairest of all fair maidens, you are surely the daughter of the king of these realms, even though you are without the palace gates, unattended, and wear not royal robes. I am the Prince of the Sunny Valleys.'

'Daughter of a king I am,' said Rosaleen, 'but not of the king who rules these realms.'

And saying this she fled, leaving the prince wondering who she could be. The prince then ordered his trumpeters to give notice of his presence out-side the palace, and in a few moments the new king and all his nobles came out to greet the prince and his warriors, and give them welcome. That night a great feast was spread in the banquet hall, and the Prince of the Sunny Valleys sat by the king, and beside the prince sat the king's beautiful daughter, and then in due order sat the nobles of the court and the warriors who had come with the prince, and on the wall behind each noble and war-rior his shield and helmet were suspended, flashing radiance through the room. During the feast the prince spoke most graciously to the lovely lady at his side, but all the time he was thinking of the unknown beauty he had met outside the palace gates, and his heart longed for another glimpse of her. When the feast was ended, and the jewelled drinking cups had gone merrily around the table, the bards sang, to the accompaniment of harps, the 'Courtship of the Lady Eimer', and as they pictured her radiant beauty outshining that of all her maidens, the prince thought that fair as Lady Eimer was there was one still fairer.

When the feast was ended the king asked the prince what brought him into his realms.

'I come to look for a bride,' said the prince, 'for it was foretold to me in my own country that here only I should find the lady who is destined to share my throne, and fame reported that in your kingdom are to be found the loveliest maidens in all the world, and I can well believe that,' added the prince, 'after what I have seen today.'

When the king's daughter heard this she hung down her head and blushed like a rose, for, of course, she thought the prince was alluding only to herself, as she did not know that he had seen Rosaleen, and she had not heard of the restoration of her beauty.

Before another word could be spoken, a great noise and the clang of arms were heard outside the palace. The king and his guests started from their seats and drew their swords, and the bards raised the song of battle; but their voices were stilled and their harps silenced when they saw at the threshold of the banquet hall a battle champion, in whose face they recognised the features of their murdered king.

''Tis Niall come back to claim his father's throne,' said the chief bard. 'Long live Niall!'

'Long live Niall!' answered all the others.

The king, white with rage and amazement, turned to the chiefs and nobles of his court, and cried out:

'Is there none loyal enough to drive that intruder from the banquet hall?'

But no one stirred, and no answer was given. Then the king rushed forward alone, but before he could reach the spot where Niall was standing he was seized by a dozen chiefs and at once disarmed.

During this scene the king's daughter had fled frightened; but Rosaleen, attracted by the noise, and hearing her brother's name and the cheers that greeted it, had entered the banquet hall unperceived by anyone. But when her presence was discovered every eye was dazzled with her beauty. Niall looked at her for a second, wondering if the radiant maiden before him could be the little sister he had been separated from for so many years. In another second she was clasped in his arms.

Then the feast was spread again, and Niall told the story of his adventures; and when the Prince of the Sunny Valley asked for the hand of Rosaleen, Niall told his lovely sister to speak for herself. With downcast eyes and smiling lips she said, 'yes,' and that very day was the gayest and brightest wedding that ever took place, and Rosaleen became the prince's bride.

In her happiness she did not forget the little robin, who was her friend in sorrow. She took him home with her to Sunny Valleys, and every day she fed him with her own hands, and every day he sang for her the sweetest songs that were ever heard in lady's bower.

This is a photograph of Steve's late father 'Pat Lally' visiting the grave of W.B Yeats. It was taken in January 1973 when Pat was working as a representative for the pharmaceutical company 'Wellcome' in Co. Sligo. Pat died on the 13th, which is also Yeats' birthday. He passed away in 1993, so this year 2018 is his 25th Anniversary. Photograph courtesey of Wellcome Trust.

HOW TO KEEP ON THE RIGHT SIDE OF THE SIDHE

If you find yourself lost in a fairy fort, ring or field, do not panic. Take your right shoe off and put it on your left foot, and vice versa, then take your coat off and put it on inside out, then turn around three times and you will find your way out. The fairy folk fear madness, hence it is wise to act a little unwise in their presence, and they will leave you well alone!

Another way to find yourself out of a fairy field is if you spot a hare – make sure to chase it as they will be heading for any available exits.

Never interfere with, damage or destroy any fairy property. This includes fairy trees, bushes, forts, mounts, paths or anything else associated with the fairy folk. For if you do you will bring a fairy curse upon yourself and your loved ones.

If you are building a house or any other structure, it is vital to make sure you are not building on a fairy path or fairy pass. For if you do, the fairies will do everything in their power to make you leave or remove the structure. In order to avoid their wrath, it is strongly advisable to place four ash rods in the corners of the foundations. Leave them overnight or for a couple of days and if the rods are damaged or removed then you know to build elsewhere.

Fairies have been known to steal children and leave one of their own in their place. These creatures are called changelings. If you have a baby or a small child make sure to place iron tongs, a crucifix or a Bible over their cradle or cot, for the fairies fear Iron and God. The iron apparently counteracts magic, and they have a grievance with God because he would not allow them into Heaven.

If you hang an iron horseshoe above your front door the fairies will never enter. (This belief may be due to the idea that fairies were driven out of their homes by the Celts, specifically in the Iron Age, hence the fear of iron and iron weapons.)

If you find a comb outside (especially a silver one) that does not belong to you, never pick it up for it may belong to the banshee – and it is inevitable that she will come looking for it.

If and when you meet the fairies, answer their questions with another question, for they enjoy trickery and they don't like it if you simply say 'yes' or 'no' as they see this as being lazy and no craic.

If you find yourself in the presence of the fairy folk, under no circumstances except any food or drink from them; if you do, you will never return to your own world again. If the fairies are adamant and unyielding (as they often are when offering you refreshments) ask them for salt and they will leave you be. This is because, like iron, salt counteracts their magic.

It is bad luck to paint a house or shed green as it offends the fairies. This is because green is 'their' colour and belongs to the land.

Smaladh or *smooring* is a good practice when dealing with the fairies. It is a process by which the fire is dampened down by covering the embers with ash. This means the fire is kept smouldering during the night for the fairies, if they happen to pay a visit. The only night the fire should be extinguished is on Bealtana on the 1st of May and Halloween on the 31st of October, for that is when the ethereal wall between the human world and the fairy world is at its thinnest, and you don't want an army of fairy folk visiting your house!

A black-hafted (handled) knife is a good thing to have on your person when you are going to where more malevolent fairies may roam. This will protect you from both physical attack and magical powers.

If and when you encounter a *Sí Gaoithe* (fairy wind) it is advised to kick dust from the ground into the wind and it will send it away. Also, if someone has been carried away by a *Sí Gaoithe*, throw some dust at the fairy wind and it will release the person.

If you want to take a walk through the woods, it is advised to carry a walking stick made of ash or rowan wood.

St John's Wort is said to provide strong protection from fairy magic and mischief.

Carrying a four-leafed clover will allow you to see the fairies – but only once.

Hang garlands of marsh marigolds over barn doors to protect the horses from being ridden to exhaustion by fairies in the night.

Spread flowers (especially primroses) on windowsills or hang them above the door-posts of your home for safety.

Red berries are believed to keep fairies at bay, especially if they are from rowan trees, ash or holly.

Daisies are often tucked into children's pockets or braided into chains to wear around their necks to prevent them from being taken away by the fairies.

When you are making a hot beverage, especially tea (a favourite of the fairies), make sure to pour a little outside your front door for them to enjoy. This is known as 'the Fairies' Share'.

If you have made fresh butter, bread or a nice cake, leave a piece outside your back door for the fairies. In return they will make sure that everything that you make will taste lovely. If you don't, be prepared for sour butter, hard bread and burnt cake.

If you cut a footing of turf in the bog, leave a few pieces in a small pile for the fairy folk.

IF YOU WANT TO KEEP FAIRIES AWAY FROM YOUR HOME

If you have fairies in your house and you don't have any of the required paraphernalia to send them on their way, just shout, 'The fairy fort is on fire!' and they will quickly depart.

Leave anything made of iron out in plain view (scissors, pins, knives, etc.) as this will frighten them away.

Fairies hate clutter, so this is a good reason not to tidy too much!

Fairies fear cats and bells, so put a bell on your cat.

If you meet a fairy, look them in the eye. It is said that you can gain control over them (especially a leprechaun) if you look him/her straight in the eye and hold their gaze. Cats also hate us staring at them straight in the eyes, so maybe they too are fairies? Cat Sidhe is a fairy creature from Celtic mythology.

Always remember to speak well of the fairies by referring to them as the 'good folk' or the 'gentle people', for they are always listening!

ACKNOWLEDGEMENTS

We would like to thank the following people who have helped us in various ways, from providing us with research material to sharing their stories:

Graham Langley, Marie McCartan, Eugene McCann, Aideen McBride, Jack Lynch, Madeline McCully, Domhnal McGinley (fiddle player with the Pox Men), Stephen McCollum (Bill Hazzard), Carol Brennan, Doreen McBride, Ronan Kelly, Lucan Library, DKIT Library, Críostóir Mac Cárthaigh (UCD National Folklore Collection), Pat Noone, Maureen O'Donoghue, Seamus Cullen, Réamonn Ó Ciaráin, Micky McGuigan, Br Charlie Conor, Frank Burgan, Ronan Kealy (Junior Brother), Charles and Andrew Hendy, Kevin Woods, Simon Young from www.fairy-ist.com, Francis McCurran, Holly Peel (Wellcome Trust), Nicola Guy, Ronan Colgan and Ele Craker (The History Press), Michael Fortune (michaelfortune.ie) Eamonn Keenan, Kerry McLean (BBC Radio Ulster), William Anderson, Eddie Lenehan, Máire Ní Dhuibh, Peadar Mac Eoin, Reggie Chamberlain-King, Sean Flynn.

We would like to especially thank Liz Weir for writing the foreword and for being a constant support to both of us.

Thanks to James Patrick Ryan for his never-ending patience and for sharing his advice and talent so willingly.

Finally, to Woody and Isabella – a constant reminder that magic still exists.

BIBLIOGRAPHY

BOOKS

Alexander, Skye, *Fairies: The Myths, Legends & Lore*, Adams Media, New York, 2014.

Beresford Ellis, Peter, *The Mammoth Book of Celtic Myths and Legends*, Robinson, London, 1999.

Briggs, Katherine, *A Dictionary of Fairies: Hobgoblins, Brownies, Bogies and other Supernatural Creatures*, Penguin Books, 1976.

Briggs, Katherine, *The Fairies in Tradition and Literature*, Routledge & Kegan Paul, London, Henley and Boston, 1967.

Bourke, Angela, *The Burning of Bridget Cleary: A True Story*, Pimlico, London, 1999.

Carleton, William, *Traits and Stories of the Irish Peasantry, Vol. 1*, Barnes & Noble, 1990. Originally published in 1830.

Colum, Padraic, *A Treasury of Irish Folklore: The Stories, Traditions, Legends, Humour, Wisdom, Ballads and Songs of the Irish People*, Crown Publishers, INC, New York, 1967.

Crawford, Michael George, *Legendary Stories of the Carlingford Lough District*, V.G. Havern, Warrenpoint, 1911.

Croker, Thomas Crofton, *Fairy Legends and Traditions of the South of Ireland*, first published in Great Britain by John Murray in 1825. This edition by the Collins Press, 1998.

Danaher, Kevin, *Folktales from the Irish Countryside*, Mercier Press, Colorado, 1967.

Danaher, Kevin, *The Children's Book of Irish Folktales*, Mercier Press, Ireland, 1984.

de Valera, Sinéad, *Irish Fairy Tales*, Macmillan Children's Books; 1st edition, 1973.

de Valera, Sinéad, *More Irish Fairy Tales*, Pan Books, 1979.

de Valera, Sinéad, *The Enchanted Lake: Classic Irish Fairy Stories*, Curragh Press, Dublin, 2005.

Glassie, Henry, *Irish Fairy Tales*, Pantheon Books, New York, 1985.

Gose Jr, Elliot B., *The Irish Wonder Tale*, University of Toronto Press, Canada, 1985.

Graves, Alfred Perceval, *The Irish Fairy Book*, A & C Black Ltd, 1909. This edition published by Senate, London, 1994.

Gregory, Lady, *Lady Gregory's Complete Irish Mythology*. Originally published by John Murray Publishers, London, in two volumes: *Gods and Fighting Men* (1904) and *Cuchulain of Muirthemme* (1902). This edition published by Bounty Books, London, 2004.

Grey, Peter, *The Irish Famine*, Thames & Hudson, London, 1995.

Jacobs, Joseph, *Celtic Fairy Tales*, David Nutt, London, 1892.

Jacobs, Joseph, *More Celtic Fairy Tales*, David Nutt, London, 1894.

Kelly, Eamon, *Ireland's Master Storyteller: The Collected Stories of Eamon Kelly*, Marino Books/Mercier Press, Ireland, 1998.

Kennedy, Patrick, *Legendary Fictions of the Irish Celts*, Macmillan & Co. Ltd, London, 1st edition, 1866.

Kroup, Ben Adam and Gmelch, George, *To Shorten the Road: Traveller Folk Tales from Ireland*, O'Brien Press Ltd, 1978.

Lally, Steve, *Down Folk Tales*, The History Press Ireland, 2013.

Lally, Steve, *Kildare Folk Tales*, The History Press Ireland, 2014.

Lally, Steve, *Monaghan Folk Tales*, The History Press Ireland, 2017.

Leamy, Edmund, *Irish Fairy Tales*. First published in 1906. This edition published by Mercier Press, 1978.

Lenihan, Edmund with Green, Carolyn Eve, *Meeting the Other Crowd: The Fairy Stories of Hidden Ireland*, Gill Books, 2003.

Lenihan, Edmund, *Long Ago by Shannon Side*, Mercier Press, 1982.

MacManus, Dermot, *The Middle Kingdom: The Faerie World of Ireland*, Colin Smythe Ltd, Buckinghamshire, 1959. This edition published 1974.

MacManus, Seamus, *Heavy Hangs the Golden Grain*, Macmillan Company, New York, 1950.

MacManus, Seamus, *Donegal Fairy Stories*, Dover Publications, Inc. New York, 1968.

McBride, Doreen, *Fermanagh Folk Tales*, The History Press Ireland, 2015.

McBride, Doreen, *Tyrone Folk Tales*, The History Press Ireland, 2016.

McGarry, Mary, *Great Folk Tales and Fairy Tales of Ireland*. First published by Muller Books, 1979. This edition published by Leopard Books. 1986.

Meehan, Cary, *A Traveller's Guide to Scared Ireland: A Guide to the Scared Places of Ireland, Her Legends, Folklore and People*, Gothic Image Publications, Somerset, 2002.

Murphy, Michael J., *At Slieve Gullion's Foot*, W. Tempest Dundalgan Press, Dundalk, 1942.

Ó hEochaidh, Seán, *Fairy Legends of Donegal*, translated by Máire Mac Neill, Comhairle Bhealoideas Eireann, UCD, Dublin, 1977.

O'Cahill, Donal, *Legends of Killarney*, self-published, Kerry, 1956. This edition published by Mac Publications, Killarney Printing Works, 1999.

O'Faoláin, Eileen, *Irish Sagas and Folk Tales*, Oxford University Press, 1954. Reprint edition 1960.

O'Sullivan, Sean, *Folk Tales of Ireland*, Routledge & Kegan Paul Ltd, 1966.

Patterson, T.G.F., *Country Cracks: Old Tales from The County Armagh*, W. Tempest Dundalgan Press, Dundalk, 1939.

Rackham, Arthur, *Fairy Tales from Many Lands*. First published as *The Allies' Fairy Book* with an Introduction by Edmund Gosse, 1916. This edition published by Pan Books, 1978.

Reader's Digest Illustrated Guide to Ireland, The Reader's Digest Association Limited, London, 1992.

Rolleston, T.W., *Myths and Legends of the Celtic Race*, Constable, London, 1911. Reprint edition 1985.

Stephens, James, *Irish Fairy Tales*, Gill & Macmillan, 1st Facsimile Edition, 1924. This edition published in Ireland by Gill & Macmillan, 1979.

Woods, Kevin J., *The Last Leprechauns of Ireland*, Original Writing Ltd, Dublin, 2011.

Yeats, W.B., *The Book of Fairy and Folk Tales of Ireland*. Originally published by John Murray Publishers, London, in two volumes: *Fairy and Folk Tales of the Irish Peasantry* (1888) and *Irish Fairy Tales* (1892). This edition published by Bounty Books, London, 2004.

JOURNAL

Young, Simon, 'True Fairy Stories? Nineteenth-Century Irish Fairylore', *Tradition Today*. 7 (2018), 1–19.

WEBSITES

www.aliisaacstoryteller.com
www.fairyist.com
www.fairyist.com/wp-content/uploads/2014/10/The-Fairy-Census-2014-2017-1.pdf
www.ringofgullion.org